D0594091

THE
UNKEPT
WOMAN

Also by Allison Montclair

The Right Sort of Man
A Royal Affair
A Rogue's Company

THE
UNKEPT
WOMAN

ALLISON MONTCLAIR

MINOTAUR BOOKS
NEW YORK

First published in the United States by Minotaur Books, an imprint of St. Martin's Publishing Group

THE UNKEPT WOMAN. Copyright © 2022 by Allison Montclair. All rights reserved. Printed in the United States of America. For information, address St. Martin's Publishing Group, 120 Broadway, New York, NY 10271.

www.minotaurbooks.com

Library of Congress Cataloging-in-Publication Data

Names: Montclair, Allison, author.
Title: The unkept woman / Allison Montclair.
Description: First edition. | New York : Minotaur Books, 2022. |
    Series: Sparks & Bainbridge mystery ; 4 |
Identifiers: LCCN 2022014263 | ISBN 9781250750341 (hardcover) |
    ISBN 9781250750358 (ebook)
Subjects: LCGFT: Detective and mystery fiction. | Novels.
Classification: LCC PS3613.O54757 U55 2022 | DDC 813/.6—dc23/
    eng/20220328
LC record available at https://lccn.loc.gov/2022014263

Our books may be purchased in bulk for promotional, educational, or business use. Please contact your local bookseller or the Macmillan Corporate and Premium Sales Department at 1-800-221-7945, extension 5442, or by email at MacmillanSpecialMarkets@macmillan.com.

First Edition: 2022

10 9 8 7 6 5 4 3 2 1

PARA HORACIO

More and more things that used to be done exclusively by men are now done by women too, and apparently sometimes done quite well. Women vote, smoke, fly, shoot (and with anti-aircraft guns, if necessary). They conduct buses and hold Cabinet portfolios, play cricket, edit newspapers, swim the Channel, practise at the Bar, wear trousers. To the anti-feminist this remorseless encroachment must be painful in the extreme. The monstrous regiment is advancing on every front, nor is there any compensating loss of territory to which its opponents can point: women still do all the things they used to do.

—LETTER TO *THE TIMES*, SEPTEMBER 25, 1946

I find myself dreaming about lovely rooms I've seen . . . But then I frighten myself by thinking of rooms where it was obvious something had gone wrong . . . How can I avoid all the traps? . . . Please help me—and as soon as you can.

—MARY SHAW, *BUYING FOR YOUR HOME: FURNISHING FABRICS*, COUNCIL FOR INDUSTRIAL DESIGN, 1946*

* Used by permission of the University of Brighton Design Archives

THE
UNKEPT
WOMAN

PROLOGUE

The black Wolseley roared down Welbeck Street and came screeching to a halt behind the two patrol cars double-parked at Number 51. Cavendish and Myrick got out of the front seat while Keller got out the back, pulling his camera from his case as he did.

There was a constable standing at the entrance. He glanced cursorily at the detectives' idents, then jerked his head towards the entrance.

"Flat thirty-one," he said.

"Thanks," said Cavendish. "Medical examiner's on his way. Any word on Godfrey?"

"Dispatcher said he's coming back from another job, so they'll turn him around straightaway."

"Good. Send him up the moment he gets here."

There was a flash from behind him as Keller took a shot of the doorway.

Cavendish went in, followed by the others. He stopped by the mailboxes, pulling out his notebook as he scanned the names.

"Thirty-one belongs to Anthony Rigby," he said. "Ian, call that name in, then meet me at the flat."

Myrick nodded and went outside in search of a call box.

Another constable stood in front of Number 31 on the third storey.

"Cavendish, Homicide and Serious Crime Command," said Cavendish. "You're PC Peterson?"

"Yes, sir," said the constable. "I was first on the scene."

"Talk to me."

"A Miss Jennifer Pelton in thirty-two called it in," said Peterson. "She was coming home about six, saw the door partly open, peeked in, and saw the body. She called from her flat. I got here at ten after. I went inside, ascertained that the woman was dead, and did a quick look around the flat to make sure no one else was hanging about. Then I secured it. I was careful not to step in any blood, sir. I recommend you keep to the right when you go in."

"Good," said Cavendish. "Stay here. Don't let anyone inside until I've done my walk-through."

"Yes, sir."

Cavendish slowly pushed the door open. The body of a young woman was immediately evident, lying in the entrance hall about eight feet from the door. There was a spray of blood droplets on the floor and lower part of the wall to the left.

"Get some shots of those," he said, pointing them out to Keller.

He stepped gingerly into the hallway, keeping to the right to avoid treading through the evidence. More blood drops made a trail from the initial group to where the woman had fallen. He had to edge around an umbrella stand on the right, noting a cricket bat nestled between two umbrellas.

The woman lay on her stomach. She was wearing a light blue blouse which set off a small amount of blood surrounding a bullet hole in the upper middle of her back. Her arms were awkwardly bent, so she must have been dead before she hit the floor, he thought. There was a small pool of blood below her left shoulder. He stepped around her, then carefully lifted the shoulder up. There was a second bullet hole in the right side of her chest. No exit wound on the other side.

He glanced about the apartment. There was a small kitchenette next to them. A vase holding a spray of chrysanthemums sat on the windowsill. They were starting to wilt.

Did Mr. Rigby give you those? he wondered.

The hall opened into a sitting room. There was a door to the right, which he assumed led to a bedroom. He looked at the wall opposite. No bullet holes visible.

He turned back to the woman, squatted down, and looked at her face. Late twenties, he guessed. Brunette, petite. Eyes still open, her last expression one of shock and pain.

"Quite the looker," commented Keller as he turned his lens towards her.

"Certainly was," agreed Cavendish, straightening.

He looked around for a handbag, saw none.

"Peterson," he called. "Did you see a bag or anything with her ident?"

"No, sir," replied Peterson. "I thought it might be a robbery. I saw some letters and bills on the table in the sitting room."

"Thanks," said Cavendish.

He stepped into the sitting room. There was a small table, large enough for an intimate dinner for two, with a stack of letters on it. He picked up the top one.

"Miss Iris Sparks," he read.

He replaced it in the stack, then looked back at the woman.

Hello, Miss Sparks, he thought. My name is Nyle Cavendish. I'm going to find the man who killed you.

CHAPTER 1

TWO DAYS EARLIER

The woman following Iris Sparks wasn't very good at it. Iris, who was trained for this sort of thing, spotted her as soon as she walked out the front door of her building. A flicker of motion off to her left, a glimpse of burgundy ducking hastily into a narrow alley.

That wasn't the following part. That was the surveillance, which wasn't necessarily directed at Iris, but did set off her alarms. The internal clanging, muted at first, increased as she realised that the burgundy blur, now resolving into a decent cloth coat belted tightly around a brunette woman in her late thirties, was in lukewarm pursuit.

This shadow was so blatant that Iris was almost ready to discount her. A professional would not have been so obviously hiding behind telephone boxes and kiosks, even lampposts that were miserably unsuited to concealing anyone thicker than—well, than a lamppost, thought Iris.

Iris kept walking south through Marylebone, taking the direct route to The Right Sort for a change. She stopped once to check her makeup, using her compact's mirror to see if she recognised the woman, but she was a stranger to her.

One of the Brigadier's new recruits, perhaps? Iris had thought she had made it clear on their last exchange that she was never going to work for him or Special Ops, or whatever they were calling themselves now, again, but she wouldn't put it past him to send one of his minions on a recruiting mission.

Or was this an operative in training? Sent on an exercise in tailing someone who knew how not to be tailed. They used to do that when Iris was first recruited during the early stages of the war. Start by following a random, unconnected pedestrian, mark everything they do and everyone they encounter, then recount it in detail back at the base, all without notes. Then move to the next level and follow someone who knew you without letting them realise you were doing it. Finally, follow someone who was expecting to be followed. Make sure they didn't spot you and make sure they didn't lose you.

It was all great fun, and many wagers were won and lost. Iris was always proud that she graduated from that course very much in the black.

She wondered if there was any money on the line for Miss Burgundy Coat. If so, the woman was going to be out a few bob. She should have turned the other way the moment Iris's hand went into her bag for the compact, or done some window-shopping or engaged in conversation with a newsboy, or availed herself of any of a half dozen ways to keep her face from being presented full on. And she openly stared when Iris stopped in front of a shop window of her own to straighten a stocking that needed no straightening, allowing her to get another look at the woman's face.

She wore her hair in a neat bob under a bright red felt slouch fedora with a cluster of yellow feathers on the left that looked like it had come from one of the better hat shops. Another bad choice—wearing something that stood out so easily in a crowd. She regarded Iris with a look of intense uncertainty, as if she was working up her courage.

To do what? thought Iris. To talk to me?

Or could this be an attack?

She resumed her commute, wondering if she should try losing the woman. It would serve her right, thought Iris. Completely amateurish job of it. She almost wanted to turn around and give her some pointers.

In the end, she trusted her circumstances. Whoever the woman was or was working for did not change the fact that Iris hadn't been involved in any Intelligence work since the war ended. She was no longer a target, no longer a person of interest to any side of whatever games were being played now. She was merely Iris Sparks, co-owner and operator of The Right Sort Marriage Bureau, and it was highly unlikely that anyone was going to attack her in the middle of Mayfair.

And if the woman did make an attempt, Iris had one or two items in her bag next to the compact that she could bring to bear.

Nothing happened. Iris crossed Oxford Street, using the blare of a car horn as an excuse to glance back. The woman stayed on the north side, watching. Iris thought about giving her a wave, but decided against it.

She passed the construction site next to the building that housed the offices of The Right Sort. Normally, she would stop and see what progress had been made. They had finally finished excavating and poured the foundation last week. A small crane had taken up residence at the corner of the lot, which meant that the noise levels for the block were about to increase considerably. She and Gwen, her partner in matchmaking, were grateful for the first time that their windows faced the rear rather than the side. That gave them some insulation from the irregular roaring by the engines next door.

But with her unexpected guest somewhere behind her, Iris didn't waste time watching the construction, which was a mild pity—some of the workers were worth a glance, one or two worth several. She blew them a kiss as the morning chorus of wolf whistles greeted her arrival, then walked straight to her building's door, glancing to her right as she opened it.

Sure enough, there was a flash of burgundy slinking around the corner behind her. Iris walked inside the small foyer, then up the steps to the first landing, which had a window overlooking the front door. She stood just out of sight and waited.

The woman came up to the building and approached the front door. From this angle, Iris had an excellent view of the crown of the fedora, its feathers pointing up at her accusingly.

Are you coming in, milady? wondered Iris. With a story of wanting to be matched, but with another purpose in mind?

But the hat rotated one hundred and eighty degrees, then the burgundy coat moved across the street to take up a position by the shoe store on the other side. She looked up at the window, and Iris ducked away.

How long is she going to wait? she wondered. Well, I'm not going to spend any more time watching her watching me. I have a job.

She trotted up the rest of the stairs to the fourth storey, poked her head into the reception room, and greeted Mrs. Billington, their secretary/receptionist, then went into her own office where Gwen was already at her desk, of course.

"Have you got a moment to look out the window with me?" asked Iris.

"I think I could squeeze you in," said Gwen. "Which window?"

"Front stairwell," said Iris. "Good morning, by the way."

"Good morning to you," returned Gwen as she came out from behind her desk.

She followed Iris to the landing. Iris took up position by the side of the window. Gwen towered behind her, peering quizzically over her partner's head.

"In front of the shoe shop," whispered Iris. "Tell me what you see."

"Do you wish me to remain unobserved, or does that matter?" asked Gwen. "And why are you whispering?"

"Just look," Iris said.

Gwen stepped to the window and gazed down at the sidewalk opposite.

"Was there something in particular you wanted me to look at?" she asked. "They have the new Waukeezis in, if you're in the market for a men's semi-brogue."

"There's nobody standing in front, keeping an eye on us?"

"Not currently. Was there such a person before?"

Iris stepped to the window, then looked as far as she could in both directions.

"She's gone," she said in chagrin. "I wanted to see if you recognised her."

"Recognised who?"

"The woman who followed me here this morning."

"Really? From where?"

"She was waiting outside my flat when I came to work this morning."

"How long has this been going on?"

"This was the first time."

"And she followed you all the way here?"

"She did."

"How very odd. What do you make of it?"

"Several different theories. It spurred my paranoia to new creative heights."

"Your paranoia can be spurred by the fall of a single leaf," said Gwen. "Are we going to spend the day here, or shall we go back to our real lives?"

"Reality is overrated."

"Which is why we are in the romance business," said Gwen. "Let's go match some people."

They returned to their office.

"Thank you, by the way," said Iris as she picked up the letters Mrs. Billington had left for her.

"For what?"

"For coming to look without questioning. I appreciate the faith you have in me despite my odd demands."

"Oh, I have questions," said Gwen. "But being your friend and business partner has subjected me to so many oddities that this was fairly run-of-the-mill. Something to do with your old job and your boss who must not be named?"

"That's my guess, or my main category of guesses, which contains a series of sub-guesses, indexed neatly in order of likelihood."

"You are a very organised paranoid," observed Gwen. "It speaks well of you. And you've never seen her before?"

"I don't think so. She certainly acted as if she knew me."

"Any read on her emotional state?"

"She seemed—" Iris hesitated.

"Yes?" prompted Gwen.

"I thought at one point that she was going to approach me. Then she changed her mind."

"Approach to do what?"

"Two subcategories: Speak or attack. Maybe both. Neither appeared friendly."

"That's disturbing," said Gwen. "Maybe you should give your old boss a call."

"I don't want to waste his time on anything this insubstantial."

"Could it be something other than espionage at play?"

"For example?"

"Something to do with Archie."

"Goodness, you've opened up an entirely new category," said Iris. "See under Gangster, hazards related to the dating of. The subheadings are multiplying like rabbits!"

"And, like espionage, they potentially involve danger."

"Hooray!" said Iris. "Something to keep me enthused."

"The work isn't doing that?" asked Gwen.

"No, no, the work continues to be great fun," said Iris. "More and more remunerative now that the summer is over. The leaves begin to turn and people start thinking, No, not another winter huddling alone in my sad little bed. I need someone with whom to share it. I know! I'll get married!"

"You are not in the proper frame of mind to match people today," said Gwen.

"How many have you done?"

Gwen picked up three pairs of file cards and passed them across.

"I wanted your opinion on these."

"Hmm," said Iris, perusing them. "Mr. Callum with Miss Eversham. Interesting. I wouldn't have thought of pairing them, but I can see it. Miss Conyers with Mr. Potts—not sure about that one. I'll have to let it simmer."

"You're just annoyed that Miss Conyers didn't hit it off with Mr. Trower, and there's tuppence at stake."

"You won't win the bet unless Miss Donnelly reels him in," said Iris. "Now as to the third, Miss Sedgewick with—oh! Mr. Daile!"

"Yes," said Gwen. "What do you think?"

"How much does she know about him?" asked Iris.

"She knows about his international background and that he's at Royal Ag," said Gwen. "She doesn't know about his connection to my father-in-law. We've been able to keep that under wraps."

"He'll have to tell her at some point," said Iris. "He is John's uncle, John is Lord Bainbridge's illegitimate son, and whoever marries Mr. Daile will have to be privy to that."

"And if they get to that point, then I am certain he will tell her," said Gwen. "There is always a moment reached in a relationship when secrets must be revealed, but they don't have to come right off the bat."

"So that's where I went wrong," said Iris. "I always held some secrets in reserve."

"And still do, I'm sure," said Gwen. "Have you told all to Archie yet?"

"Oh, no," said Iris. "It's fun parcelling them out. Maybe I'll present a new one to him tonight."

"You have a date?"

"We do. Dinner and dancing. I'll be running home to change."

"Your poor pursuer. She'll be completely worn out."

"Serves her right. Anyhow, yes to Sedgewick and Daile. Shall we have Mrs. Billington send him a letter?"

"He's coming in this Friday to visit John for the weekend," said Gwen. "I thought I'd deliver it personally. We're taking the boys to see the *Britain Can Make It* exhibition at the V and A Saturday. Would you like to come?"

"Love to. I've been wanting to see that, and I haven't seen the boys since the school term began."

There was a knock on the door. They looked to see Mrs. Billington standing there with an expression of great moment. She cleared her throat.

"Ladies," she announced. "Mr. Salvatore Danielli wishes to be granted an audience."

"Hello," said Sally, looming behind her, trilby in hand.

"Goodness, Sally, come in," said Gwen, laughing. "You don't need to be announced."

"But I love being announced," said Sally as he ducked through the doorway. "It makes me feel grand."

"You're already six foot eleven," said Iris, coming around her desk to hug him. "How much grander do you need to be?"

"I'm still a small, whimpering child on the inside," said Sally.

"Aren't we all?" said Gwen, embracing him in her turn. "Mrs. Billington, how long before our next appointment?"

"There's a Mrs. Jablonska at ten thirty," said Mrs. Billington.

"Mrs. Jablonska? Not Miss? Is she coming for herself or someone else?"

"Herself," said Mrs. Billington. "Widow, I suppose. I'll take her basics and let you know. Good day, Mr. Danielli."

"And a very good day to you, my dear Mrs. Billington," said Sally. "Thank you for boosting my self-esteem."

Mrs. Billington went back to her office and Sally sat on one of the guest chairs.

"I have much news," he said. "First, I got the tickets to opening night for the new Priestley play. Upper circle, but in the front."

"Marvellous!" said Iris. "That's next Tuesday?"

"Right, the first. Six thirty curtain so the press can make deadline, so a late dinner after?"

"Lovely," said Gwen, jotting it on her calendar. "What do we owe you for the tickets?"

"My dear Gwen, this is my party," said Sally, offended. "Besides, I got them from a friend. Remember Alec from the play reading you did for me? He's with the Old Vic."

"Well, thank him from us," said Gwen. "It should be a treat. I haven't been to the theatre since—"

She stopped momentarily, then forced a bright smile.

"Since before the war," she said.

With the late Ronald Bainbridge, no doubt, thought Iris.

"What's the other news?" she asked Sally.

"I picked up an interesting job," he said. "I've been doing occasional work over at BBC Television since they started up again. Mostly assistant stage managing, which mostly means figuring out how to get everything moved in and out of Ally Pally when we have no room for any of it. Quite the variety—one night it's *School for Scandal,* the next is Jack Billings tapping away in front of a dance band with me out in the corridor wrangling a dozen chorines clutching their giant feathery fans, waiting for their cue to prance in. It was like being surrounded by a flock of wiggling red ostriches, all cooing, 'Ooo, 'e's a big one, innee?'"

"You sound quite distressed about the situation," said Gwen.

"It made me appreciate why I fought for this country," said Sally solemnly. "So, a couple of weeks ago, the Prime Minister swings by for a reccy, along with Mrs. Attlee. Big to-do, of course. Ashbridge comes over from the main office, and Burnham gives them the tour personally. They watch *Serenade in Sepia* with the audience and Lord Edric Connor has a magnificent voice. Then they all trooped up to the control room to watch a completely different Priestley play, *The Rose and Crown*."

"Any good?" asked Iris.

"It was all right," conceded Sally. "He set it in a bar so nobody had to move around much, which is perfect for television but too static for my taste. Anyhow, Priestley was there, naturally, pipe and all, pontificating away. They had a Russian chap with them, come over for some chat with the PM, and the interpreter they brought over was trying to explain the play to him, and getting it terribly wrong, so I, um—"

"You jumped in and corrected him," said Iris.

"I did," Sally confessed shamefacedly. "Wasn't my job, wasn't my place, but as an aspiring playwright and champion of the arts, I couldn't let it go by with such a bad impression. So Priestley was intrigued that the behemoth hulking in the background could speak Russian, and asked me a few questions, and before you know it, they signed me up to be a guide for a Russian cultural delegation coming in for the premiere of the new play!"

"Amazing," said Gwen. "Why are they coming in for this one?"

"It had its premiere in Moscow," said Sally. "Lord knows Priestley has his reddish side, and he said he didn't want to do it in London until Richardson was available. Imagine that, holding on to a play until one of the best actors in England is ready for it, and getting it done! I'd be lucky to get mine done in a local pub with the resident drunks performing it for a pint each."

"Maybe you should offer two pints," suggested Iris. "It sounds like a blast, but be careful, Sally. Half of them are bound to be spies."

"And the other half will be informing on them," said Sally. "Don't worry, I won't be saying anything political. If I play my cards right, I might be able to wangle us passes to the opening gala."

"That would be great fun," said Gwen. "Let us know, and we'll dust off our gala frocks."

"Easy for you to say," grumbled Iris. "You actually have some."

"Wear that short black number, Sparks," advised Sally. "I promise your dance card will be full."

"Assuming we go," said Iris. "All right, Sally. Thanks, and keep us posted. I'll brush up on my Russian and practice my kazotsky, just in case."

"Until then, ladies," he said, kissing each of their hands in turn.

"Goodbye, Sally," said Gwen, waving as he left.

Then she turned to Iris.

"Three of us," she said.

"Yes," replied Iris.

"On a theatre date."

"Yes."

"Don't you dare pull out at the last second, shamming a headache," said Gwen as she resumed her seat. "I will not be the target of any romantic plots. If Sally intends to ask me out, he'll have to wait until I'm done with my custody litigation and then ask me directly."

"I want to see the play, too, you know," said Iris. "Relax. It will be three friends going to the theatre. I want to hear everyone sitting behind the two of you complaining about the obstructed view."

"Tall jokes, hooray," said Gwen with a sigh.

"Since you mentioned it, how is the custody battle going? I thought you brought the in-laws over to your side after our last adventure."

"Carolyne is in my corner," said Gwen. "Possibly because she's still furious at Harold over his infidelities, although she adores John in spite of it all. I thought Harold would finally back down once he was forced into convalescence, but as he's regained his strength, he's regained his orneriness. He felt he did enough by letting Ronnie stay in London for his schooling, but now he's worried I might move out and take Ronnie with me if I finally get him back. In any case, there's a step I must take before all of that."

"What's that?"

Gwen looked down at her lap.

"Legally, I am still under the control of a guardian," she said. "In other words, in the eyes of the court, I am still a lunatic, as I have been ever since I was first committed."

"But you were released! I mean, I know that you're still a ward of the court, but I thought that was just about your inheritance from your husband."

"I was released from the sanatorium, but under conditions of guardianship under which I have remained to this day. I see Dr. Milford not only because I need him, but because I'm required to."

"Wait a moment," said Iris. "You signed contracts with me. For the loan, for the lease, for—good Lord, for every single client we've taken on! Were you legally allowed to do any of that?"

"I thought you might ask that one day," said Gwen, opening her drawer.

She pulled out a folder, opened it, and removed three pages stapled together at the top corner.

"When I first told Dr. Milford about wanting to start up The Right Sort, he was very much in favour of the idea," she said. "He thought it would be therapeutic."

"Has it been?"

"The parts in between the murders, yes. The parts with the murders, less so. Anyhow, remember when we finally got a bank loan, I said that I needed to run it by my solicitor before I signed?"

"Yes."

"It wasn't my solicitor. Or rather, he is a solicitor, but he was my court-appointed guardian. The one who won't grant me access to my inheritance. Because I'm a lunatic."

"I don't like that word, I must say."

"Try having it next to your name on a court document," said Gwen. "So I presented the loan application to him along with Dr. Milford's letter detailing what a good idea this would be, and my guardian hemmed and hawed, then reluctantly, very reluctantly, drafted and signed a document giving me his permission and authority to enter into these agreements, which I then took back to the bank."

"You did all of that without telling me," said Iris.

"Secrets in reserve, remember? So, here is a copy of that authorisation should you wish to verify it. It's only fair."

"Put it away," said Iris.

"You don't want to look at it? Cross-examine me? I could use some practice being cross-examined with my hearing coming up."

"Put it away," repeated Iris. "What holds true is that I trust you. I trusted you even after finding out you were in a sanatorium. I don't need a legal document to assure me of that."

"Well, all right," said Gwen, replacing the papers in their folder. "I'm hoping to make it all moot soon. I'm meeting with an attorney tomorrow morning to work out strategy."

"Not your guardian this time."

"Oh, no," said Gwen. "This is someone Sir Geoffrey recommended. An expert in this area."

"A lawyer for lunatics," said Iris. "I wonder how he ended up specialising in that?"

"We're in England. Lunacy is a general practise here. I have a nine o'clock appointment with him. I should be back at the office by eleven. Can you manage?"

"Of course. Take your time to recover after."

"I may need it," said Gwen. She glanced at her watch. "Almost ten thirty. Shall we shift from lunacy back to love again?"

"'Love is merely a madness; and, I tell you, deserves as well a dark house and a whip as madmen do,'" said Iris.

"Rosalind?" guessed Gwen.

"Right in one. Full marks."

"I've been in the dark house," said Gwen. "They've replaced the whips with drugs and leather restraints, but otherwise, very much the same."

"Sorry. I shouldn't have said anything. For a woman who keeps secrets, I do turn my mouth loose too much."

Mrs. Billington appeared in the doorway, clutching a pair of forms.

"Mrs. Jablonska is here," she said. "She pronounces it Yablonska, although it's a funny sort of 'Y' that I can't quite wrap my mouth around. And I was right about her being a widow. Whose turn for the carbon?"

"Mine," said Gwen, holding out her hand for it. "Give us a few minutes, then we'll buzz."

Mrs. Billington gave her the copy and the original to Iris, then went back to the reception office.

"A widow," said Iris. "Shall I take the lead?"

"Are you afraid I might join her in a prolonged weep?" asked Gwen. "I'm stronger than that."

"Fine, you take the lead," said Iris, skimming over the form. "Mrs. Helena Jablonska. From Poland. Works at the Mars factory in Slough."

"Twenty-seven," read Gwen. "Lives out in Iver in Buckingham-shire. I wonder. Isn't that where one of the resettlement camps is?"

"No idea," said Iris. "They're stashing them all over the place. There are Poles here who want to go back to Poland, Poles who want to go anywhere but Poland, Poles who want to stay here, and Germans in Poland who have to get out of Poland to make room for the Poles coming back. And everyone is still at odds over what is Poland now that the war is over. Stalin took a huge bite out of the eastern half, and the German border is still unsettled."

"How do you know so much about it?"

"Can't tell you," said Iris, grinning.

"Spies," said Gwen with a groan. "Why couldn't I have gone into business with a normal person?"

She buzzed Mrs. Billington. A minute later, a young, brunette woman stood at the door.

"How do you do, Mrs. Jablonska?" said Mrs. Bainbridge as she came around her desk to greet her. "I am Mrs. Bainbridge, and this is my partner, Miss Sparks. Welcome to The Right Sort Marriage Bureau."

"Hello," said Mrs. Jablonska, tentatively taking the proffered hand, looking up at her with an almost childlike expression of wonder.

Short like me, thought Sparks, as she shook the woman's hand in turn, giving her a quick, reassuring smile. Short women always seemed surprised that tall women like Gwen existed.

"Please take a seat," she said.

"Thank you," said Mrs. Jablonska, sitting primly on the guest chair in the centre of the room. She looked back and forth uncertainly at the other two as they took their places.

Her clothes were worn but clean. She wore a moss green twill coat that was a size or two too big over a simple light pink blouse with a white jabot, and a floral print skirt that was tight at the waist.

She seems so much younger than she is, thought Sparks. She would be pretty if she didn't look so tired. But so would we all. The world does wear you out some days.

"Now, we have your basics from Mrs. Billington," said Mrs. Bainbridge as she picked up her copy of the form. "You are with us now for the more extensive part of the interview. It gives us a chance to get to know you and get an idea of the sort of man you're looking for. I understand that you were married previously."

"Yes," said Mrs. Jablonska softly. "To Jerzy. We were married very young. He joined army before everything happened, then escaped here after invasion."

"Leaving you behind?"

"Yes," said Mrs. Jablonska, a fleeting glimpse of anguish crossing her face. "He fought for General Anders. *Trzeci Karpacki Batalion Saperów*, eh, Third Karpathian—I don't know how in English. Something with explosives."

"Sappers?" guessed Sparks.

"Yes!" she said, her face lighting up. "Sappers! Boom! He always would say 'Boom!' when he talked about it."

"When did you get the chance to talk to him about it?" asked Sparks.

"After war ended, he sent for me," she said.

"He survived the war?"

"He survived, but he was ill," she said, her face retreating back to melancholy. "He had been wounded, there was infection, there was weakness of heart. He did not want to go back to Poland, not with what is happening there now. They put his unit in camp in Grove Park Iver. It was army camp during war, all Nissen huts. We call them *beczki,* eh—"

She held her arms out suddenly, shaping them into a circle in front of her with a ballerina's grace.

"Barrels," guessed Mrs. Bainbridge.

"Yes!" said Mrs. Jablonska. "We shared with another family. Nice family, three children, but our half was only Jerzy and me. And he was sick, but had no one but me to take care of him. I got job in factory, was able to pay to another woman to watch him, but he never got better. Then he died."

"I'm so sorry," said Mrs. Bainbridge. "How long ago?"

"It is one year last month," said Mrs. Jablonska. "They moved me into another hut, all single women without families, and all they do is talk about boys, and how they will find local boys and become English. And I thought I don't want to live there. I don't want to live where he died. I read about you in newspaper. You helped a man in jail!"

"We did," said Mrs. Bainbridge. "Although that was by happenstance."

Mrs. Jablonska looked at her in puzzlement.

"Happenstance, oh dear," said Mrs. Bainbridge hastily. "I mean to say, that was an accident. We don't do that kind of thing normally."

"But you help people," said Mrs. Jablonska earnestly. "You help people who are alone."

"We try."

"And you will help me?"

"I'm so sorry," said Mrs. Bainbridge. "But I'm afraid we can't."

Sparks turned and looked at her in shock.

CHAPTER 2

Mrs. Jablonska gaped at her, the tears forming immediately. Mrs. Bainbridge looked back at her with compassion mixed with sadness.

"But I don't understand," said Mrs. Jablonska.

"I think you do," said Mrs. Bainbridge.

"But I filled out form! I have fee. I have been saving for this."

"In order for you to retain our services, you have to be approved by both of us," said Mrs. Bainbridge. "And I cannot approve you under these circumstances."

What circumstances? wondered Sparks. But her partner was so certain in her disapproval that she held back the question, not wanting to show dissension to their new client. Well, not yet a client.

"I have come all this way," wailed Mrs. Jablonska, the sobs openly gushing from her.

"I know," said Mrs. Bainbridge kindly, grabbing a tissue from a box on her desk and coming around to give it to her. "I can only imagine what you're going through. Come, let me walk you out."

"Should I—" Sparks began, but she stopped as her partner gave her a quick shake of her head.

She watched as Mrs. Bainbridge guided her out the door.

Mrs. Bainbridge led her down to the storey below, which still lacked any tenants.

"No one can hear us here," said Mrs. Bainbridge. "We can speak freely. Let me explain further, and maybe I can still help you in some fashion."

"The only help you can give me you won't give me," said Mrs. Jablonska bitterly, wiping her face with the tissue.

"And for a very good reason," said Mrs. Bainbridge. "You understand, don't you, that the men who come here do so because they want to start a new life."

"So do I."

"Of course. And those who are young enough also seek to start families."

"I know, but—"

"It would be a shame if the family they started was not truly their own, wouldn't it?"

Mrs. Jablonska looked up at her, her face turning pale.

"How far along are you?" asked Mrs. Bainbridge gently.

"How—how do you know this?" asked Mrs. Jablonska.

"I can tell with some women," said Mrs. Bainbridge. "You, I'm sorry to say, are one of them. I don't wish you ill, Mrs. Jablonska, but we do have standards to meet at The Right Sort. We take clients from all classes, all religions, all nationalities, but there are still some lines we cannot cross, and you are standing on the other side of one."

"I see," said Mrs. Jablonska heavily. "I must go."

"There are agencies that can help women in your situation," said Mrs. Bainbridge. "If you like—"

"No, no," said Mrs. Jablonska, turning to descend the stairs. "You have done enough. I am sorry to bring such unpleasantness to your happy establishment."

Mrs. Bainbridge watched until she vanished, then looked out the window to see her trudge desolately away from the building.

She glanced across at the sidewalk in front of the shoe store just in case, but there was no one watching.

She walked back up to the office where Iris was patiently waiting for her return and plopped herself down in her chair with a sigh.

"I feel absolutely wretched," she said.

"Are you going to tell me what that was all about?" asked Iris.

"She's pregnant, Iris," said Gwen. "I would guess two to three months."

"How on earth did you know that?"

"The tightness of her skirt's waist—no one's gaining weight with rationing. Then there's the fullness of her cheeks, and a few other places. No wonder she was so desperate. God only knows how she managed to scrape together our fee working in a candy factory."

"Poor thing," said Iris, looking out the door. "What can she do?"

"I offered to help her, but she refused," said Gwen. "I can't blame her. It must have been a shock to be found out so quickly."

"Two to three months, you think."

"Yes."

"And her husband died a year ago."

"Yes."

"Poor thing," said Iris again. "There but for the grace of God and plain dumb luck go I."

"You understand why I had to refuse her," said Gwen.

"Yes," said Iris. "Although—"

"What?"

"There may be men who would welcome a child, no matter where it came from," said Iris. "Men who, you know—"

"Know what?"

"Who can't have children."

"None of our candidates has ever mentioned that," said Gwen.

"No," said Iris. "I doubt that they would."

"Have you ever thought about it?" asked Gwen.

"About having children? Of course. Especially after meeting your Ronnie, who is as wonderful an example of a child as I have ever seen. But that's all tied into the other very large question of marriage."

"Ronnie still plans on marrying you when he grows up," said Gwen.

"There you have it, then. I'll have to wait a few years. When does he come of age?"

"1958."

"That should be enough time for me to assemble my trousseau, don't you think? And how about you?"

"How about me what?"

"Children. More of them."

"As you said, tied into that other large question, only I have several more large questions in front of that one."

"We're not doing our part to replenish the species, are we?" said Iris.

"I hope this doesn't put a damper on your date with Archie," said Gwen.

"That's hours away," said Iris. "Ample time for me to cheer up."

But the day passed, and they remained gloomy throughout.

"Well, let's hope for better things tonight," said Iris as she retrieved her hat from the coat-tree.

"May your date be free of surveillance," said Gwen.

"I almost forgot about that," said Iris. "I wonder if she's waiting for me outside."

"Would you like me to follow you to see if she is following you?" offered Gwen. "Then follow her?"

"That is very sweet of you, but no," said Iris. "If she's still there, I'll ditch her this time. Show her how a real spy does it. I will see you tomorrow. Oh, you're coming in late, aren't you?"

"Yes," said Gwen.

"Good luck with that. Tell me all about it at lunch."

"I will," promised Gwen as they walked out.

She locked the door behind them. Mrs. Billington came out and did the same with her door.

"Turned Mrs. Jablonska down, did you?" she commented.

"Yes," said Gwen.

"Thought you might," said Mrs. Billington. "She's got a bun in the oven, doesn't she?"

"Why am I the only one who didn't see that?" complained Iris. "Usually, I'm the observant one."

Iris and Gwen walked together to Oxford Street.

"Good so far?" asked Gwen.

"Honestly, I can't see her, but I have the sense that she's watching," said Iris. "She has improved since this morning, but it's only been a few blocks."

"I don't like this, Iris."

"I'll be fine. Tell you what—I'm not going to walk west with you. It will be much easier for me to lose her in Mayfair where it's still busy. Do you mind?"

"Not at all," said Gwen. "But call when you get home so I won't be worried."

"I will," promised Iris. "See you tomorrow. The world must be peopled!"

"The world must be peopled," echoed Gwen. "But legitimately."

They parted. Iris watched fondly as Gwen headed west with her long strides on her walk to Kensington, her head bobbing above most of the crowd. Then the light changed. Iris crossed to the other side of Oxford Street, then turned right, thinking about her pursuer.

If I'm her and I'm following me and I knew what I was about and knew that the woman I'm following, who is still me, knew what she was about, I wouldn't be crossing right now, she thought. I would take a parallel route on the other side.

She risked a quick, surreptitious glance to her right, but saw no burgundy coats or yellow plumes looming among the crowd of pedestrians shopping or making their assorted ways home.

She could have changed, thought Iris. That would have been smart. Lock the bright image into my mind, then switch to something drab to blend into the drab world.

She was touched and amused by Gwen's offer to tail her tail. Gwen was many things, but stealthy wasn't one of them. She was noticed wherever she went. It wasn't the height so much as the beauty. Gwen's face drew the eye immediately. There was a natural loveliness, of course, but it had been tempered by so many contributing factors—joy, loss, despair, revival—that every expression of hers, every glance, told a story, and it was one you wanted to hear.

Iris's face, on the other hand, kept secrets. The hint of mystery behind the carefully guarded masks she presented to the world intrigued men who liked their women mysterious, who saw them as a series of puzzles to be solved, hidden doorways to be unlocked, or traps to be negotiated, with the promise of some glorious treasure at the end, should one survive to see it.

Or so she liked to flatter herself. Her recent forays into her psyche with Dr. Milford were showing that there might not be any treasure at the end, that the walls and traps she had constructed were themselves the essence of who she was.

And that it was no accident that her most recent relationships as a result were with Andrew and Archie, a spy and a spiv. Men who had dangerous secrets and walls of their own.

The funny part was that Archie, the gangster and master of spivs, was still the best relationship she had had in her life, though certainly not the sort of man one brings home to meet Mum.

Although Mum was terrifying in her own way, thought Iris. Maybe she should introduce them, just to see their reactions.

Then she could recount the event to Sally, and he could write a play about it, and she could watch it and pretend it was all fiction.

She was coming up on Oxford Circus. Right, she thought. Let's see if my shadow can keep up.

She crossed back over Oxford, continued down Regent Street, then took the next left on Little Argyll. A right put her onto Argyll with the Palladium looming on her left. She stopped in front of it, perusing the bill and the publicity photos. A variety show called *High Time*, which didn't look promising. The featured performers were Bob Bromley, a marionetter, which always gave her the creeps; Tessie O'Shea, who she rather liked; Halama and Konarski, a Polish dance act; and Nat Jackley, an eccentric dancer who she found even creepier than the marionettes.

She watched the reflection in the glass covering the photos. There! Someone popped around the corner, then back again, too quickly for Iris to make out who it was. No burgundy, no feathered hat, so she had indeed changed while Iris was spending the day arranging love between strangers.

Very good, Miss Formerly Known as Burgundy Coat, thought Iris. Now, the acid test.

Across from the Palladium was the Argyll Arms, a pub she knew well enough. She gazed at its sign with the expression of a woman longing for a drink (which she was), then apparently came to a decision and walked inside.

There were legends of a tunnel under the Argyll Arms, connecting it to the Palladium, but Iris needed nothing so dramatic. The entryway led to a long corridor with etched mirrors on the left and partitioned snugs concealed by etched glass panels on the right. Overhead was a patterned Lincrusta ceiling, painted to match the carved mahogany framing the mirrors and windows. She passed by the snugs, continuing to the larger lounge at the rear. Anyone coming in behind her would be exposed to view, and she had her compact out the moment her feet hit the corridor.

No one followed her, which meant her shadow was outside, waiting for her to reemerge.

Anyone who knew Iris at all knew that waiting for her to re-emerge from a pub would be a long wait.

There was a crowd of post-work, pre-commute businessmen, mixed with uniformed officers from various services, some getting a start on the evening's drinking, others clearly in continuation from liquid luncheons. A stout, red-faced American army captain lurched towards her, bellowing, "About time you got here, gorgeous! What'll you have?"

"Hold that thought, handsome," she said, stopping him with a finger to his chin. "I will be right back."

She knew the toilets were upstairs by the dining room, but they weren't her destination. She watched the bartender moving about the lengthy servery. When he was at the other end, she ducked through the gap in the bar and scooted through a door to the kitchen. A pair of cooks looked at her in irritated surprise.

"You lost, love?" said one of them.

"Please, I'm fleeing a bad date," she said, her voice high and breathy. "If a drunk American captain comes looking, tell him you haven't seen me. Could you let me out the back door?"

"Righto, dearie," said one of them. "You'd best come along with me."

He beckoned to her and walked her through the back to the delivery entrance.

"You're a lifesaver," she said as he opened it.

"Bloody Yanks should leave our girls for our boys," he said with a wink. "Give a local lad the next one, eh?"

"Will do," she promised.

The alley let her out on Little Argyll. She walked quickly back to Oxford Circus, zipped down the stairs and through the station just to be certain, then headed north, took her next left, stepped into a doorway, and waited for a few minutes.

No one followed her.

She walked home to Welbeck Street, checking periodically to

make sure she had truly lost her pursuer. But there was no one, not even waiting in the alley across the street where she had caught her first glimpse of burgundy.

And that's how we do it where I come from, she thought smugly as she climbed the stairs to her flat and opened her door to find Andrew sitting on her sofa.

"Hello, Sparks," he said. "I was wondering when you'd be getting in."

She took a few quick steps back, then came forward slowly, taking him in, the reality of him, the weight of him pressing against her cushions. He wasn't in uniform, and his civvies were threadbare and decidedly un-English in make and style. She would have gone so far as to say they were from somewhere far to the east of the fashions she knew. He looked tired, riddled with weariness far beyond the fatigue of travel or work. There was underneath the forced jauntiness of his greeting something that she had never seen in him before.

Fear.

"What in God's name are you doing in my flat?" she asked, her mind racing to assemble the thousand questions she had into some semblance of order.

"Technically, it's my flat," he said. "I paid for it. I'm still paying for it."

"And when we split—"

"When you threw me out."

"When I severed the fraying ties that bound us, you said right before you left, and I am quoting to the best of my memory, 'The rent on the flat is paid for through the end of the year.' It is still September."

"I also said I would be hanging on to my key, if you'll recall," he said, holding it up. "And where we left things was in a state of uncertainty, not finality."

"That is not where we left them. A state of uncertainty ran

through the entire course of our sordid affair. Certainty finally showed up when I put an end to it."

"You never quite said that."

"So in your self-centred world, I am still yours because of some linguistic ambiguity that your ego resolves in your favour?"

"I offered you time to reconsider."

"Generous of you."

"What was generous of me was paying for the flat," he said.

"Let's not be coy about why you did that," she said.

"No, let's not. I paid for this flat so that we could make love together as much as circumstances permitted. It was, and I am being absolutely truthful when I say this, the best experience that life has given me. And I think you may have enjoyed it a little, didn't you?"

"Why are you here, Andrew?" she asked, refusing the bait. "I haven't heard a word from you, then suddenly, you're here."

"I wasn't in a position to communicate," he said.

"You know forty different ways to sneak a message out of anywhere."

"What did you want? A sonnet on a square of silk rolled inside a lipstick? A Valentine on microfilm?"

"None of that. But to have you show up on my doorstep—"

"On your sofa."

"Figuratively speaking, out of the blue, without one word of warning—"

"No one knows I'm here," he said abruptly.

"In my flat?"

"In London," he said. "In England, for that matter."

"No one?" she asked, his fear beginning to find its way over to her. "Not your wife?"

"Poppy? Be serious."

"Not even—"

"No one," he repeated. "Especially not him. No one knows, no one needs to know, no one can know. I need to lie low for a while."

"Lie low? You don't mean here?"

"My flat, Sparks. Remember?"

"Out of the question. What's going on, Andrew?"

"Can't tell you," he said, with a brief flash of his old wolfish grin.

"The hell you can't!" she snapped. "It was one thing when we were together, and God knows I'm stretching the definition of that word, but it's been three, no, three and a half months—"

"You've been counting the days. I'm touched."

"And if you're on the outs with the office, if you have in any way crossed over—"

"I'm not, and I haven't."

"There is something in the Official Secrets Act about harbouring offenders. Section Seven, I believe."

"First, if it's my flat, then you're not harbouring anyone," said Andrew. "If anything, I've been harbouring you, and your only offense has been against conventional morality. Second, Section Seven is only a misdemeanour, and I've never known the lighter crimes to scare you off."

"For God's sake, Andrew! Get out! Now!"

"No," he said. "There is nowhere else I can go at the moment. I don't know why you're putting up such a fuss, Sparks. It's not like I haven't been here before."

"But you're talking about being here around the clock, not just sneaking in for the occasional bit of slap and tickle. People will notice you clumping about while I'm at work."

"I don't clump about, Sparks, and it won't be for long. Your reputation will be no worse than it already was."

"Oh, that was a low blow. I'm sorry, Andrew, but I really need you to leave."

"I refuse, and there you have it," he said. "What are you going to do? Walk out? It's your turn."

"Please, Andrew, will you go away now?" she asked desperately. "There's something you don't know about. A complication."

"And what would that be?" he asked, smirking slightly.

"That would be me," said Archie, stepping into the doorway behind her.

He had dressed up, she saw with dismay. A newly pressed shirt, a clean collar, and in his hand was a spray of chrysanthemums, at the moment being clutched much harder about their stems than normally would be healthy. He had shaved and was wearing cologne, something he only did for her.

"Mind if I come in?" he asked in a light tone that carried undercurrents of imminent violence.

"Please do," she said automatically. She gestured hopelessly with an arm towards each. "Current, meet ex. Ex, current."

"No names, is it?" commented Archie as he came up behind her.

He didn't put his arm around her, she noticed gratefully. She didn't need any more masculine assertions of ownership.

"No names," agreed Andrew affably as he stood up, shifting his weight to a stance she knew all too well. "I take it you're the gangster."

"You told 'im about that?" Archie asked her.

"As a matter of fact, I haven't," said Iris. "Of course, my old boss knows about you. I guess word does travel to wherever when it needs to. I don't know why it needed to."

"And you're in the same line of work that Sparks used to be in," said Archie.

"Actually, I'm The Right Sort's first travelling employee," said Andrew. "I recruit marital prospects from the Continent. I've just returned with a fresh list."

"What's 'e doing 'ere?" asked Archie.

"Showed up unexpectedly," said Iris. "Very unexpectedly. Oh, are those for me? How lovely! Thank you!"

She prised the flowers from his grip, found a vase to put them in, and ran some water from the kitchen faucet into it.

"I remember that vase," said Andrew. "I brought it home for you last February."

"You're lucky I haven't chucked it at your head by now," said Iris as she put it on her windowsill, fanning the flowers out.

"That's my girl," said Archie approvingly. "Shall I show the gentleman out?"

"I'd like to see you try," said Andrew.

"You might get your wish," said Archie.

"Please stand down," said Iris. "Unfortunately, he has certain claims."

"On you?"

"On the flat," she said. "Although he's treating me as a fixture when he knows very well I'm a movable."

"Is 'e evicting you?"

"Not exactly. You aren't, are you?"

"Not at all," said Andrew.

"Then what's going on?" asked Archie.

"He wishes to stay here. Temporarily."

"'Ow long is temporarily?"

"We hadn't got to that part of the discussion," said Iris.

"And where exactly would 'e be sleeping?" asked Archie.

"The sofa will suit me fine," said Andrew.

"Do you trust 'im to stay there?" asked Archie.

Iris hesitated.

"Right, that's enough for me," said Archie. "You're leaving."

"I'm afraid not," said Andrew.

"I wasn't offering you a choice."

"Nor was I making one," said Andrew.

They glowered at each other, tensing their muscles.

Iris stepped between them, reached into her umbrella stand, and pulled out a cricket bat.

"Both of you stop," she said, holding it up. "I will have no violence in here. This may be your flat, but the furniture is hired and

I will be the one stuck for damages. The next man who makes a hostile move will get a broken kneecap."

"I'm on your side 'ere, remember?" said Archie.

"Yes, but I didn't ask to be rescued."

"So what are we going to do about this, Sparks?" asked Andrew.

"I'm thinking," she said.

The telephone jangled. They all turned to look at it.

"Were you expecting a call?" asked Andrew.

"Oh, dear God," said Iris, picking it up. "Hello?"

"Iris? Thank goodness," said Gwen. "You were supposed to ring me up when you got home safely. Were you followed?"

"No, I was preceded," said Iris.

"What? You mean she was waiting for you at your flat?"

"No, but—Look, it's very complicated, and I can't explain it to you over the telephone."

She glanced back and forth at the two men, then came to a decision.

"May I beg an enormous favour of you?" she asked.

"Yes?" replied Gwen.

"Could I stay with you for a couple of nights? I promise to keep out of the way, and you don't have to worry about feeding me—"

"Done," said Gwen. "How soon will you be here?"

"Half an hour?"

"I'll have them make up a room for you."

"Thank you, darling. You have no idea what this means to me."

"Ronnie will be over the moon," said Gwen. "See you shortly."

Iris hung up.

"I'm going to pack my bag," she said. "Archie, could you give me a lift? Sorry about the date, but you see how things are."

"You used my name," complained Archie.

"So I did," said Iris. "His is Andrew. Now you're even."

"Damn you," said Andrew irritably.

She stuck her tongue out at him, headed for her bedroom, then turned to face Andrew again.

"I want you to know that I will be spending the next few nights at the house of a lovely young man who wants to marry me," she informed him. "I will check back here periodically to see whether or not you've gone. Do not mess with a single item in this flat. If I find so much as a stocking out of place, both of your kneecaps will pay."

She brandished the bat for emphasis, then vanished into her bedroom, slamming the door closed.

The two men stared at the door, then at each other.

"We have some competition, it appears," said Andrew.

"Just you," said Archie, chuckling. "I'm not worried about 'im."

CHAPTER 3

Archie put Iris's suitcase in the boot, closed the lid, then held the door for her.

"It's a fifteen-minute drive to the Bainbridges'," she said as she got in. "Will that be enough time to apologise?"

"Apologise for what?" asked Archie as he got behind the wheel. "For 'aving an ex-boyfriend? You've 'ad more than one, and I've got a list of ladies 'ose last memory of me was of my 'eels as the door swung shut after me."

"Any of them likely to show up tonight?" asked Iris, staring glumly out the window as Marylebone receded from view. "It would make the night complete. There are too few chances to have a decent date in one's life, and I've just squandered one. Oh, damn! I left the flowers behind."

"Good. It will give 'im something to remind 'im you're with me," said Archie. "Why do you think 'e picked tonight to make an appearance?"

"I don't like to speculate."

"You love to speculate."

"All right, I do. But I don't know why he showed up at all, much less tonight. My knowledge of his comings and goings was restricted even when we were together, especially after I left—"

"Go on, say it," said Archie with a grin. "Left being a spy."

"Left my previous employment," she finished.

"Well, it answers my question about what the last boyfriend looked like," said Archie. "You undercover types don't leave pictures lying about. Tougher-looking bloke than I imagined. I thought 'e'd be one of them pencil-moustached, thin-waisted, pipe-smoking, trench coat types. This one looked like 'e knew 'is way around a pub fight."

"He does."

"Think I could take 'im?" he asked, giving her a sidelong glance.

"I don't know, and I hope never to find out," she said.

"Which of us would you wager on?"

"I've never seen you fight," she said.

"I 'aven't lost one yet."

"Your nose has lost a couple."

"I didn't say I never got 'urt. It's what you do after you get 'urt that shows what you're made of."

"Which one of us are we talking about now?"

"Whichever you like. Broken date aside, I noticed you didn't ask if you could stay with me."

"You didn't offer."

"I'm offering now."

"I don't think I'm ready to live in sin full-time just yet," she said slowly, considering. "Dating sin is fun, don't get me wrong, but committing to it . . ."

"You didn't mind Mr. Secret Agent keeping you stashed away for fun and frolic."

"No," she said. "I didn't mind. Only I did, but I wasn't paying any attention to myself. I don't want to make that mistake again."

"I'm a mistake now, am I?"

"No, no, no, darling. What I meant was I don't want to make that mistake about me and mess things up with you. I need to figure things out before—"

She stopped, staring straight ahead, refusing to meet his glance.

"Before what?" asked Archie quietly. "Before you marry me? Before you drop me?"

"Before I do whatever I do. And I don't know what that is going to be."

"So you don't want to marry me."

"Not tonight, Archie. I hope you weren't expecting me to."

"Nah, not tonight," he said. "Tonight was gonna be Italian food and whatever we could manage after with full stomachs and too much wine."

"It all sounds divine," she said, smiling at him ruefully. "I will make it up to you, Archie. I promise."

They drove on in silence until he pulled into the driveway of the Bainbridge town house.

"They letting you in the front, or are you sneaking around to the kitchen?" he asked.

"I don't know," she said. "There wasn't time to negotiate the terms of my surrender."

The question was answered when the front door opened and Gwen came out, waving.

"Hello, Archie," she said, leaning through the driver's door window to kiss him on the cheek. "So sorry about the date. I was looking forward to hearing Iris stop short of all the sordid details tomorrow."

"You talk about me, then?" he said, trying not to look pleased.

"Talk, break down each word for every possible meaning, plot, strategise," she said. "We women are a very analytical bunch when it comes to romance."

"I am duly warned," he said.

He got out, held the door for Iris, then removed her suitcase from the boot.

"Thanks for the lift," said Iris.

She stood on her tiptoes and kissed him as Gwen considerately looked in the other direction.

"The offer still stands, Sparks," he said.

"Thank you, Archie. It means a great deal. Good night."

He got back in the car, waved to Gwen, then backed out of the driveway and drove into the night.

"There was an offer?" asked Gwen.

"There was an offer," said Iris.

"We must dissect and examine this offer," declared Gwen as she led her into the house. "But not on an empty stomach. Have you eaten?"

"Snacked on gall, supped on wormwood."

"Oh dear, I was afraid that might be the case. Well, I'm glad to see that things were cordial between the two of you. He wasn't the source of the problem, I take it."

"No."

"Good. And here's Percival to take your suitcase."

"Good evening, Miss Sparks," said Percival, standing by the main staircase. "It is good to see you again. You will be staying in the same room as the last time, if you remember."

"That will be perfect, Percival, thank you," said Iris. "You are looking fit, I must say."

"The resumption of my boxing regimen has proved a boon to my physique," he said proudly.

"Percival has been giving the boys lessons," said Gwen.

"How are they doing?"

"Improving daily," said Percival. "One thing you should know, Miss Sparks."

"Yes?"

"You won't be the only person in the guest wing. We put His Lordship there so that he could be isolated from the rest of the household while he is convalescing. We would ask of you the courtesy of quiet while you are there."

"I will be a veritable mouse, Percival," promised Iris.

"Mice squeak, Miss Sparks," said Percival.

"Then I will be—Heavens, I have no idea what creature would be quieter than a mouse. A squid, perhaps? Whatever it is, I will be that creature."

"Very good, Miss Sparks. I believe Prudence has set out a light repast for you in the kitchen. Enjoy the rest of your evening."

"Thank you, Percival."

The two walked through the hall.

"I should pay my respects to Lady Bainbridge," said Iris.

"She's usually in the library this time of evening," said Gwen.

She stopped and rapped lightly on the door.

"Come in," called Lady Bainbridge.

Gwen opened the door and leaned in.

"Iris Sparks is here, Carolyne," she said. "She would like to say hello."

"By all means," said Lady Bainbridge.

She rose from her seat and came forward as Iris followed Gwen into the library. Lady Bainbridge was dressed simply for an evening at home, wearing a light blue muslin blouse over a tweed skirt. A half-empty glass of sherry and a small, crystal dish of glacé cherries sat by an open book on the small table by the fireplace.

"I hope I'm not interrupting," said Iris, shaking her hand. "I wanted to thank you for putting me up."

"Not at all," said Lady Bainbridge. "It's good to have another woman here for reinforcement. Between Ronnie and John tearing through the house reenacting every battle of the war and Harold's constant demands, I feel like we're under siege, only from the inside. This room has become my refuge. I come here for the quiet. And the sherry. Would you care for a glass?"

"Maybe later, thanks," said Iris. "I'm en route to the kitchen. How goes Lord Bainbridge's recovery?"

"Slowly and petulantly," said Lady Bainbridge. "It's like having another child, only not quite so adorable. He wants to be waited on hand and foot."

"At least his demands are confined to one room, Carolyne," said Gwen, patting her mother-in-law's hand. "Think what it will be like when he's up and about stomping through the place again. Misery will run rampant!"

"I never thought I would be grateful for someone's heart attack," said Lady Bainbridge. "Uncharitable of me, but there it is. Well, I don't want to keep you from your dinner, Miss Sparks. Stop by later. We promised each other a good old-fashioned whisky binge, and we still haven't done it."

"Not with work waiting for me in the morning," said Iris reluctantly. "I'll have one glass with you later, and save the binge for some weekend evening."

"I will hold you to that," said Lady Bainbridge, pointing a finger at her.

Prudence was not in the kitchen when they arrived, but a plate of cold chicken and pickles sat on the table.

"Water or something stronger?" asked Gwen.

"Water, please," said Iris. "I'd be presuming on your generosity to ask for anything more. Besides, I have Lady Bainbridge to keep up with later."

"No one can keep up with Carolyne, I'm afraid," said Gwen as she poured Iris a glass.

"Has it been very awful? I thought she seemed all right just now."

"It's still early," said Gwen as they sat down at the table. "That was only her first sherry. There will be more, followed by a whisky chaser. And there was wine at dinner. Percival has helped her up the stairs more than a few times lately."

"It must be hard, having John around as a constant reminder of how Harold betrayed her."

"The remarkable thing is that she and John quite like each

other," said Gwen. "That surprised me. But she doesn't blame John for being who he is, and I think she likes having him around to let Harold know that she has the upper hand in the morals game."

"And you get to watch it all from the sidelines."

"The middle of the scrum, more often than not," said Gwen.

"How is John settling in?"

"It's been difficult," said Gwen. "Understandably. Losing his mother at such a young age, being transplanted from one continent to another, and then being thrust into this house where most of the staff don't know why he's here or how to treat him."

"The story about him being Lord Bainbridge's charity project isn't holding up?"

"It is with the outside world, but the household staff is suspicious. Percival knows the truth, of course, but he is the soul of discretion. Still, it's been hard. John cries at night. Ronnie wanted to have them room together, bless him, but—"

"But what?"

"But Harold asserted himself, weak heart and all. 'The boy must have his own room,' he declared. 'He must learn to manage his grief and get on with it like we all did.'"

"How very English of him. What about the school?"

"John's the only black child there. It would have been good if he and Ronnie had been in the same class, but John's a year older. He didn't know anyone, and some of the children—they've been despicable. Then there was the marmalade incident."

"The what?"

"We forget the everyday things, the ones that are constantly with us yet invisible. It takes someone who hasn't grown up here to see them."

"Marmalade?"

"Marmalade. Golden Shred marmalade. With the picture of Golly on the label."

"Oh dear. I forgot all about that."

"Some of the schoolchildren started calling him Golly. He didn't know what they meant. Then he was having his tea with Ronnie and he saw the label with that horrid little black caricature on it and he stared and he stared, then asked, 'What is that?' And Prudence without thinking said, 'Oh, that's just the Golly.' And he realised why those children were calling him that. I made Prudence throw it out. She protested. It was nearly a full jar. As if that mattered more."

"At least Ronnie likes him."

"Ronnie adores him. He sees him as the brother he never had. He's even learning Chitumbuka from him. He thinks it's a secret language, and he can't wait for Simon to visit so he can show it off. Do you know who else speaks it around here?"

"Harold?"

"Of course, Harold. One of his smattering of African languages. He has the boys come and visit every afternoon after school, and they chat away."

"What do they talk about?"

"Who knows? It's an exclusive boys club. Of course, that drives Carolyne mad, too."

"How about with you? Has he become a second son yet?"

Anguish flashed across Gwen's face.

"What?" asked Iris.

"I want to say yes," said Gwen. "But he was raised by his mother, and now she's gone. I can't possibly replace her, and—he's not my son, Iris. I didn't bring him into the world, and I didn't bring him here. He's been thrust upon me in a house where the lord and master doesn't want me to be a mother to my own son; and all of a sudden I'm expected to step up for someone else's, all while I'm trying to take control of my life so I can move out of here with Ronnie. Ronnie wants to be brothers with John, and if I become the one who separates them, I don't know what will happen to Ronnie and me. I want to leave here, Iris. I want to get out from under the thumb of the Bainbridges, and John has become another hurdle to overcome. It's not his fault, he's a seven-year-old boy, but every time I see him, this runs through my head."

"All these complications, and now I've crashed into them. Sorry."

"It makes me envy you, sometimes, living on your own."

"My situation is not as enviable as you think," said Iris.

"Right, we should be talking about that. What happened tonight?"

"Where do I start?" said Iris, leaning back and staring at the ceiling. "Remember when you suspected me of carrying on with a married man?"

"Yes. You broke it off in June, you said, but there wasn't much else."

"There was more. Much more. It started during the war, when I was doing the things I can't talk about for the men who can't be named."

"Including the one I met. The Brigadier, you called him. He wasn't the one, was he?"

"God, no," said Iris with a shudder. "It was someone else, and yes, he was married. And had money. Have you ever wondered how I could afford a flat in Marylebone on my own?"

"I had guessed it was something along those lines."

"I'm amazed at times at how much you tolerate me," said Iris.

"Likewise. You're with the crazy lady, remember? So: married man, long-term affair, complete with rented love nest, and then?"

"As you said, I broke it off in June and segued almost immediately into dating Archie. Then tonight I walk into my flat to find the ex sitting on my sofa like he owns the place. Well, like he rents the place. Which, unfortunately, he does."

"He came back for you?"

"That's the thing—I don't think he did. He said he needed to lie low, and any more of what he said goes straight into classified territory."

"I am going to have to join the Secret Service if we're ever to have a complete conversation. Are you saying the gentleman is also a spy?"

"I will neither confirm nor deny that he is a spy. I have my doubts as to whether he's a gentleman. But there he was, staking his claim to my flat. Words were exchanged, then in walks Archie."

"And I thought I was in the middle of a scrum. Was violence threatened?"

"Yes. Mostly by me. And what with Andrew—"

"Ah! A name at last."

"It does make the narrative easier. Andrew is staying in my flat, so I now need to be anywhere but in my flat."

"And the offer from Archie?"

"Was to stay with him."

"I'm surprised you didn't take him up on it."

"So am I, to tell you the truth. It's not as if I have taken great pains to maintain my reputation—"

"You have kept your relationship out of the public eye."

"Yes, although all the gangs know about me."

"About both of us by now," said Gwen. "Word travels fast in the underworld. And we thought Mayfair was a gossipy place."

She got up, collected the dishes, and washed them in the sink.

"Andrew and Archie," she mused as she dried them and placed them in the rack. "All of this trouble with men, and you're still only in the A's."

"I shall career through the alphabet of love until I meet a zoologist from Zanzibar named Zoltan, then I will settle down for good," said Iris. "Just him, me, and the lower primates."

"That's not what we call children," said Gwen sternly. "Speaking of which, you should come with me to say good night to the boys. They'll be delighted."

"And Harold? Should I visit him?"

"Let me speak with him first, then we'll see."

"The last time I saw him, he ended up having a heart attack," said Iris. "I'm supposed to mend hearts, not break them. I should confine myself to the office. I've become a curse everywhere else."

They went up to the family wing. Agnes, the governess, was coming out of Ronnie's room. She looked over to Gwen with a smile, which grew larger as she caught sight of Iris.

"Miss Sparks," she said, coming forward to shake her hand. "What a lovely surprise! Ronnie has just settled down with a book, so he should still be awake."

"What is he reading?" asked Iris.

"*The Magic Faraway Tree*," said Agnes.

"I can't say I know it."

"You are, alas, too old for it," said Agnes.

"I will never be too old for anything," said Iris.

"That's what gets you into trouble," said Gwen, knocking on Ronnie's door. She poked her head inside. "Ronnie, I have a surprise for you!"

"What is it?" piped Ronnie's voice.

"Ta-da!" she cried, opening the door to reveal Iris.

"Iris!" exclaimed Ronnie.

He was sitting up in his bed, the lamp on his nightstand, which was decorated with knights on horseback, still lit. The walls were covered with his drawings. On the dresser opposite was a framed photograph of his father, Ronald, Senior, wearing the dress uniform of the Royal Fusiliers.

"I want to hug him," Iris said to Gwen. "May I hug him?"

"You may," said Gwen.

Iris perched on the side of the bed and gathered him into her arms. He clung to her tightly.

"You are getting strong," she said, laughing. "How nice to see you."

"Have you come to stay?" he asked, his voice muffled as he buried his head against her shoulder.

"For a few nights," she said. "Just for fun. Maybe you could read to me."

"They've just got to the Land of Do-As-You-Please," he said.

"Now, that sounds like my kind of place," said Iris.

"And you have to say good night," added Gwen. "We don't want you staying up late. You have school."

"You're coming with us on Saturday," said Ronnie, finally relinquishing his hold.

"I am, and I am so looking forward to it," said Iris.

"Uncle Simon is coming!"

"So I hear."

"Have you and Mummy matched him yet?"

"We're working on it, I promise."

"All right. Good night, Iris. Good night, Mummy."

"Shall we do the double kiss?" asked Iris.

"What's that?"

Gwen came over, bent down, and kissed him on his left cheek as Iris kissed his right. Ronnie giggled with delight.

"Go to sleep, my darling boy," said Gwen, tousling his hair. "Mummy loves you."

"I love you, Mummy," said Ronnie. "And I love you, too, Iris."

Iris smiled, but didn't reply. The smile vanished as they left the room.

"What's wrong?" asked Gwen, noticing it.

"The declaration of love," said Iris. "So easy to make when you're young and have no idea what it means."

"He knows what it means," said Gwen. "They all do. We're the ones who've forgot."

She went to the room next to Ronnie's and knocked lightly.

"It's me, John," she called softly. "May I come say good night?"

"All right," said a boy from inside.

She opened the door.

"I have Miss Sparks with me," she said. "She would like to say hello. Is that all right?"

"Yes, Mrs. Bainbridge," said John.

John was a year and a month older than Ronnie. He was a light-skinned young man, his complexion somewhere near the halfway point between his late mother and Lord Bainbridge. He had much of his mother in his features, thought Iris, glancing at the small photograph of the two of them taken outside the house Harold kept in Northern Rhodesia when he visited the holdings of Bainbridge, Limited. Used to visit, she corrected herself, his travelling days having been cut short by a recalcitrant ticker.

But John had Harold in his face as well. More than enough for people to see the resemblance, maybe to make the connection between father and son without being willing to admit it. He had in particular his father's expression upon meeting people. A way of assessing them, wondering what they wanted from him, and what he could get from them in return. At the moment, he was sitting up in his bed, laying the book he was reading beside him while his eyes measured Iris.

The servants must see it, thought Iris. How could they not?

"Hello, John," she said, coming up to sit by him. "I'm staying a few nights, and I wanted to come by. What are you reading tonight?"

"*Treasure Island,*" he said, holding it up. "It's about a boy who meets some pirates."

"Sounds quite thrilling," said Iris.

"It was one of my husband's favourites," said Gwen. "This was his copy. He has his name written inside the cover."

"How delightful!" said Iris. "I hear your uncle Simon is coming in this weekend."

"Yes," said John. "Ronnie says you are finding him a wife."

"With luck," said Iris. "That's what we do for people."

"I don't want him to get married," said John.

"Why not, dear?" asked Gwen.

"Because then he won't have time for me," said John. "He's my only family here."

"That's—that's not true, dear," said Gwen. "You know we're all your family."

"I would like to finish this chapter before I go to sleep, Mrs. Bainbridge," said John. "May I?"

"Of course, dear," said Gwen, patting his hand. "Sleep well. I'll see you before Agnes takes you to school tomorrow. Good night, John."

"Good night, Mrs. Bainbridge. Good night, Miss Sparks."

He turned back to his reading before they left.

"Let me walk you to your room," said Gwen.

They didn't speak until they reached the hall with the guest rooms.

"He calls you Mrs. Bainbridge," said Iris.

"What else can he call me? I'm not his mother. I'm his half sister-in-law."

"He could call you Gwen."

"He's seven. And Ronnie doesn't call me that, so why should he?"

"It's all so formal," said Iris. "Well, here's my room."

"One moment," said Gwen.

She walked to the middle of the corridor. She paused at the door to the room. No light shined through the crack at the base of the door. She returned without knocking.

"I think Harold must have retired for the night," she whispered. "I'll leave him a note that you're staying with us. Maybe you could see him tomorrow."

"Only if he wishes to."

"Then I'm going to read for a while," said Gwen. "Will you be joining Carolyne for a nightcap?"

"The younger me would love to," said Iris. "But the older and wiser me has decided to turn in. How sad! See you in the morning."

Gwen stepped forward and gave her a quick, impulsive hug which Iris, after a moment of surprise, returned.

"I'm really glad you're here," said Gwen. "I want to sneak into the attic with a pair of torches and you and read our fortunes in the cards and stay up all night talking about boys."

"Get yourself a boy to talk about, and we will," said Iris.

"Get me my sanity back, my fortune back, my son back, and my life back," said Gwen, "then I'll take the next step."

She released Iris and suddenly began whirling about the hall, her arms out, her head back.

"Sanity, fortune, son, life!" she chanted. "Freedom! Freedom from the Bainbridges!"

"You'll wake His Lordship if you keep that up," warned Iris.

Gwen slowed to a halt, panting from the momentary effort.

"I don't know why I did that," she said, gasping. "But it felt glorious."

"You were a wonder to behold," said Iris.

Gwen gave her a brief, sad smile, then turned and walked away. Iris stood by her doorway, watching her until she turned at the end of the hallway and vanished.

But don't call upon me to testify at the sanity hearing, thought Iris as she went into her room. I'm not sure which way I'd go on that at the moment.

Gwen stopped by Ronnie's room again. Quietly, she opened the door and peeked in. His lamp was still on, but he was fast asleep, *The Magic Faraway Tree* lying next to him, still open. She eased it from his grasp, placed a bookmark where he had stopped, closed the covers, and placed it on his nightstand.

She gazed at him fondly, reaching down to brush a wayward lock of soft blond hair back from his forehead, a colour she remembered from another Ronnie whose hair also had a habit of drifting into his face. She leaned over her son and kissed him gently, then turned off the lamp and left the room.

She closed the door. John's room was next, and some empty rooms after that before hers. Rooms that she and her husband thought they would fill, once upon a time. How many children were they going to have? Four, she thought. Or was it five? Lots, in other words, and she would have been a happy Lady of Her Nest, bustling about with all the other mums and their flocks.

Instead, she was a widow of twenty-eight. Even if everything went right, would she ever be the woman she planned to be? If she found someone new, if she had more children, would it be the same? She was twenty-two when Little Ronnie was born. She would be in her thirties for the next one. If there ever was a next one. Could she give a new baby the same love she gave the first one, having been through war and loss and insanity?

She wasn't sure.

She started to walk to her room, then paused as she passed John's door.

He was crying.

He's not my son, she thought.

But he's a child, and he's crying, and I'm here.

She knocked softly on the door, then turned the handle and went in.

"Hi," she whispered.

"Mrs. Bainbridge?" he said, looking up at her through tearful eyes.

"Gwen," she said, sitting by him and pulling him into her arms. "Call me Gwen."

Iris lay in bed, staring up at the ceiling, waiting for it to fall in.

Last time I slept here, all hell was breaking loose with the Bainbridges, she thought. Tonight, it's my turn.

And Andrew is sleeping in my bed, curse him.

She made a mental note to launder the sheets immediately once she retook possession of the flat. Maybe burn them.

Thoughts of Andrew sleeping in her bed progressed quickly and easily to memories of Andrew in her bed. With her.

Not helpful, Iris, she thought. Not conducive to falling asleep, or easing your conscience over your broken date with Archie. Put Andrew out of your mind.

Which she had been doing. Successfully, she thought, especially the last few weeks. He hadn't popped into her daydreams once, and her times with Archie were fully focused on Archie.

Yet all Andrew had to do was show up, and now her bloody brain refused to do anything but summon up their torrid history together.

"So you're going to improve my German, are you?" he asked when they were introduced.

"Yes, Captain Sutton," she replied. "I'll handle the German, and Lieutenant Waleski the Polish."

"Dobry wieczór, Kapitanie Sutton," said Waleski, saluting him with his left hand.

"Dobry wieczór, Poruczniku," replied Sutton. "What happened to your right arm?"

"Paralysed, courtesy of the Luftwaffe," said Waleski. "Where did you learn Polish, sir?"

"I had some ambitions to become a concert pianist when I was younger," said Sutton. "I studied with Michalowski at the Warsaw Conservatory. Know him?"

"I was a mechanic in Poznan who learned to fly planes," said Waleski. "Now I can do neither. You sound like an Englishman who studied piano in Warsaw. I don't know your piano teacher, and I don't care."

"Fair enough," said Sutton. "Do you like music, Lieutenant Sparks?"

"Sie könnten für mich bevor Ihre Abreise spielen, Kapitän," *she said.*

"Berlin?" he guessed.

"Ja, Kapitän."

"Well, I place myself in your hands, Lieutenants. Turn me into a native."

They drilled him intensively for weeks, surprising him with questions, screaming at him, flirting with him, until his responses were automatic and easy. One afternoon, while Waleski was elsewhere, Andrew, or Andrzej as they now were calling him, looked at her across the table in the small room they were using.

"I heard you were supposed to go over," he said quietly. "Then something went wrong."

"I failed parachute training," she said lightly.

"Usually that means splat," he said.

"Not quite. Broke an ankle."

"You don't limp."

"Not anymore," she said.

"But," he prompted.

"But if you ever try to put me on a plane, I'll claw your eyes out."

"I won't ever do that."

She rested her chin between her palms, her elbows on the table, contemplating his face.

"I heard you were going over," she said.

"I passed parachute training," he said. "And my Polish and German have been ruled acceptable. Danke."

"Bitte. *How soon?"*

"Soon," he said.

"How do you feel?"

"Most of us don't come back from these missions."

"I know," she said.

"I'm scared, of course."

"I know."

"*Particularly of not seeing you again.*"

"*I know,*" she said. "*Which is why I asked Waleski to take today off. Let's go, Andrzej.*"

"*Where to, Sparks?*"

"*My place. I told you I wanted you to play for me before you went.*"

"*You have a piano?*"

She smiled.

"*Who said anything about a piano?*" she asked.

Bemused, he followed her.

It was one night, one intense parting gift from her to him, a reward for his courage, penance for her failure. Then he went over. Occupied Poland was his destination. He made contact with a network of Polish informants and relayed what they knew. She became one of his handlers on their irregularly scheduled radio contacts, and she lived for those brief moments of hearing his voice through the static, his German impeccable.

Then the contacts ceased.

They gave him up for dead. It was late in 1943, and when they closed his file, Iris went out with Waleski and drank to his memory.

So when he showed up, pale and thin and grinning at her door shortly after Poland was retaken, she screamed in shock, then hauled him inside, the door not even closed as they tumbled into bed.

She knew he had a wife somewhere. She didn't care. Not then. Not for a long while after that.

It was Gwen who made her realise that she should end it. Not that anything specific was said, but it was Gwen's life, her great passion for her late husband, that made Iris look at her second-hand affair with Andrew and at last find herself wanting more.

Gwen wanted more, too, thought Iris. She couldn't have what she had before, so she had to have more now to make up for what she had lost.

Freedom from the Bainbridges. With a fortune allowing her to live however she wanted.

No longer needing The Right Sort to fill in the emptiness of her current existence.

I hope you get your freedom, Gwen, she thought. Only what happens to me if you do?

CHAPTER 4

G wen was early for her appointment, the result of a more than usual amount of morning energy. She had woken early, and taken advantage of that to grab a solitary session with the heavy bag hanging in the playroom, practising the various blows and kicks she had been taught by Mr. Macaulay in her self-defence course.

No one other than Iris knew that she had named the heavy bag "Lord Harold."

She took a faster pace than her normal brisk one on her commute, so much so that poor Iris had to scamper on several occasions to keep up. Gwen slowed marginally after repeated protests from her partner, but resumed her rapid trot immediately when their paths diverged, Iris's shouted "Good luck!" trailing after her.

The office was on the third storey of a building on Elm Court. The stairs presented no obstacle whatsoever to Gwen, who had been bounding up the four flights to The Right Sort for months now, but the door to the office was locked. She glanced at her watch. It was ten minutes to nine. She looked at the sign on the door to make sure she was in the right place. Yes, there was his name: Rawlins Stronach, K.C., Attorney-at-Law. All civil and criminal matters.

From the stairwell came the sounds of someone else taking the stairs even faster than she had. Two at a time, it sounded like.

A man popped out of the stairwell into the hallway, landing on the floor as if he had been catapulted. He was sorting through his keys as he appeared, not looking up until he found the one he wanted. Then he glanced up to see her standing by the door.

"Mrs. Bainbridge?" he asked.

She nodded.

"I would apologise for keeping you waiting," he said as he brushed by her to unlock the door, "only you're early."

"Should I apologise for that?" she asked.

"It's not a fault," he said, holding the door for her. "Wait, let me get the lights. My girl's out ill and my clerk is serving papers, so I'm on my own for the moment."

He led her through a small waiting room with a pair of desks and a quartet of narrow chairs crammed into it, opening another door opposite the entry.

"More light," he said, hitting the switches, then striding across to draw back the curtains. "Sit, please. I'll be with you in a moment."

Brown accordion files were precariously stacked on every available surface: desk, windowsills, sheet metal cabinets whose drawers could not be closed, stuffed as they were. On a coat-tree in the corner hung a set of silks with a white barrister's wig carelessly tossed on the top hook. He threw his derby on top of it as he passed by, then sat in his chair while swooping up a file in a practised motion.

Late forties, she guessed as he put on a pair of half spectacles. Ruddy complexion, not yet jowly but on the way. Short, wavy black hair. She suspected some grey had run into some dye along the way.

"Right," he said as he ran his eyes across the file. "Sir Geoffrey Calisher referred you."

"Yes."

"You wish to petition the Master of Lunacy for a change in your status."

"Yes."

"How did you end up being judged a lunatic, Mrs. Bainbridge?"

"I don't like that term," she said.

"It could have been worse," he said. "They used to call people like you feebleminded."

"My mind is anything but feeble, thank you," she said. "I accept 'lunatic' with honours."

"Then we'll stay with that," he said. "You were so adjudged on the seventeenth of March 1944, and sent to an asylum. Why? What was the precipitating event?"

"My husband was killed in battle."

"Many women's husbands were killed in battle," he said, looking over his spectacles at her. "Those women didn't crack when they lost them. What made yours so special?"

"Because this one was mine!" she said hotly. "Maybe I loved him more."

He leaned back in his chair, appraising her.

"Good answer," he said. "Now, when you're being questioned, same answer, same passion, less volume."

She stared at him, wrestling with her fury.

"You were testing me," she said finally.

"Yes."

"You could have told me."

"It wouldn't have been much of a test if I had, would it?"

"Was that necessary?"

"You are retaining my services for representation in court, Mrs. Bainbridge," he said. "Things may go easily, but then again, they may not. My job is to prepare you for all contingencies. I like to know from the outset if a client is capable of being an adequate witness on her own behalf, especially given her unreliable past history."

"I see. Will there be more tests?"

"Why would I tell you? When were you and the late Mr. Bainbridge—"

"Captain Bainbridge, please."

"Even better," he said, scribbling it down. "When were you married?"

"The third of June 1939."

"And when and where did Captain Bainbridge give his life for king and country?"

"The third of March 1944. Monte Cassino."

"When did you learn of his death?"

"The tenth of that month."

"And do you remember what happened immediately after?"

"I—I," she said, stammering. She swallowed hard. "I don't have a coherent memory of it. I remember screams—first my own, then of the servants."

"Why were the servants screaming?"

"I was told later, much later, that I tried to kill myself."

"By what method?"

"By stabbing myself in the heart. It turns out that I was not an effective suicide."

"Fortunately, for all concerned."

"Yes. Lucky me."

"We'll have no answers like that," he said, giving her a sharp glance. "No bitterness, no sarcasm."

"Are those marks of insanity, Mr. Stronach? Because I know many bitter and sarcastic people freely wandering the upper echelons of London society."

"We'll get to them in due course, Mrs. Bainbridge, but unfortunately there is a backlog in the courts," he said. "Continuing on. There was another suicide attempt while you were institutionalised?"

"Yes. I tried to hang myself with a bedsheet. I got closer that time."

"What prompted you to do that?"

"I learned that my husband's parents had taken legal custody of our son. I was still—fragile, I could call it."

"As good a word as any."

"No comments on other mothers losing custody of their children and why is mine special?"

"All children are special to their mothers, Mrs. Bainbridge," he said. "It would have been questionable if you hadn't reacted to that news."

"Well done me, then."

"Is your reason for petitioning the court for the change in status so you can regain custody of your son?"

"Primarily that."

"Secondarily?"

She hesitated.

"Go on," he said. "Say it."

"I would like to regain control of my finances," she said.

"Which are substantial," he said.

"They are. My husband was part of a wealthy family and left his share to me. It has been managed on my behalf by my guardian—"

"Committee is the proper legal term," he said.

"Committee, yes. That word never sounds right when it involves only one man."

"Nevertheless, it's the person to whom the Master of Lunacy committed your property and finances while you were deemed incapable of managing them for yourself. Your committee is Oliver Parson."

"Yes," she said in what she hoped was a measured tone.

"You don't like him," he commented, picking up on it immediately.

"No," said Mrs. Bainbridge. "He alternates between brusque and condescending in our dealings, except when he manages to be both."

"I myself have often been described in that manner," said Stronach.

"No," she said, considering him. "You're not condescending."

A quick, appreciative smile flashed across his face.

"Well, at least Mr. Parson has approved my fee," he said. "So you wish to be rich. Secondarily."

"I am rich," she said. "I wish to have access to my wealth. Is it crass to want that?"

"Greed is fine," he said. "It's considered a perfectly acceptable desire in the Courts of Lunacy. Rejection of a fortune would be regarded as insane."

"Jesus would not fare well in those courts."

"He would not," agreed Stronach. "For many reasons. Very well. Do you understand that the issue of the custody of the child will not be part of these proceedings?"

"Why not?"

"Separate jurisdiction. It would be routine once you've been restored to normality with control of your finances for the subsequent restoration of custody to be granted, assuming the sole ground for revoking it in the first place had been the lunacy adjudication. We'll petition for that when we resolve the lunacy case in your favour."

"How long will this take?"

"Have you any upcoming event that requires a deadline?"

"Hard to say," she said. "I persuaded my in-laws to keep Ronnie—that's my son, by the way."

"I know."

"To keep him in school locally for this term. My father-in-law wanted to send him away to a boarding school that was part of an antiquated family tradition."

"Impressive that you prevailed. So you're concerned about the spring term? Or autumn of 1947?"

"Both," she said. "Each day is a new fight. It's wearing me down, to be frank. I would rather have started this application during the summer, but my psychiatrist felt I wasn't ready yet."

"Then you weren't," said Stronach. "No point in doing anything during the summer, anyhow. The Vacation Court was in session, and they would simply have deferred the matter to the resumption of Lunacy Court. Let's get back to your case. Your initial suicide attempt allowed your in-laws to petition to have you declared a lunatic. They did so as your nearest relatives, yet you have a mother and an older brother, correct?"

"I do," she said.

"Why didn't they get involved?"

"My brother, Thurmond, was serving with the Royal Navy in the Pacific. But I doubt that he would have stepped into the fray had he known."

"Why not?"

"Let's just say that he and I have not had the best of relations, and it became considerably worse when our father died and he inherited the estate. He said to me shortly after, 'You married your fortune. I'll be keeping this one.' And there hasn't been so much as a letter exchanged since, not even after he was demobbed. I heard he was completely content with leaving me in the sanatorium once he found out."

"And your mother?"

"Dependent on Thurmond now, thanks to the entailment. She didn't want to rock the boat, especially given that the only way she could see her grandson was by permission of my in-laws."

"Lovely," he said, grimacing. "So you were in for half a year or so."

"Yes. It was fairly awful."

"It could have been worse."

"How so?"

"You could have been poor. You at least were treated in a private facility with decent care."

"True enough," she said, looking down at her lap where her hands were folded but clenched so tightly that they were white.

"You were released at the behest of your doctors," he said, consulting his notes. "Not because of any outside intervention. That's a positive."

"I like to think it was because of the progress I had made," she said, "but I suspect it was because there were soldiers returning from the war with combat neurosis, and they wanted to free up the room."

"And you've been living with your in-laws ever since."

"I have to. My son is there."

"You've continued with psychiatric treatment?"

"Yes. My doctor is Edwin Milford."

"I know him. Excellent man. How has that worked out for you?"

"It took me a long time to come to trust him, but I have. He's been very helpful."

"Good to hear. Medications?"

"Veronal. I've been weaning myself from it. Slowly."

"No more suicide attempts?"

"None."

"Thought about it?"

"Initially. When I was released, and the custody and living situations were so overwhelming. But not for over a year now."

"What about violence towards others? Any thoughts or tendencies in that direction?"

She didn't answer. He looked up from his notepad.

"Mrs. Bainbridge, is there something you wish to tell me?" he asked.

"This conversation is completely confidential, correct?" she responded.

"Attorney-client privilege applies," he said. "But this is a question that could come up in the courtroom. If there is any response to that question other than no, then I need to hear it now."

"Yes, of course you do," she said. "Violence towards others. Does justifiable violence count?"

"That depends on who's doing the justifying," he said wryly.

"This will sound strange," she said.

"Mrs. Bainbridge, I have been in this practise for twenty-three years. There is nothing that you can say that would shock me."

"Very well. Several weeks ago, I was in a car with my father-in-law, and we were waylaid."

"Waylaid? How so?"

"Swarmed by men with guns. I'm afraid I assaulted one of them."

"Assaulted? You attacked a man with a gun?"

"Well, I saw an opening—"

"You attacked a man with a gun?" he repeated, looking at her incredulously.

"Yes."

"And was this—attack, as you call it, successful?"

"Not entirely," she said. "Although I got close, I must say. Then things became—complicated."

"I'm sure they did," said Stronach. "Do you have police reports to validate this incident?"

"I'm afraid not," she said. "We had to keep things quiet."

"Why on earth was that?"

"Family complications. But I assure you, it was entirely in self-defence."

"Your assurance does not assure me, Mrs. Bainbridge. Would your father-in-law be a witness to this?"

"He is presently indisposed, I'm afraid. In convalescence, recovering from a heart attack."

"Relating to this incident?"

"Not directly. It's— Oh dear, it would take hours to explain it properly, and I'm really not at liberty—"

"And that's the only time that you've been violent?"

"Yes," she said, then she hesitated.

"There's something more?" he asked.

"Do threats of violence matter?" she asked in a small voice.

"I'm afraid they do. Have there been any such threats?"

"I may have—"

"'May have,' Mrs. Bainbridge? Please be definite."

"I threatened a man," she said.

"How?"

"Verbally."

"Well, I suppose—"

"And with a gun."

"What?" he exclaimed.

"Well, he had been using it to threaten us, so it seemed only fair!" she said indignantly.

"And this was when?"

"July."

"And did this have anything to do with the men who waylaid you?"

"Oh, no," she said. "This was a completely separate investigation."

"Investigation? What were you investigating?"

"I really can't tell you much about it," she said, practically in tears. "There are confidences and matters of state!"

"Matters of state?"

"It's all been hushed up, you see," she said, her words pouring out in a torrent. "Because of the involvement of Scotland Yard and—I'm sorry, are you by any chance a signatory to the Official Secrets Act?"

"Good Lord! Why would I need to be?"

"Because British Intelligence and, and, and—and the royal family were involved."

"The king? The king knows about this?"

"Well, I don't know for sure," she said, considering the question. "I'd like to think the queen would have told him—"

"The queen?"

"But you never know how much real conversation happens in a marriage, do you?"

"And I suppose the royal family can give you references for all this."

"I could write them, I guess," she said. "I don't like to trouble them about such matters."

"To be sure," he said. "How is it that you've managed to get caught up in these bizarre situations?"

"They somehow keep finding us," she said.

"Us? You and who else?"

"Miss Iris Sparks," she said. "My partner at The Right Sort."

"Has she ever been committed to an asylum?"

"Not yet," said Mrs. Bainbridge. "Look, I know this must all sound quite—"

"Insane, Mrs. Bainbridge?"

"Strange, please? I know it's not the usual experience one has in life, but ever since the first murder—"

"Murder now?"

"Yes, perhaps I should have brought that up earlier," said Mrs. Bainbridge. "But you were asking me about my own acts of violence—"

"You said 'first murder,'" he said. "Have there been others?"

"We've investigated—"

"By 'we,' you mean Miss Sparks and yourself?"

"Yes. So there have been four to date."

"Four."

"Yes."

"Four separate murders."

"Yes. That sounds like rather a lot when I say it out loud. And let me emphasise that we didn't commit any of them. We only helped catch those responsible."

"The Yard must be very grateful."

"They were resentful at first, I must admit," she said. "But I think they're coming round. In fact, you should call Detective Superintendent Philip Parham of the Homicide and Serious Crime Command. He could verify much of this."

He sat silently for a slow count of twenty, looking at his notes while rubbing the bridge of his nose between his thumb and forefinger.

"Mrs. Bainbridge," he said finally, "I told you before that there was nothing you could say that would shock me. I stand corrected. This is odd. Very odd indeed. At the moment, I'm ready to have you recommitted myself."

"Mr. Stronach, you must see that it is my circumstances that have taken an insane turn, not I," she said. "I beg you, please call Mr. Parham for a start. Call Iris. If you aren't certain about my mental competence after speaking with them, then you can refuse my case. I'm not making any of this up. In fact, the first case was reported in the newspapers with Iris and me prominently mentioned. That should give you some confidence, if nothing else."

"I don't rely upon the press for evidence of sanity in the world," he said. "If anything, they provide constant proof that the world has gone mad."

"Please," she began.

He held up a hand to stop her.

"However," he said, "I don't find your reactions to what has happened to you to be beyond the realm of retrievability. Those who haven't cracked under the weight of recent events aren't sane. They're oblivious. I will give Detective Superintendent Parham a call, but I anticipate he will answer in your favour. So I will take your case, Mrs. Bainbridge."

"Thank you," she said, making no effort to stop the tears.

"Now, we need two doctors to assess you and provide favourable opinions to the Master of Lunacy," he said. "That may be difficult in light of these revelations."

"Dr. Milford knows about all of the investigations, and still thinks I'm ready," she said.

"Very well. Speak to him about testifying," he said, jotting down some names and numbers on an index card and handing it to her. "Here are some others I've worked with. See them at your convenience. Once we have the reports in hand, we'll file the petition and schedule your court appearance."

"I will get right on that," she said.

"One more thing."

"Yes?"

He looked at her so seriously that she trembled for a moment.

"There is to be no more of this investigation nonsense," he instructed her sternly. "No matter how well-meaning it was, no matter how necessary you thought it to be, it presents to the outside world behaviour that is, to put it mildly, aberrant. You won't be helping your case if you continue."

"I won't," she promised quickly. "Fortunately, there are currently no such matters that require my attentions, and I doubt that there will be."

"Don't go looking for any," he cautioned her as he rose and came around the desk to shake her hand. "I will have my clerk type up the contract and put it in the afternoon post. I look forward to restoring you to normality, Mrs. Bainbridge."

"I look forward to finding out what that is, Mr. Stronach," she replied.

Iris glanced up as Gwen came through the door.

"Welcome to The Right Sort Marriage Bureau," she chirped. "What size husband are you looking for?"

"One large enough to carry me for the rest of my days," said Gwen as she unpinned her hat.

"I know one," said Iris.

"Stop," said Gwen wearily. "It's been a long morning."

"That bad?"

"Did you know that doing good is considered a symptom of insanity?" responded Gwen.

"At last, all of my evil impulses have been validated," said Iris. "What do-gooding are you referring to?"

"Our extracurricular activities," said Gwen. "The attorney is of the opinion that crime solving is not normal behaviour for people in our position."

"He is not wrong," said Iris. "Is this going to be a major problem?"

"I hope not," said Gwen. "I'm afraid I raised his eyebrows practically to his hairline. He may be calling you for verification of our adventures."

"What do you want me to tell him?" asked Iris.

"The truth, naturally."

"The whole truth? Are you sure about that? I could slap a few coats of varnish on it before we show it to the public."

"No, no, that will only make things worse," said Gwen. "I did suggest that he call Parham first."

"Good," said Iris. "Parham almost likes us now. Unlike a certain former fiancé and current detective sergeant working for him."

"Mike hasn't forgiven you yet?" asked Gwen. "Even after getting married?"

"There were things that happened that are not easily forgiven," said Iris. "I don't blame him. We've moved on. Let him live his life undisturbed, or as undisturbed as a homicide detective can live. Why is investigating murders considered a sane activity when you choose to go into it professionally?"

"Beats me," said Gwen. "In any case, my investigatory proclivities shall be a thing of the past. I will walk a narrow path from now until my fortunes are restored."

"And then we'll have a right old bash to celebrate, won't we?" said Iris with a grin.

"Oh, yes," said Gwen. "We certainly will."

They worked through the rest of the day.

"Coming straight back with me?" asked Gwen as they got ready to leave.

"I want to swing by my flat first," said Iris. "There were one or two items I left behind in my haste to flee the scene."

"Would you like me to come with you?"

"No, no. Go home, attend to your son. I should be half an hour behind you."

"Are you allowing for eluding your shadow along the way?"

"Blast, I forgot about her," said Iris. "Make it forty minutes, then. See you at dinner!"

This time Sparks turned right out the front door, venturing a few blocks south before looping back. No hairs prickled on the back of her neck this time, nor did any suspicious silhouettes dart away from her peripheral view.

Nevertheless, she took more than the necessary cautions, this time using a department store's loading dock to accomplish her latest disappearing act. By the time she reached Marylebone, she was confident that she had made the trip unaccompanied. She reached into her bag for her keys.

"Miss Sparks?" came a woman's voice from behind her. "May I have a moment of your time?"

She spun to see Helena Jablonska standing there.

This was not the hopeful then distraught visitor of the previous morning, thought Sparks. This was a woman who was coolly assessing a potential adversary.

As I am now doing with her, she thought.

"I don't usually let myself get followed," said Sparks.

"I don't usually lose people when I follow them," returned Jablonska.

"That was you yesterday afternoon?"

"Yes. You were very good. That's how I knew you had to be working with British Intelligence."

"So we're one even," said Sparks. "Your English has improved considerably since our first conversation. Who do you work for?"

"I'm looking for Andrew," said Jablonska.

"Who?"

"Andrew. Major Andrew Sutton," said Jablonska. "He told me about you. He said, 'Find Iris Sparks. She will help you.'"

"I don't know any Andrew or why anyone would think I will help anyone other than finding them a match for a five-pound fee," said Sparks. "I may have done some work along your lines for a few years during the war, but I was demobbed over a year ago and I haven't looked back. I think you had better go peddle your story to someone who's actually buying."

To her surprise, Jablonska abruptly burst into tears, immediately turning away from her and grabbing a handkerchief from her coat pocket.

"Really?" said Sparks in exasperation. "Do you actually think that sort of thing would work on someone like me?"

"Shut up," said Jablonska, wiping her eyes furiously. "Just shut up for a minute. God, it comes out of nowhere."

"What are you talking about?"

"You think it's all under control," sobbed Jablonska. "You tail the target successfully, you plan every word you were going to say, and then this stupid, stupid thing inside of you flutters and your emotions—I must look so unprofessional to you."

"The baby," said Sparks in wonderment. "You're talking about the baby. It's not a subterfuge. It's real."

"It's real," said Jablonska, the tears subsiding at last. "It's real. And it's Andrew's."

Boom, thought Sparks.

CHAPTER 5

W hat did this man Andrew tell you about me?" asked Sparks.
"Why do you keep pretending you don't know him?"
replied Jablonska. "Aren't we past that game?"

"Who do you work for?" asked Sparks.

Jablonska didn't answer.

"Fine," said Sparks, turning to go inside.

Jablonska grabbed her left arm. Sparks spun towards her, pulling
her arm down and to her side to break the other woman's grip, ready
to strike with her right. Jablonska was already on the move, stepping
back to slip the blow.

Sparks stopped short and pulled away, relaxing her hand and
letting it go palm up.

"Sorry," she said. "I've never struck a pregnant woman. I'm not
about to start."

"You wouldn't have struck this one," retorted Jablonska.

"I am not taking that bait," said Sparks. "Have you had anything to eat this afternoon, or have you been watching the office
the whole time?"

"I had an apple."

"That's all?" said Sparks. "And you're eating for two. Let's get some tea and talk things over. There's a decent shop two blocks from here."

Jablonska looked at her, then slowly nodded.

"You wouldn't rather go somewhere private to talk?" she asked.

"If you think for one second I'm letting you into my flat after this, you're mad," said Sparks. "Besides, I don't have enough food. This way."

They walked to the corner. As they passed a telephone box, Sparks stopped.

"Hang on," she said, stepping into it and closing the door.

Jablonska watched warily as she dialled a number. Sparks turned so that the other woman couldn't read her lips.

"Bainbridge residence," answered Percival after the third ring.

"Percival, it's Iris Sparks. Something has come up and I won't be joining you for supper. Would you please let Mrs. Bainbridge know?"

"I will, Miss Sparks," said Percival. "Is everything all right?"

"Everything is not all right," she replied. "But I am in no immediate danger for a change, so don't worry anyone. I will see you later."

"Very well, Miss Sparks."

She hung up, then came back out.

"I had to break a date, thanks to you," she said. "I'm not planning on treating you, so I hope you're able to pay for your own tea."

"I can pay," said Jablonska.

It was five thirty when the two women walked through the gold and white entrance of a J. Lyons at the corner of Bulstrode and Thayer. High tea was in progress. Jablonska eyed the plates of sandwiches and cakes greedily.

"It's self-serve at this one," said Sparks as she grabbed a tray. "No Nippies anymore."

"Nippies?" asked Jablonska as she trailed her.

"That's the name for the waitresses in J. Lyons," said Sparks. "You used to see them all over, but now they're mostly in the big corner shops. Black uniforms with double columns of pearl buttons down the front, white collars, caps, and aprons. They used to say more men married Nippies than they did anyone else. Get a well-mannered woman who already knows how to serve, and you have the makings of a reliable housewife. I suppose that made some kind of sense. Do they have anything like that where you're from?"

"Where I'm from, we barely have food," said Jablonska, placing a sandwich and a bun with margarine on her plate. "Why are they called Nippies?"

"Because they nipped about, I suppose," said Sparks. "I hope that's the reason. They used to call them Gladyses before that."

"Why Gladyses?"

"I guess it sounded like a waitress's name," said Sparks as they paid the cashier and found a free table. "Who knows why? What's in a name? Is yours really Helena Jablonska?"

"Is yours really Iris Sparks?" asked Jablonska.

"It is, in fact," said Sparks as she bit into her sandwich. "But it's been other things at times."

"My name is Helena Jablonska."

"And the late Jerzy? Did he exist?"

"He was my brother," she said. "Everything I told you about him was true."

"Except for him being married to you, of course," said Sparks. "Sorry for your loss. Smart of you to use him for your cover. He would have checked out as legitimate, and there would have been no way for us to track down his records in Poland to see if the marriage was real or not. Who do you work for?"

"No one," said Jablonska. "Not anymore."

"Who did you work for?"

"How much do you know about what Andrew did during the war?"

"Assume nothing. Assume I don't know Andrew. Assume that the only way I'm going to help you is if you level with me."

"'Level'?"

"If you tell me the truth," Sparks explained. "Keep things on the level."

She quickly mimed it with her right forearm coming to a horizontal line in front of her.

"Level," repeated Jablonska. "I must remember that. The truth. Andrew, or Andrzej as I knew him first, made contact with us in August of 1943. I was a forced labourer in a factory in Mielec, but also working for the underground of *Armia Krajowa,* sending them intelligence, falsifying factory records so we could divert supplies to them. Then a group of us were transferred to the V-2 testing site at Blizna after Peenemünde was bombed."

Blizna was part of Andrew's mission, remembered Sparks.

"Andrzej collected the information we obtained on the V-2 launchings and on German troop movements. He had a radio he kept buried in the forest, moving it after each transmission. We took turns sheltering him, bringing him food. He was—"

She stopped to wipe her eyes again.

"He was very brave, and very handsome, as I'm sure you remember," she continued.

Sparks remained expressionless.

"You became lovers," she said.

"Yes," said Jablonska. "Not right away. I couldn't let myself take the risk. But there was a mission—it went badly, and he was wounded. We kept him in a woodsman's hut. I nursed him, changed his bandages, cleaned his wounds."

His wounds. The scars on the left side of his abdomen that Sparks knew so well. The ones that made him flinch whenever she trailed her fingers over them.

"Eventually, he got stronger," said Jablonska. "Eventually, I weakened."

"Very romantic story," said Sparks. "But the war ended."

"The war ended, but Poland—it continued to be terrible there," said Jablonska. "In many ways worse. Those of us who worked with the *Armia Krajowa* have been targeted by the NKVD and the Polish puppet government. But Andrzej came back when the war ended. He called himself Andrew now, still working for British Intelligence. He sought me out."

So that's where he's been, thought Sparks.

"That still doesn't explain why you're here now," she said. "Or why you came to me."

"Because I was in danger," said Jablonska. "He couldn't bring me himself. Too risky, he said. He made arrangements. I had papers made saying I was Jerzy's wife so that I would have some claim to come to England. Andrew told me about you, said to contact you at your funny little marriage bureau—"

"Funny!" exclaimed Sparks indignantly.

"He thought it was," said Jablonska. "It does seem a strange occupation for one who has done what you did."

"What else did this Andrew tell you about me?" asked Sparks.

"That you and he had been lovers," Jablonska said simply. "That does not bother me."

"Big of you," said Sparks. "Did he tell you anything else about his life here?"

"That he has a wife."

"That doesn't bother you, either, I take it."

"It didn't bother you," said Jablonska.

"What's the plan for you now that you're here?"

"He finds a place for me. He leaves his wife. Maybe we go somewhere new. Become family together."

"Just like that."

"No," said Jablonska. "Not just like that. But after so many terrible years, I have hope at last. He gave me hope."

"Hope," said Sparks. "Powerful force when you have none. One glimmer on the horizon is all you need sometimes."

"You understand how I feel, then."

"I don't, actually," said Sparks. "I lost my hope during the war. And when it came back, it turned out to be a shabby, hollow imitation version that I finally discarded."

"You mean Andrew now."

"How far along are you, if I may ask?"

"Three months, I think," said Jablonska.

"Have you seen a doctor?"

"What are those?" asked Jablonska. "Where are they to be found? Do they treat refugees?"

"Here," said Sparks, shoving the uneaten half of her sandwich across the table. "I have no appetite, it seems. Why did he send you to me?"

"He said you were the most resourceful person he knew," said Jablonska, taking the half sandwich and devouring it as she spoke. "He said he trusted you."

"When did he say this?" asked Sparks.

"A month ago," said Jablonska. "When he told me the plan to get me out."

"After he found out you were pregnant."

"No," said Jablonska. "He still doesn't know."

"He doesn't?" exclaimed Sparks, her head jerking up. "Yet you're telling me."

"I wasn't going to, but your Mrs. Bainbridge guessed, and I knew she would tell you."

"My Mrs. Bainbridge has a knack for these things," said Sparks.

"You have to help me find Andrew," said Jablonska urgently. "He has to know. You are the only person in England who can help me. You are my last hope."

"Hope again," muttered Sparks. "The truly funny thing is that I have become a purveyor of hope, even to someone I should—"

She caught herself.

"Who you should hate?" finished Jablonska. "Maybe that's why he sent me to you. Because he knew you would do what was right even if you hated doing it."

"Maybe," said Sparks. "Well, then here it is. I don't know where he is."

Jablonska looked distraught. Sparks held up a hand to forestall further tears.

"But I may know some people who may know some people," she continued. "Give me a number where I can reach you. I'll make some calls. I won't know anything for certain until tomorrow."

Jablonska took a pencil from her bag and wrote a number on a paper napkin, then gave it to Sparks. Sparks looked at it, then folded it and tucked it inside her bag.

"What name should I ask for?"

"The one that I gave you," said Jablonska. "Thank you, Miss Sparks."

She got up from the table and walked out of the shop. Sparks toyed with the idea of tailing her, but she was tired and dispirited. And she didn't want to find out that the other woman was better at avoiding tails than she was.

She finished her tea, then left the shop and walked back to Welbeck Street. She climbed the stairs to her flat, unlocked the door, and went in.

Andrew stood in the living room, pointing a Browning semiautomatic at her. Slowly, too slowly for her liking, he lowered it.

"This is why domestic life with you wouldn't have worked," she said. "Who were you expecting?"

"No one," he replied, tucking the weapon into his waistband. "Hence the precautions. I thought you had fled to your partner's place. Have you been thrown out of there already?"

"Not in the least. But I forgot some things. I didn't bother calling because I knew you wouldn't answer."

"You could have at least used the knock."

"Use a coded knock on my own door?" she said. "All the neighbours would be wondering why. It's bad enough that I'm hiding a man in here. Have you kept yourself entertained?"

"I've been reading," he said. "Couldn't listen to the radio while you were out. You're appallingly low on food, by the way. I had to sneak out the back to shop."

"I will accept no complaints from a flat-crashing bore like you," she said, passing by him to get to the bedroom, which was now showing distinctive signs of masculine invasion. "And you didn't make the bed. Shall I send for the maid? Oh, wait—I don't have one."

"Get your things and get out," he said wearily as he followed her in. "Did you notice anyone watching the building when you came in?"

"Well, there was the woman who followed me here," she said, rummaging through her bureau for additional items of clothing.

"Don't joke," he said.

"I'm not joking. Does the name Helena Jablonska mean anything to you?"

She had positioned herself in front of the mirror so she could monitor his reaction. She was disappointed. He merely shook his head.

"Not a thing," he said. "Was that who followed you?"

"It was," she said, stuffing the clothes into a horn blue train case that sat by the bureau. "She knew a lot about you."

"Did she? I wonder how she came by that information."

Iris swept her remaining makeup and perfume bottles onto the clothes in the bag, plopped the bag on top of the bureau, then turned abruptly and slapped him hard across the face. He reeled back, more stunned than hurt.

"I didn't see that coming," he said, rubbing his cheek.

"You don't see anything coming," she said. "You just do as you please and damn the consequences. Helena Jablonska came to The Right Sort yesterday, seeking our services. We refused."

"Did you? Why?"

"Because she's pregnant, Andrew."

"Pregnant? What do you mean, she's pregnant?"

This time she saw him react, an involuntary stiffening of his jaw, no matter how hard he tried to suppress it.

"As in with child," she said. "Three months pregnant. Interesting period of time, that. Three and a half months ago, we split up and you walked out this door, and two weeks later, you're making the beast with two backs with a pretty Polish piece."

"You think she's pretty, then?"

"You do have a type, don't you?" she said bitterly. "I thought I was unique, but here comes another short brunette, damn you. Have you got one stashed in all your ports of call? Is there a Berlin *flittchen* coming to visit next week?"

"In Berlin, I've got four—one in each occupied zone, of course. What did this Jablonska woman want?"

"She, pregnant. You, father. Me, patsy."

"My, my, you do seem upset," he said. "One might almost suppose you still had feelings for me."

"I do have feelings for you, Andrew, and they are entirely negative. You came back from the war and we embarked on our torrid, tawdry, two-year affair. You've been going back and forth ever since VE Day. And the entire time you were cheating on me."

"No, the entire time I was cheating with you. Remember?"

"Then what was she?"

"Someone I knew in the war."

"I was someone you knew in the war."

"No, you weren't," he said thoughtfully. "Not really. I knew you, and the war was happening when I knew you, but you were never in it. Not like I was. And certainly not like she was."

"You heartless bastard. You don't know what I went through."

"Oh, you went through things, I'm sure," he said. "I've got an inkling of what you did, and thank you for your service."

"Don't condescend."

"Then don't compare what you did in London to what I did, or anyone did, over there. Yes, you lived through the Blitz. You had your clandestine adventures, even got your hands bloodied, I hear. But at the end of the day, so long as the sirens weren't sounding, you went home to a flat with a bed, ate your rations, and went to sleep with the absolute knowledge that the Gestapo wouldn't come barging through your door in the middle of the night to carry you off to a windowless room with fresh blood drying on the walls. You didn't wonder if each casual conversation you had was with an informer, or if the people in whose hands you placed your life would sell you out to save their own. Or if you would have to kill people you had come to care for, because you found out they were working for the other side. Or worse, kill them because you only suspected they might be, and it was too dangerous to give them the benefit of the doubt. You experienced none of that because you had one bad jump in parachute training."

"I nearly died."

"But you didn't," he said. "You could have chalked it up to bad luck, figured out what went wrong, made sure it wouldn't happen again, and got on the next plane. Instead, you let a convenient phobia stop you from becoming what you were meant to be."

"That isn't fair," Iris said softly.

"None of this is fair," he said with a shrug. "Helena lived through what I lived through, only she did it longer. By the time I showed up, she had survived being in the underground for three years. She cared for me after I was wounded. The smart thing to do would have been to kill me and bury me in the woods. But she risked her life to protect me, and nursed me back to health. Would you have done that for me, Sparks?"

"Would you have done that for her?"

"I'd like to think so," he said. "We'll never know, will we? All I can do is what I'm doing for her now."

"She is under the impression that she's going to make a life with you here."

"Maybe she will," he said, drifting over to the window and peering through the curtain.

"You'd leave your wife for her? Destroy your career?"

"There is a baby, if what you're telling me is true," he said. "That makes a difference."

"So if you and I had been more careless during our intermittent debaucheries, I might have been the lucky one to pull you away from your wife?"

"Again, we'll never know," he said, turning back to her.

"It was cruel of you, sending her to me for help," said Iris. "Why did you do that? Why me, of all people?"

"Because I did this on my own," he said. "I couldn't go to the Brigadier. I couldn't go to anyone on the inside. You're the only one I know on the outside who could help."

"And if I say no?"

"Are you saying no, Sparks?"

She folded her arms across her chest, hugging herself slightly. Then she dropped them to her sides.

"I've always had a problem saying no to you," she said. "I thought throwing you out was a step forward in my life."

"It was a step in some direction. I'm not sure that dating a gangster reflects forward movement."

"You are in no position to judge me, Andrew. At the moment, I could cheerfully shove you out that window and have a bottle of wine open to celebrate before you hit the pavement."

"I should probably move away a few paces," he said, glancing outside.

"However, there is a baby to consider, as you pointed out," she continued. "I expect you'll be a terrible father."

"Thank you."

"But the baby won't know that for a long while," she said. "So we'll give her the benefit of a good start. Perhaps she'll inherit her mother's survival instincts."

"Let's hope so."

There's that word again, she thought.

"How do you want her to make contact?" she asked. "I told her I would call her in the morning. Would you rather do that?"

"If she's expecting you to call, let's keep to that," he said.

"What shall I tell her?"

"Tell her to come here."

"All right. I'll send her over in the morning."

"And do me a favour," he said.

"I haven't done enough of them already?"

"You've done many, and if you will accept the gratitude of a lout like me, I offer it to you."

"The favour, Andrew, without the snivelling, if you don't mind."

"Quite right. The favour is make sure you have everything you need now, and give this place a wide berth for a few days."

"Putting the love nest back to use, are you?"

"Had it become an anchorite's cell since I left? Your flower-bearing spiv seemed familiar enough with the premises."

"Right," she said, scanning the room for anything else she needed. "Ah, almost forgot."

She walked to the nightstand by the head of the bed and picked up an Allingham book lying on top of it.

"Pity," he said. "I was just getting interested in that."

"Get your own books," she said irritably. "Damn you, you lost my place."

"Sorry," he said.

"That's the only thing for which you've apologised," she said. "Two days, Andrew. That's all I'm giving you. I still have a normal life. I want it back."

"You'll get it."

She stuck the book inside the train case and slammed it shut.

"And make the damn bed," she said as she walked to the front door. "You're a disgrace to the Royal Army."

"In so many ways," he said. "Good night, Sparks."

She stormed out. He locked the door behind her.

Percival opened the door as she was reaching for the bell.

"I heard the cab," he said.

"And you just happened to be waiting by the door, listening for it," she said as she crossed the threshold. "Thank you for being so considerate, Percival. It's a great thing to be considerate."

"It shouldn't have to be," he said. "Let me take your bag up to your room."

"It's not necessary. I can manage."

"It's my function, Miss Sparks," he said, holding his hand out.

"Thank you again," she said, handing the train case to him. "Where is everyone?"

"Lord Bainbridge remains sequestered," he replied. "Lady Bainbridge is having her after-dinner sherry in the library, and Mrs. Bainbridge is reading to the boys."

"Both of them?"

"Yes. It's a special treat."

"I don't want to interrupt that," said Iris. "I'll go say hello to Lady Bainbridge."

"Very good, Miss Sparks."

Iris walked down the corridor and knocked lightly on the library door.

"Come in," said Lady Bainbridge.

She looked up as Iris entered. Something in the younger woman's eyes struck her.

"I was having sherry," she said, indicating the decanter on the low table. "But I renew my offer of whisky, if you are more inclined to it this evening."

"God, yes," said Iris.

Gwen tiptoed out of John's room, having walked the very sleepy child over from Ronnie's room after she finished reading to them. She passed her mother-in-law, who was tottering towards her room.

"Good night, Carolyne," Gwen whispered.

Lady Bainbridge stopped and beckoned to her.

"Go talk to Iris," she said, the alcohol heavy on her breath. "I don't know what happened, but she's in a bad way."

Gwen immediately turned and walked to the guest wing. She paused at Iris's door to listen for a moment. To her consternation, she heard her partner sobbing from inside the room.

What is it about this house that causes so many tears? she thought. And why does it fall upon me of all people to be the source of comfort?

She had no answer, nor time to consider the question. She knocked on the door.

The crying stopped. A moment later, she heard Iris padding to the door.

"Yes?" came her voice.

"It's me," said Gwen.

"Go away," said Iris. "I can't take anyone being nice to me right now."

"Too bad," said Gwen. "Tell you what, if you open the door, I promise I'll be mean."

There was a pause, then the door opened. Iris looked up at her, the streaks from her mascara striping her cheeks.

"You look awful," said Gwen.

"That's a start," said Iris, turning and walking back into the room. "Keep going. Tell me I'm a failure and a coward and that I deserve to live a lonely life and die alone and be found half-eaten by an excessive number of cats who only pretended to love me because I fed them."

"Wait, I need to write all that down," said Gwen as Iris threw herself facedown on her bed. "What have you failed at?"

"Everything," said Iris.

"Move over," said Gwen, climbing onto the bed next to her. "What brought this on?"

"Your mother-in-law's whisky."

"And what brought that on?"

"Your mother-in-law."

"Iris, what happened when you went back to your flat tonight?"

Iris rolled to her side, casting a bleak, bleary-eyed stare in Gwen's direction.

"I can't tell you," she said. "There is so much I want to tell you, but I can't. There are entire categories of I can't tell you, plus subcategories, footnotes, and scribblings in the margins, and it all adds up to me being a failure and a coward."

"As to the second, I seem to recall that not six weeks ago, you walked alone into a roomful of armed ruffians to save me."

"There were only four of them, and I think only two were armed at the time. And I had Sally waiting in the wings. And it turned out you didn't need saving."

"Nevertheless, you didn't know any of that when you went in. I call that the opposite of cowardice."

"I call it a small, foolhardy event compared to what everyone else went through."

"Everyone?"

"Everyone I worked with."

"Iris Sparks, the war years," said Gwen, "which you can't tell me about, except that you trained as a spy—no, operative, that was the word. And then you didn't go over because you broke your ankle in parachute training."

"I told you about that?"

"It was during a previous fit of despair," said Gwen. "Don't worry, your secret is safe with me. Did this Andrew know about it? Did he throw it in your face tonight? Is that what's going on?"

"Stop being intuitive."

"I can't. It's a curse. What else happened?"

"No, no, no, no, no. I won't. It's too humiliating."

"Have you ever been tied to a bed and force-fed through a tube up your nose?"

"Please don't use your terrifying sanatorium anecdotes to minimise my pain. Let me wallow."

"Fine, wallow away," said Gwen. "But I will wake you for breakfast tomorrow morning and drag you off to work regardless. We are seeing Dr. Milford afterwards."

"Because I'm falling apart?"

"Because tomorrow is Thursday," Gwen reminded her, "and that's when we see Dr. Milford. You may unburden yourself to him of those secret categories. Until then, remember that you threw this Andrew out of your life for what I assume were very good reasons, so don't let him make you feel this way now."

"That's it?"

"That's it," she said, getting up. "Good night, darling."

"You're a terrible comfort and a terrible friend," Iris called after her.

"You're welcome," said Gwen as she closed the door behind her.

Iris buried her face back in her pillow, but the tears weren't coming this time.

Damn you, Gwen, she thought. Why can't you let a woman wallow uninterrupted?

She sighed, feeling foolish and overdramatic now. It was because she wasn't in her own bed, she thought. If she was home, she could bury her feelings by picking up the phone and calling Archie if he wasn't out looting a warehouse somewhere, or Sally if he had the funds to spare for a decent carousal.

Which she was trying to cut back on doing, she remembered.

Forgive me, Dr. Milford, for I have strayed. It has been not even one day since my last drunken binge. All it took was my ex cheating on me.

She could smell her own breath, the whisky turning stale. She grabbed her toothbrush, tooth powder, and a hand towel and walked into the corridor down to the loo.

Which was occupied, as it turned out. She waited patiently. There was a flush, followed by the sound of running water in the sink. Then the door opened and Lord Bainbridge emerged. He looked at her with barely concealed loathing.

"Good evening, Lord Bainbridge," she said.

He had never been a tall man, but now, standing in the doorway in a flannel bathrobe over a pair of light blue pyjamas and leaning on a cane, he seemed diminished, like an elderly, arthritic hound with rheumy eyes.

"I heard you were lurking about," he said. "Didn't know we were taking in strays."

"The YHA said I was too old for them," she replied. "I was devastated. How are you feeling?"

"Weak," he said. "I've never been weak before. I don't like it."

"A heart attack will do that. On the bright side, you're not dead, divorced, broke, or homeless, all of which you deserve to be."

He grimaced in response, then noticed the condition of her makeup.

"You've been crying," he observed.

"I have."

"You should wash your face."

"That was my plan, but thank you for the suggestion."

"Can't stand women who cry," he said.

"You don't like women much at all," she said.

"Not women like you."

"You're missing out. But thank you for sparing us your attentions."

"Why are you here?"

"I'm fleeing my past," she said. "Something you should know about."

"Mine lives with us now," he said, glancing down the hall.

"Well, mine is only visiting for a few days," she said. "I will be out of what's left of your hair after that. I promise I'll be more careful to avoid you while I'm here."

"No need," he said. "I'm not as fragile as I look. I can stand the sight of you, or will once you clean that mess off your face."

"Step aside, sir, and I will commence."

He moved out of her way. She walked past him, then turned.

"I am washing my face for my own purposes, not to please you," she informed him.

Then she closed the door.

He almost smiled.

She woke immediately at the light tap on the door. The sun was just beginning to come up. She put on her robe, then opened it to see Gwen standing there, wearing exercise togs.

"You can't be serious," said Iris.

"Throw something on," said Gwen. "We'll beat up Lord Harold together."

It did feel good to pummel the heavy bag, Iris thought a few minutes later. She whirled and kicked, alternating legs, each time connecting higher than the last. Gwen held the bag from the other side, grunting occasionally under the force of the kicks.

"You're almost at the level of my chin," she observed.

Iris bounced on the balls of her feet, then jumped high, spinning into an airborne kick that made Gwen flinch and reel back involuntarily.

"And that was above the level of my chin," she said. "I'm glad you're on my side."

"Likewise, partner," said Iris. "Thanks, I needed this."

"Let's wash up and get to work. I'll meet you at the foot of the steps in fifteen minutes."

Gwen came down at the appointed time. She heard Iris's voice from down the hallway where the house telephone was located. She walked in that direction.

"Fifty-one Welbeck Street," Iris was saying. "Number thirty-one. He's expecting you. He knows, by the way. Yes, I told him. If he hasn't run away by the time you get there, maybe you'll have a chance. No, don't thank me. I don't want your thanks, or anything else from you."

She hung up.

"Who on earth were you talking to?" asked Gwen.

"Someone I should hate," said Iris. "Let's go."

CHAPTER 6

Gwen came into Dr. Milford's office with a more determined expression than he was used to seeing. He waved her to the chair in front of his desk.

"You have to do something about Iris," she said immediately upon sitting. "She's spiralling rapidly downward, and she won't talk to me about it."

"I will talk to Miss Sparks when it's her time to talk to me," he said. "This is your time."

"But you'll help her?"

"I try to help everyone," he said. "At the moment, it's time to help you."

"All right," she said. "I met with the attorney yesterday."

"Ah. And what are you going to do?"

"I'm going to petition for a change in status. For the restoration of my—of my everything."

"What were you about to say?"

"Restoration of my life," she said. "But it isn't that. Not really."

"Why not?"

"Because my life isn't being restored. Too many things have happened."

"Then what is being restored? What does that word mean to you?"

"I get to be a mother again."

"You were a mother all along, Mrs. Bainbridge."

"I get to be a mother without interference from my in-laws."

"Do you really believe that their interference will cease? From your descriptions and, indeed, from what I know of your mother-in-law, they will be a constant intrusion in your son's life. He's the next Lord Bainbridge, no matter what your status is."

"Why does something that sounds so grand seem so bleak?"

"You tell me."

"You're challenging me a lot this session," she observed.

"What else is being restored, Mrs. Bainbridge?"

"My independence."

"Were you independent before this all happened?"

"Actually, no," she said, considering the question. "I lived with my family, then I married Ronnie and lived with his. I never really have been independent, have I? I shouldn't complain about it. There are plenty of people who haven't had the advantages I've had."

"Most, I should think," he said drily. "So what will you do with this newfound independence of yours?"

"I haven't really thought about it."

"Nonsense. Of course you have."

"All right. I want to move out of the Bainbridge house. I want to have my own home."

"What will your son think about that?"

"He will be upset at being uprooted, I'm sure."

"How do you feel about upsetting your son?"

"I'm his mother," she said. "I have to make the decisions. He'll have to adjust."

"Good," he said. "Nothing wrong with that. There's not a person alive who hasn't been upset by their parents during childhood. Or adulthood."

"That keeps business steady for you lot," she said.

"Don't tell anyone," he whispered, "or everyone will want in."

She laughed.

"So what's left?" he asked. "What else will be restored?"

"My sense of myself as a person, I suppose."

"Really? And what is that?"

"I'll have to find out. This lunatic label has been a constant weight since I came out of the sanatorium. I want to live without the constant stares and whispers."

"Do you think those will stop merely because a judge issues an order?"

"No, of course not," she said, looking down at her lap. "I will always be the Woman Who Cracked."

"But," he prompted her.

"But what?"

"But you don't have to be among those people," he said.

"Those are my people," she said. "Those are the people I've grown up with. To whom I'm related. I can't simply vanish from that world."

"Since you've come back from the sanatorium, how much time have you spent among those people?"

"Not much," she said. "Of course, society was shunted aside by the war."

"Yet people still socialised, and the war is over. You've been out for two years, and you've chosen not to mingle. Who are your friends currently, Mrs. Bainbridge?"

"There's Iris."

"Your business partner."

"And friend."

"Who besides her?"

"Sally, although I really only know him through Iris."

"And outside of Iris's circle? Any of your prewar set? Have you made any new friends recently?"

"I've met some very nice gangsters."

"Apart from gangsters."

"I've been busy," she said defensively. "I started up The Right Sort."

"Yes. You did," he said, leaning back in his chair.

"You say that like I did something strange," she said.

"Strange indeed," he said. "In the sense of unusual. Remarkable."

"It's just a small business," she said.

"Yet how many of your rank and, let's be frank, your sex have done anything remotely similar?"

"I know many women who did amazing things in the war," she said. "Flew planes, became doctors, journalists . . ."

"But to start a business—that's unusual," he said.

"You're being very encouraging," she said. "I'm starting to get suspicious."

"What haven't you talked about with this restoration of yours? Come on, Gwen. Be honest. What was the biggest piece of your life?"

"Ronnie," she said reluctantly. "My husband."

"Exactly."

"The reason I fell apart. And even if all the king's horses and all the king's men do their very best, that piece will never be put back."

"No. So what ultimately is being restored by this petition?"

"Nothing," she said. "It's not a restoration at all, is it? Humpty-Dumpty stays broken for life."

"Or becomes something new," he said.

"Like an omelette?"

"Let's be more optimistic," he said, leaning forward, his voice forceful. "Life isn't static. It's ever changing, and you have to adjust to each change. When you don't, there is resistance. And when there's too much resistance, things can break."

"Are you saying I should have adjusted to my husband's death? Taken it in stride and moved on?"

"I am going to ask you a question, and I don't want you to answer it today. I want you to think about it."

"That sounds terrifying. What's the question?"

"You say you fell apart when your husband died. But was it because he died?"

"I—" she began, the colour rising in her cheeks.

He held up his hand to stop her.

"Answer me next week," he said. "Work on it until then. And I want you to start reaching out to more people. Contact old friends, make new ones. See what happens. Now, let's talk about the upcoming legalities. Your attorney told you what you need."

"Yes," she replied, still flustered. "I need two doctors to assess me. You would be one, of course."

"Are you certain about that?" he asked.

"Of course," she said, puzzled. "Why wouldn't you be? You know me better than anyone."

"Did your attorney explain the legal consequences of my testifying on your behalf?"

"Not specifically."

"I have been a witness in the Courts of Lunacy many times," he said. "I am quite familiar with their procedures. For a medical expert to certify the status of a patient, he must have no financial incentive in the matter. In other words, if I am going to testify on your behalf, I would have to give up treating you."

"What?" she exclaimed. "But that's unfair!"

"It's the law," he said. "Do you want me to be one of your certifiers, knowing that?"

"I don't know," she said. "If I'm well, then I shouldn't need further treatment. But if I'm not well, then I can't prevail in the court. I'm—I don't know."

"Legal lunacy is at the extreme end of a vast human scale," he reminded her. "Continuing treatment doesn't mean you're a lunatic, Mrs. Bainbridge. It only means you need help."

"I'll have to think about this some more," she said, sighing. "This would mean convincing two other psychiatrists that I'm competent, not one. Lord, I wish the attorney had told me about that."

"I'm surprised he didn't."

"I may have thrown him off when he learned about my various adventures with Iris."

"I don't doubt it," said Dr. Milford.

"He didn't regard them as the proper pursuit of an ordered mind," she said. "He's suggested that I avoid such activities in the future."

"I happen to agree with him on that point," said Dr. Milford. "If they come up in court, the Master will be hard put to loosen your restraints."

"Then I had better keep to myself until the hearing," she said. "It's been such an odd and eventful year. I never could have imagined my life would turn out this way."

"It has been a series of unlikely occurrences," he agreed. "Fortunately, the odds are very much against anything like them happening again."

"God, I hope not," she said, shuddering.

Detective Sergeant Michael Kinsey sat at his desk in his large shared office at the Homicide and Serious Crime Command at New Scotland Yard, pecking away at his typewriter, memorialising his interview notes from witnesses to an armed robbery at a jewellery store that left a recklessly brave salesclerk in hospital with a bullet in his hip. The last witness had been a woman who apparently had been waiting her entire life for the chance to tell her story to someone, and he had taken considerable pains to separate the wheat from the copious amounts of chaff, ranging from anecdotes from her childhood to her opinions on the morality of American film stars.

He finished, unrolled the last page from the typewriter, and signed it with a flourish. He glanced at the clock. Another half hour to end of shift. He wanted to get home. Beryl had promised him something special when he got there, and she had left it ambiguous as to whether she meant dinner or something else.

He stretched in his seat, thinking either way, it would be something nice to come home to.

Godfrey came in, his camera bag slung over his shoulder. He went to his desk and opened a drawer, rummaging through it for unused rolls of film.

"Done for the day, mate?" asked Kinsey.

"No rest for the wicked," said Godfrey, grabbing his coat from the rack. "Got a murder scene. Cavendish needs prints, so there goes my evening."

"Lucky you. Who got killed?"

"Some woman," said Godfrey. "Don't know the details."

"Whereabouts?"

"Em, Marylebone somewhere, I think," said Godfrey. "Where'd I put it?"

He searched his pockets, then pulled out a scrap of paper.

"Yeah, Marylebone," he said. "Fifty-one Welbeck Street."

"Welbeck?" repeated Kinsey, his chest suddenly tight. "Did you say Fifty-one Welbeck?"

"Yeah. Why?"

"Mind if I tag along?" asked Kinsey.

"Cavendish has it. He wasn't asking for help."

"I know the location," said Kinsey, putting on his coat and hat. "I'm hoping I don't know the woman."

* * *

Gwen emerged from Dr. Milford's office looking stunned. She plopped down next to Iris and said, "You're up."

"How's he bowling?"

"Mostly fast, with the occasional spinner."

"Right," said Iris, getting to her feet. "Back in a bit."

She went through the door to his office, feeling like she was passing through a veil between dimensions, shedding layers of skin as she did so. By the time she reached the chair, she was shaking.

"What did she tell you?" she asked.

"Please sit, Miss Sparks," said Dr. Milford.

She sat in the chair, hugging herself, rocking back and forth.

"What's that all about?" he asked.

"It's chilly in here."

"It's not in the slightest," he said.

"Fine. Where should I start?"

"How old were you when you first started hugging yourself?"

She looked up, surprised by the question.

"Don't you want to know about what happened with my ex this week?" she asked.

"Yes, but we'll get to that. Answer my question, Miss Sparks."

"Why is that important?"

"Let's find out together, shall we?"

"I hate this," she said. "I hate every second of it."

"Yet here you are. I am not the cause of your self-embrace, Miss Sparks, and neither is the temperature. When did you first start doing it?"

"Last night," she said.

"No," he said. "The first time."

"Thirteen, maybe?" she said. "No. Fourteen. I was reading in bed. I remember the book was *All Passion Spent,* by Vita Sackville-West.

My mother came in without knocking, which was unlike her. She always was good about respecting my privacy. Too good, sometimes. She pulled my desk chair over to the bed, straddled it the wrong way, and leaned on the back, looking at me like I was some oddity preserved in a jar. I knew something was wrong. More wrong than usual, I should say. Things had been wrong for a while, and I couldn't—I couldn't make them right."

"Did you try to make them right?"

"I didn't know how. There were no books on how to make one's parents love each other again. Are there now?"

"It's not the job of the child to take care of the parents."

"Maybe it should be. Maybe there should be courses given early on. More useful than Latin, I should think."

"You're avoiding, Miss Sparks."

"So I am," she said. "Where did I veer off? Oh, yes. My mother straddling the chair. 'Your dad's gone,' she said. 'Gone where?' I asked. 'Gone for good,' she said. 'Well, maybe not for good. But we're done, he and I. He's moved out. So it's just you and me now. I thought I should tell you.' And with that, she got up and walked out of my room."

She stopped, drawing her knees further up in the chair, making herself smaller.

"What was the first thing that you thought when she did that?" asked Dr. Milford.

"That Daddy didn't say goodbye," she said. "He was a drunk, and a terrible businessman, but when I was a little girl, he would always give me a big hug before going off to work in the morning, and another when he came home, and one more when he came in to say good night. Now he was gone, and no one was going to hug me anymore. So I hugged myself. I was fourteen. It was a childish thing to do, I knew that. But it helped a little."

"Your mother never hugged you?"

"Not after I turned ten. She told me I had to stop acting like a child, so she was going to stop treating me like one. She was never an affectionate woman."

"So I see. And did you see your father after that?"

"Occasionally. I was handed over like a parcel one weekend a month."

"Did he hug you then?"

"Not always, and not like he used to. It was as if he had lost the knack. It never felt the same."

"You were maturing by then," Dr. Milford pointed out. "He may have felt awkward about it."

"He may have," said Iris. "But I felt absolutely miserable."

"What happened with your ex this week?"

"We're back to that now?"

"Yes. Tell me everything."

Kinsey and Sparks had parted on horrendously bad terms years before. He had caught her being unfaithful, or so he thought. He later suspected her of murder, but that he would never prove. He had driven her from his thoughts, fallen in love with and married Beryl. Married her two months ago, and was blissfully happy.

Or so he thought.

He and Godfrey were almost in Marylebone when it occurred to him that he hadn't told Parham he was going to someone else's crime scene.

Then it occurred to him that he hadn't called Beryl to say he'd be late for dinner, or for whatever she was cooking up for him.

Fifty-one Welbeck was a narrow brick Victorian-era building, four storeys and a garret. Large windows on the left bowed out from the vertical. Must be nice inside, he thought idly. There was a plaque by the entrance to the building, boasting of its history as a military hospital during the previous war and the site of the removal of Edward VII's royal appendix, which delayed his coronation for a few months in 1902. It was retired as a hospital after the

First World War, and converted into apartments for singles and young marrieds unburdened by children.

He stopped by the mailboxes as Godfrey started up the stairs. Sparks's name wasn't on 31. Somebody named Anthony Rigby. Not the name of the spiv she was seeing now, he thought. Another lover? Or just the previous tenant?

DI Cavendish was a rank above and a few years ahead of him in Homicide and Serious Crime Command. He was a solidly built chunk of a man with fine, thin blond hair that he kept slicked back with brilliantine. He was in the hallway in front of the flat, talking to Godfrey.

"The whole place—bureaus, kitchen, bath," he was saying. "I don't want a surface left clean."

"Yes, sir," said Godfrey. "I'll begin with where she was found, then work my way out from that."

"Right, better make a start," said Cavendish.

Then he saw Kinsey.

"Mike, what are you doing here?" he asked. "We picked this one up. Does Parham think we need help?"

"No," said Kinsey. "I recognised the address. I may know the victim. What have you got?"

"Female, white, mid- to late twenties," said Cavendish. "Short brunette. Rather a looker when she was alive."

Each word sank a dagger into Kinsey.

"Name?" he asked, his heart pounding.

"No bag, no ident on her," said Cavendish, glancing at his notebook. "A few letters and bills in the flat addressed to an Iris Sparks—I say, Mike, are you all right?"

Kinsey was hoping against hope for some other name. He wasn't expecting it to hit him as hard as it did. He folded involuntarily into a squat, great, heaving gasps bursting from his chest, his knees not quite hitting the floor.

"Who was she to you?" asked Cavendish, coming over to put a hand on Mike's shoulder.

"A friend," choked out Kinsey.

"A friend," repeated Cavendish sceptically.

"More than a friend once," said Kinsey, pulling himself back up. "We were engaged for a while."

"I'm so sorry, old man," said Cavendish.

"May I see her?" asked Kinsey.

"She's already been carted off to the doc," said Cavendish.

"How did it happen?"

"Shot. Twice. Seriously, Mike, are you up to this?"

Kinsey nodded, still pale from the shock. Cavendish motioned him to the doorway.

"Best I can reconstruct, she opened the door, takes the first bullet to the right side of her chest, spinning her around," he said, pointing to the spray of droplets to the left. "She takes a few steps away from the door, then the second one catches her dead centre in her upper back, and down she goes. She was lying facedown right there."

"When?" asked Kinsey.

"We'll have to let the doc figure that one out," said Cavendish.

"No one heard anything?"

"Everyone here was at work, so far as we can tell," said Cavendish. "Which puts it any time between nine and six until the doc narrows it down. We're still canvassing the building."

"Who called it in?"

"A Jennifer Pelton in Number thirty-two. I was just going over to talk with her. If you've got your wind back, you can join me."

"I'm all right," said Kinsey.

They walked down the hallway to the next flat. Cavendish rapped on the door. It was opened right away by a brunette woman in a tan suit. She had her hair in a neat bun, and wore tortoiseshell frame glasses. She looked at them expectantly.

"Are you Miss Jennifer Pelton?" asked Cavendish.

"I am," she said.

"I am Detective Inspector Cavendish, and this is Detective Sergeant Kinsey. We're with the CID. May we come in?"

"Of course. I've been waiting for you."

She showed them into a small living room, which held a small sofa covered with floral-patterned chintz. There was a cabinet holding dishes and glasses against one wall and a pair of high-backed chairs against the other. She sat on one of the chairs and gestured to the sofa, on which the two detectives sat uncomfortably close to each other.

"I understand you called in the alarm," said Cavendish.

"Yes," she said. "I was getting back in around six, and I noticed that her door was ajar, which was unusual. I knocked, but there was no reply, so I became concerned and opened it further. And there she was."

"Did you go in?"

"No," she said. "I should have, I suppose, but I could see right away that she was dead. I didn't know if the killer was still in there, and I didn't care to find out. I thought the best course of action was to get inside my flat as quickly as I could, throw the bolts, and ring up the police. Or at least, that's what I found myself doing. I don't think I put much actual thought into it until the phone was in my hand."

"When was the last time you saw Miss Sparks alive?"

"Is that her name? I never knew."

"Really? How long have you been living here?"

"About eight months. I moved in at the beginning of February. She was already here, but she kept to herself for the most part. She'd say hello if we passed in the hall or on the stairs, but I don't think we ever had a real conversation."

"The apartment is under the name of Anthony Rigby," said Kinsey. "Do you know him?"

"I know the name from the letter boxes, of course," she said. "There was a gentleman who would visit her occasionally. I assumed that was him."

"How often would he visit?" asked Kinsey, trying to keep his voice flat and neutral.

"Every couple of months or so. It wasn't a regular pattern. Sometimes he'd spend the night; sometimes he would visit and then slip out late."

"How did you know this?" asked Cavendish.

By way of reply, she reached behind her and rapped on the wall. The sound was high and thin.

"One hears things," she said, one eyebrow slightly arched.

"Is that allowed?" asked Cavendish. "Having men up?"

"Allowed or not, it's done," said Miss Pelton. "No one kicks up a fuss. Why shouldn't a girl grab a little happiness when she can?"

"Did you ever see Rigby? Can you describe him?"

"The man I saw earlier in the year was in his mid-thirties, I should think. Five-ten, very fit, black hair and moustache."

"Earlier in the year," said Cavendish. "Has he not been around recently?"

A slow, cagey smile spread across her face.

"There's been another man recently," she said, leaning forward and dropping her voice conspiratorially. "A much different type. Dresses nice, but acts like he's not used to dressing nice. Acts like he's not used to acting nice, either."

"How so?"

"His face has taken more than a few poundings in his life," she said. "Especially the nose. Big man, six feet and a bruiser. East Ender from his voice, sneaking around with his betters, if you ask me."

Archie Spelling, thought Kinsey.

"So he's the new boyfriend?" asked Cavendish.

"He's the new something," she said.

"And he's also been visiting her on the sly?"

"Hmm. Only there's a difference."

"What's that?"

"Him, she goes out with," she said. "The first man, when he'd show up, would never take her anywhere. He'd just go in, the door would close, time would pass, however long it was, and he'd leave again. I never saw them together outside the flat. But the second man she steps out with. Or did."

"Any idea if the two men knew about each other?"

"I thought they were sequential from what little I saw," she replied.

You saw a lot, thought Kinsey. Won't have to edit the chaff out of your report.

"What changed your mind?" asked Cavendish.

"The other night, there was a bit of a row," she said.

"Which night?"

"Tuesday. I came home, heard her talking to someone. It sounded like the first man, which surprised me. He hadn't been around since June, and I thought they were over and done with. I passed on to unlock my door, then out of the corner of my eye I see the bruiser come up, stop, and listen. He sees me watching, puts his finger to his lips, then waves goodbye to me."

"And then?"

"I went inside," she said primly. "It was none of my business, I'm sure."

"Was there a fight?"

"Raised voices, including hers," she said. "I couldn't catch the words. But they didn't come to blows."

"Who stayed, who left?" asked Kinsey.

"I don't know," she said. "I put the radio on to drown them out. I haven't heard anyone talking inside since then, so that would be the last time I saw or heard her."

"Have you heard any kind of noise from the flat since then?"

asked Cavendish. "And don't pretend you don't know what I'm talking about."

"No," she said. "Not while I've been here."

"But you were working regular business hours, so you can't account for what went on during the daytime."

"No, I can't."

Cavendish glanced at Kinsey, who shook his head. The two got to their feet.

"We'll need you to come in and give a full statement," said Cavendish. "You've been very helpful, Miss Pelton. Thank you."

"I wish I had taken the time to know her better," said Miss Pelton as she showed them out.

Me, too, thought Kinsey.

"You consider yourself a failure and a coward because you didn't go over as an operative," said Dr. Milford.

"I had trained so hard for it," said Iris. "Then came that fatal parachute jump. Not fatal. Near fatal. Shattering—that's a good word for it. It shattered my ego more than my ankle, and I've never caught up."

"What happened to the women you trained with?"

"They went over. They didn't come back."

"What happened?"

"There was a betrayal. They were caught and executed."

"And you lived."

"I lived. Here, on the safe side of the war."

"You made other contributions to the war effort, certainly."

"Nothing heroic."

"And that's what you wanted? To be a heroine?"

"I wanted to show them."

She stopped. He waited. Neither said anything for a long time.

"Show who?" he finally asked, breaking the impasse.

"Everyone," she said. "Every damn one of them. But I didn't.

All I did was survive. And surviving is much easier when you're the only survivor. When another survivor shows up who actually did something dangerous and courageous, it makes you realise how small a person you really were. How little you accomplished by surviving. Andrew was the brave one."

"Is that why you gave yourself to him?"

"Is that what I did?" she asked, more to herself than him. "If I did, I don't know if I ever got myself back again."

"Do you still think he's a brave man?"

"I—" she began.

He held up his hand to stop her.

"You were about to answer too quickly," he said. "No flippancy, Miss Sparks. Do you still think he's a brave man?"

"No," she replied. "Not anymore."

"Because of this new woman?"

"No," she said. "And she's not a new woman. He was three-timing with her while he was two-timing with me."

"But you only found that out this week. When did you decide he wasn't a brave man?"

"When I asked him if he would divorce Poppy and marry me. He started mumbling about complications and his position. Then I called him a coward and broke it off."

"Did you get yourself back when you did that? The part that you gave him?"

"Maybe some of it," she said. "I did feel better."

"You stopped idolising him."

"No question."

"Did you ever think that you had been casting your own wish fulfilment onto Andrew because he did what you could not? That that was the source of your attraction to him?"

She stared at him. He watched as she unlocked her embrace of her knees, allowing her legs to slip from the chair until her feet once again met with the carpet.

"Take a deep breath," he suggested. "Hold it. Let it out. Take in the fact that you're not shaking anymore."

"Wow," she said, holding up her hands as if she had never seen them before.

"And I'm afraid our time is up," he said.

"Right when things were getting interesting," she said.

She got up from the chair unsteadily, but found her balance by the time she reached the door. She stopped and turned back to him.

"If tipping were allowed in psychotherapy, I'd double yours," she said.

"Thank you for the thought," he replied. "See you next Thursday."

"Myrick is tracking down the building manager to see if they can give us a lead on this Rigby chap," said Cavendish. "Sounds like he was keeping her for—damn, I'm sorry. I forgot for a moment."

"No, talk away," said Kinsey. "You were about to say it sounds like a flat paid by a bloke for the other woman in his life. I think so, too."

"I had the sense of recent male occupation on my initial look-see," said Cavendish. "Scent of cologne in the bathroom, bed still unmade. But no clothes, toiletries, shaving kit. If he was there, he cleared out. So let's say she broke up with Rigby, starts with the second man, and then Rigby shows up again. Maybe he wants her back, maybe it's something else."

"I'm with you so far."

"Then along comes the second man," continued Cavendish. "Jealousy, confrontation, argument—as good a recipe for murder as any. One returns later with a gun."

"I can give you a lead on the bruiser," said Kinsey.

"Can you? So you've kept track of her after you split?"

"Not really, but she showed up in an investigation a few months ago."

"Which one?"

"The La Salle murder."

"The one where the two women saved the CID from eternal damnation?" asked Cavendish in amusement. Then his expression shifted to dismay. "Was she one of them?"

"I'm afraid so."

"Pity," said Cavendish, shaking his head. "They did good work there. Who do you think is the bruiser?"

"Parham ran into the two women again while working on another case," he said. "He mentioned it to me when I got back from my honeymoon. Apparently our Miss Sparks developed a connection with Archie Spelling."

Cavendish gave a low, astonished whistle.

"That's a bruiser if ever there was one," he said. "And I wouldn't put something like this past him. I'll send a car around to bring him in."

"Let me," said Kinsey.

"Not a chance. You're too close to this one. What would the papers say? 'Victim's Ex Arrests Gangster Lover.' Too lurid by half. Tell you what, though. We still need someone to identify the body. Don't volunteer, mate, it has to be someone outside the force. Do you happen to know where to find her family?"

"Lost touch, I'm afraid. Her mum is Florence Sparks."

"The Labour MP?" exclaimed Cavendish. "Bloody hell, that's going to be a mess. I'd rather not drag her into it until we have confirmation from someone else. Who was the other woman she was working with?"

"Mrs. Gwendolyn Bainbridge," said Kinsey.

"Do you have a lead on her?"

"I still have her address at the office. Kensington somewhere. I can call in and get it."

"Be a good fellow and see if you can bring her around," said Cavendish. "I'll work on Archie Spelling."

"All right," said Kinsey reluctantly.

"I say, it was very decent of you to come over," said Cavendish, clapping Kinsey on the shoulder. "Saved me hours."

"Put it in the report," said Kinsey, "I may need backup with the wife later."

He went down to the street. There was a telephone box on the corner. He went to it and called Beryl with the news that he'd be home later than expected. He could practically hear her pouting on the other end of the line. Then he called in and got someone to look up the Bainbridge address.

It was five past eight when the driver pulled up in front of the house.

"I may be a few minutes," said Kinsey. "There's bound to be some tears shed."

"Take your time," said the constable.

Kinsey got out, walked to the front door, and rang the bell. A butler answered.

"Detective Sergeant Michael Kinsey, Metropolitan Police," said Kinsey, holding up his identification. "Is Mrs. Gwendolyn Bainbridge in?"

"She is at dinner with the family," replied the butler.

"I'm sorry to interrupt, but I'm afraid I must speak with her."

"Please come in," said the butler.

He showed him to the front parlour.

"I will bring her shortly," said the butler. "Please wait here."

Kinsey stood in the parlour, contemplating the portraits of various Bainbridges through the ages. He turned when he heard footsteps.

"Good evening, Detective Sergeant Kinsey," said Mrs. Bainbridge, coming in to shake his hand. "To what do I owe the pleasure?"

"Bad news, I'm afraid," he said. "Won't you sit?"

Puzzled and apprehensive, she sat in one of the armchairs by the fireplace and indicated that he take the other.

"We received word of a shooting," he said. "A woman was killed. There's no easy way to say this, so I'll get straight to it. We have reason to believe that the victim is my—that is to say, your friend Iris Sparks."

He was expecting tears, wailing screams, some form of feminine shock. What he didn't expect was her immediate shift into anger.

"Is this some kind of joke?" she said, her colour rising. "If so, I fail to see the humour in it."

"Mrs. Bainbridge, I have just come from her flat," he said hurriedly. "I assure you that I am completely serious."

"Iris Sparks is dead, you say."

"We found her body in her flat."

"Did you?" she asked. "Did you indeed? And you saw her?"

"Not directly, no," he said. "But I was subsequently brought into, or rather, I decided—I got there after."

"I see," she said, calming down slightly. "What do you drink, DS Kinsey?"

"Excuse me, Mrs. Bainbridge?"

"Drink, as in alcohol."

"Mrs. Bainbridge, I'm on duty."

"Rest assured, you're going to want a drink very soon," she said, standing and moving to the hall. "Whisky? Let's say whisky. I'll go fetch it for you."

"Mrs. Bainbridge, we need you to come to the morgue and identify the body," he said, desperation creeping into the voice.

"Drinks first," she insisted. "Back in a tick."

Well, people react differently, he thought. Although he'd rather not have the body identified by someone who had been drinking. He was going to have to be firmer about it with—

"Hello, Mike," came a voice from the doorway.

A voice he knew all too well. A voice that had been sounding on the edges of his memories for the last few hours. He slowly stood and turned in its direction, shock and relief coursing through him in equal measures.

"What's wrong, Mike?" asked Iris, looking at him with concern and, it had to be said, amusement. "You look like you've seen a ghost."

CHAPTER 7

Gwen, who was trailing Iris down the hall to the parlour, a bottle of whisky in one hand and three tumblers in the other, was to her everlasting regret not in position to see Kinsey's expression when Iris appeared in the doorway. What she did see a moment later was him swoop into her field of view to sweep Iris into a massive hug.

The most astonishing thing was that Iris allowed it. More than allowed—her body, rather than tensing to repel the onslaught, relaxed and fitted itself comfortably into the contours of his with a familiarity Gwen had never seen before. Iris's eyes closed as she rested her face against his chest. She inhaled deeply, gathering in his scent, letting the breath out again in a soft sigh, a tear escaping from under one eyelid to trickle down her cheek.

They stayed like that for a long moment. Gwen should have looked politely away, like she did the day before with Iris and Archie, but she couldn't stop watching.

"I'm awfully glad you're alive, Sparks," murmured Kinsey. "I'm probably going to have to arrest you for something now."

"In a minute, Mike," she said, sliding her arms around him. "You have no idea how badly I need this."

Gwen involuntarily rattled the tumblers, and they glanced over at her.

"You're right," said Kinsey. "A whisky would be very welcome."

"I should let you go," said Iris reluctantly. "I've been trying to cut down on married men."

Neither moved.

"Since no one is embracing me, I am going to have a drink," said Gwen, stepping around them into the parlour. "Join me when you're done."

They disengaged and followed her, sitting side by side on a sofa while she poured.

"As your hostess, I shall make the toast," she said, holding up her tumbler. "To the late Iris Sparks, long may she live."

"Hear, hear," said Iris, clinking her glass against Gwen's. "Now, Mike, will you kindly tell us what the hell is going on?"

"I really don't know anymore," he said, taking a healthy swig. "I came here to fetch Mrs. Bainbridge to come identify your body."

"Is this it?" asked Iris, standing and twirling in front of Gwen.

"It appears to be," said Gwen. "What next, Detective Sergeant?"

"We now have to figure out whose body we found," he replied.

He finished his drink and stood.

"Iris Sparks, by authority of the Metropolitan Police, I am arresting you on suspicion of murder of a person unknown sometime earlier today, and must ask that you accompany me to Scotland Yard."

"You can't do that!" protested Gwen. "She couldn't have killed anyone. She was—"

"Gwen, stop," said Iris. "This is clearly a mistake, and it will all be straightened out. Mike, let me get my bag and I'll join you. Will there be handcuffs involved?"

"I'm afraid so," said Kinsey.

"Then I want to touch up my makeup, too," said Iris. "I wasn't expecting to be going out tonight."

"That's what worries you?" asked Gwen.

"One unflattering mug shot can absolutely ruin one's future prospects," said Iris, downing her drink in a gulp. She looked at the empty glass sadly. "That was worth sipping. What a waste. Be right back, Mike."

"You're not planning on doing a runner, I hope," he said. "We have the place surrounded."

"No, you don't," she replied. "But don't worry. I'm as curious to find out what's going on as you are. Gwen, come with me, would you?"

They walked up to Iris's room. Gwen closed the door behind them.

"Shouldn't we be calling a solicitor?" she asked.

"Not yet," said Iris as she put on fresh lipstick and checked her makeup. "But if I'm not back by morning, assume I've been formally charged. Or in a small room being interrogated."

"And then call a solicitor?"

"No. Call the old man."

"You said I should call him only for extreme emergencies," said Gwen nervously.

"If I'm charged, this will qualify," said Iris. "Remember—don't call him from here."

"Iris, why did you stop me from telling Mike you were working with me all day?"

"Because you and I both know I was out of the office running errands for an hour this afternoon. Ample time to pop by the flat and knock off whoever I found there."

"Oh dear. I forgot about that. Any ideas as to who they found?"

"One," said Iris, dabbing on some powder. "And I can't tell you about it."

"That old song again," said Gwen.

Iris stood and grabbed her bag.

"Let's go face the music," she said.

They went back down. Just before they reached the parlour, Iris pulled up short, stopping Gwen with her hand.

"Almost forgot," she said, opening her bag. "I'm going to have to leave a few things with you. I can't be bringing them into the heart of the constabulary."

"Things? What— Oh!" said Gwen as Iris handed over a set of lockpicks, her metal knuckles, and her knife.

"Keep them away from the boys," Iris instructed her. "How do I look?"

"You're the prettiest suspect of them all," said Gwen.

"Engrave that on my headstone after the hanging, would you?" said Iris. "Here we go."

She stepped into the parlour and extended her arms in front of her.

"Clap me in irons and haul me off to the brig, Cap'n," she said. "I'm ready."

"Sorry about this," said Kinsey as he handcuffed her.

"Like old times, eh?" she said with a wink.

"That never happened," he said. "Thanks for the drink, Mrs. Bainbridge."

"Anytime," said Gwen, holding her hands awkwardly behind her.

She walked them to the door. Kinsey slipped off his coat and draped it over the handcuffs to conceal them from passersby.

"Thanks," said Iris as he walked her to the car.

The driver got out, looking confused.

"Is that the Mrs. Bainbridge you were talking about?" he asked.

"No," said Kinsey as he opened the door for her.

"You arresting her?"

"Yes."

"What for?"

"For being a common scold," said Iris. "Right, Detective Sergeant?"

"Something like that."

Gwen watched the car drive off, then looked down at the odd objects clutched in her hands. Slowly, she slid on the metal knuckles and pounded them into her palm.

Archie Spelling sat alone on a chair at a small table in an interrogation room in the basement of Scotland Yard North, wondering what was up. He was familiar with the surroundings. The usual windowless room, with a metal bar bolted to one wall. A padded door to muffle the sounds. A small metal table with a wooden chair opposite where he was sitting, and another chair in the corner of the room behind him.

He didn't know this particular detective, but he knew the type. He figured at some point the coat would come off, the tie would be loosened, the shirtsleeves would be rolled up, and then the real fun would begin.

The door opened, and Archie realised he had underestimated the impatience of his adversary. The detective came in with his coat already off and the sleeves already rolled up, revealing an impressively muscled set of forearms. The tie was still knotted. Archie hoped that was a good sign.

"I'm Detective Inspector Cavendish," said his interrogator, placing his chair so that he could sit nearly knee to knee with Archie. "You're probably wondering what this is all about."

"I don't really care," said Archie. "Have your say and be done with it."

"This will be either bad news or no news at all," said Cavendish. "A woman named Iris Sparks was murdered in her flat earlier today."

"Was she?" said Archie softly. "Mind telling me 'oo did it?"

"That's what we're here to find out," said Cavendish. "We know you and she were close."

"Close," said Archie. "Yeah. We were close. So you figure me for the deed."

"Likely a man as any," said Cavendish. "Where were you all day?"

"With unreliable witnesses of bad character," said Archie. "So I won't waste your time with their names."

"Location?"

"Why don't we skip the preliminaries and agree that I can't prove my time, place, or company to any degree that will satisfy you?" suggested Archie. "And while we're at it, that I won't bother confessing to anything, because I didn't do anything."

"You were seen at her flat on Tuesday evening by a neighbour," said Cavendish. "You were heard arguing with another man there. What can you tell me about that?"

"I can tell you that if you turn me loose, I will 'appily turn over what's left of 'im to you when I'm done with 'im," said Archie.

"Do you know where he is?"

"No," said Archie. "But I'll find out. Long before you ever will."

"Very gallant portrayal of the aggrieved lover," commented Cavendish. "Too bad I don't believe a word of it."

He reached up and loosened his tie.

"'Ere we go," said Archie. "You want to send for a couple of constables to 'old me down?"

"Now, now, Spelling," said Cavendish. "Why don't you tell me what really happened? There's no need to work you over."

"There never is," agreed Archie. "But you lads enjoy doing it anyway."

"You shot your girl twice in her flat, Spelling," said Cavendish, getting to his feet and moving the chair to the far wall by the other. "I don't like men who kill defenceless women."

"You say that like you think it makes you different from the rest of us," said Archie.

Cavendish walked back towards him, shaking his arms and hands to loosen them up.

"You box?" asked Archie, watching him with interest.

"Won the Lafone Cup last year," said Cavendish. "Light heavyweight. You?"

Before he could close in, the door opened and a uniformed constable beckoned to him.

"Can't you see I'm questioning a suspect?" barked Cavendish, glaring at him.

"I'm here straight from Parham," said the constable nervously. "Could we speak outside, sir?"

"We'll continue this conversation in a moment, Spelling," said Cavendish. "Don't go anywhere."

"Take all the time you need," said Archie.

Cavendish stepped outside with the constable and shut the door. The padded door kept most of the sound from coming through, so Cavendish's shouted "WHAT?" must have been very loud indeed for Archie to make it out.

A moment later, the door opened and Cavendish walked back in, looking like a boiler trying to force the steam back in.

"Get up," he said with an almost spastic gesture. "You're free to leave."

"What changed your mind?" asked Archie.

"It turns out that Miss Sparks is still alive," said Cavendish, retightening his tie. "That was some other dead woman we found in her flat."

"Well, that's good news for everybody but 'er, innit?" said Archie.

He retrieved his hat from the table, then walked to the open door. Right before reaching it, he turned so that his face was inches from Cavendish's.

"The answer, by the way, is no," he said.

"No? To what?" asked Cavendish, leaning back with an expression of distaste.

"No, I don't box," said Archie. "You 'ad me alone in 'ere, with your covey of coppers 'overing in the 'allway, so you 'ad the advantage. But that's just in 'ere. Outside, out there, we got the advantage, and we're very patient. You're gonna find yourself alone some night, and you might just 'appen to bump into me. I don't box. I fight. I'll teach you the difference."

"I look forward to it," said Cavendish. "You can find your way out, I assume."

Archie smirked, then walked out into the hallway.

"Archie?" came Sparks's voice from the other end.

She was between two women police constables, her hands cuffed in front, looking completely unconcerned.

"Small world," he said.

"What are you doing here?" she asked.

"They thought I might 'ave murdered you," he said.

"Clearly, you didn't," she said. "Tell you what, I'll put in a good word for you. Maybe that will help."

"No need. They've turned me loose," he said, glancing at Cavendish, who was standing in the doorway, watching them. "I guess they needed the room. We still on for tomorrow night?"

"Don't know yet," said Sparks. "I'll ring you up when I do."

"Then I'll leave you to it," he said. "Don't fret about the grasshopper. 'E's nothing much."

"Noted," said Sparks as she was led inside. "Give my love to the lads!"

Archie watched as the door closed behind her, then looked at Cavendish.

"About those defenceless women," said Archie.

"Yeah?" said the detective.

"She ain't one of them."

He put his hat on and left.

Cavendish clenched his fists in frustration, then stormed up the stairs to Parham's office.

Detective Superintendent Philip Parham was seated behind his desk when Cavendish came in.

"This won't take long," said Parham, pointing to one of the chairs in front of his desk.

Kinsey was sitting in the other one, looking profoundly unhappy.

"He can't be on this one," Cavendish said, indicating Kinsey. "He's too close."

"I agree," said Parham. "But it was lucky for you he did get involved before you went charging too far in the wrong direction. Have we identified the deceased yet?"

"No, sir," said Kinsey. "Her pictures just came over from the morgue. Along with Myrick's notes from his interview with the landlord."

He handed a folder over. Parham opened it and looked impassively at the dead woman.

"Pretty when she was alive," he said, handing the folder to Cavendish. "Go home, Mike. You're done with this one. Thanks for averting disaster."

"But, sir," began Kinsey.

"That was an order, not a suggestion," said Parham. "Leave now."

Kinsey got up and walked out, closing the door behind him.

"This is my case," said Cavendish.

"Of course it's your case," said Parham. "Which is why I am talking to you about it with Mike gone. You knew he and Miss Sparks were engaged once?"

"He told me," said Cavendish. "It hit him pretty hard when he thought she was dead."

"He's been through the wringer tonight," said Parham. "It will be a miracle if he can pay any attention to his bride when he gets home."

"At least he gets to go home," said Cavendish. "Anything else you want to tell me?"

"Yes," said Parham. "About Miss Sparks."

"I know about her and Archie Spelling," said Cavendish wearily.

"What you don't know is that Miss Sparks is a very intelligent and resourceful young woman," said Parham. "Cambridge educated. If she is your murderess, she'll be a difficult nut to crack."

"That little bit of a thing?" scoffed Cavendish. "I'll have her done and in tears in no time."

"I would advise against physical intimidation," said Parham. "It will only put her back up."

"You want me to go easy on her because she got lucky and solved a murder case."

"Four murder cases," said Parham. "It's beginning to look like something more than luck by now. Don't go easy, but be wary. Softly, softly, and all that."

"What aren't you telling me?" asked Cavendish.

"Things that I can't tell you," said Parham.

"But there are such things?"

Parham shrugged.

"Wonderful," said Cavendish. "I'll check in with you when I'm done."

"Oh, I'm going home," said Parham. "Have fun."

Sparks glanced up when Cavendish entered the room.

"Archie Spelling didn't murder me," she said immediately. "I thought we should get that out of the way at the start. Any further need for these?" She held up her manacled wrists. "I told Constable Linden over there I'd be as meek as a lamb, but she doesn't believe me."

"You can take them off," said Cavendish to the constable, who was sitting in the corner.

Linden got up, removed the handcuffs, and placed them on the table, then returned to her seat. Cavendish took the chair across the table from Sparks.

"My name's Iris Sparks," she said, massaging her wrists. "What's yours?"

"Detective Inspector Nyle Cavendish," he said. "Homicide and Serious Crime Command."

"Nice to meet you, Detective Inspector. You got to tell two different men I've loved that I'd been murdered. How did they take it?"

"Kinsey was pretty broken up about it," he said, sitting across from her at the table. "Spelling was ready to break someone else."

"Sounds about right," she said. "Interesting. If I gave you a list of all my ex-boyfriends, do you think you could go around telling them I was dead and record their reactions? Solely for scientific interests."

"I hear it's a long list," he said.

"Rude!"

"Who's the dead woman, Miss Sparks?"

"I don't know," she said. "I haven't seen—"

He threw the photographs onto the table in front of her. Her animation faded as she looked at them.

"Poor thing," said Sparks.

"Do you know her?"

"Her name is Helena Jablonska."

"How do you know her?"

"She came to The Right Sort two days ago."

"That's the marriage bureau you run with Mrs. Bainbridge?" he asked, taking a notebook out of his jacket and opening it.

"Yes."

"Why did she come there?"

"She said she wanted to sign up as a client."

"So you interviewed her. What did she tell you?"

"That she was a Polish refugee and a widow. She said she was working at the Mars candy factory in Slough, and gave us an address in Buckinghamshire. I don't recall the exact address, but we probably still have it at the office."

"Probably? Why wouldn't you have a client's address?"

"We didn't take her on as a client," said Sparks. "So I don't know if we kept her application form or not. I could check with our secretary and provide it to you."

"I'll send a man to get it from her in the morning," said Cavendish.

"Ah," said Sparks. "It sounds like you don't expect me to be at liberty by then."

"Do you?"

"I didn't kill her," said Sparks.

"Why did you turn her down as a client?"

"We don't accept everyone who walks through the door. We vet them, and if one of us thinks the candidate is unsuitable, we reject them. Mrs. Bainbridge vetoed her."

"Did she tell you why?"

"Yes," said Sparks. "Mrs. Jablonska was pregnant."

She was watching Cavendish for a reaction as intently as he was watching her, and was rewarded by a wince.

"She told you that at the interview?" he asked.

"No," said Sparks. "But Mrs. Bainbridge saw the signs and made the decision."

"How did Mrs. Jablonska take the rejection?"

"She seemed distressed."

"What about being confronted over the pregnancy?"

"I didn't see that. Mrs. Bainbridge walked her out, and told me after she came back."

"Was that the last time you saw her?"

"No," said Sparks. "She stopped me in front of my building on Welbeck yesterday."

"When was this?"

"After work. Maybe five thirty or so."

"Why was she there?"

Sparks looked at him steadily, then shook her head.

"What's that all about?" he asked.

"There are limits," she said. "I will give you what I can, but only up to a point."

"Why?"

She shook her head again.

"All right," he said. "Let's try another topic. Who is Anthony Rigby?"

"Let me think. No, that's another limit."

"He paid for the flat you live in. A full year's rent in advance. In cash. Very curious."

"I suppose it would look that way to a suspicious mind."

"But not to you."

She shrugged.

"If you were to give me that list of ex-boyfriends, would his name be on it?" he asked.

"No," she said.

"I agree," he said. "Because that wasn't his real name, was it?"

"No, it wasn't. I'm telling you that so you don't waste time looking for him."

"What is Rigby's real name?"

"Oh dear, we've hit that wall again."

"Was it love, Miss Sparks? Or a financial exchange for services rendered?"

"You say that as if the two were mutually exclusive," said Sparks. "We kept women have feelings, too."

"How long have you been running The Right Sort?"

"We started in March."

"What did you do to support yourself before that?"

"Mostly secretarial and clerical work since the war."

"And during the war?"

"The same, only with a uniform on."

"Seems a waste of your education," he said. "Cambridge, I hear."

"One did what was required without whinging," she said.

"When's the last time you saw this Rigby fellow?"

She shook her head.

"Was he the other man at your flat when you and Spelling had the row?"

"What row would that be, Detective Inspector?" she asked, smiling.

"You were at the Bainbridge house when Kinsey went there. Why?"

"I was having dinner with the Bainbridges."

"Where were you prior to that?"

"At a medical appointment, which Mrs. Bainbridge can verify. We went together. Prior to that, at our offices in Mayfair."

"Convenient how Mrs. Bainbridge is your alibi for everything. Was there any point at which you weren't together?"

"I was out of the office for maybe an hour in the afternoon."

"Doing what?"

"Running errands. Buying some ladies' things. Not killing Helena Jablonska."

"But you would agree that an hour would give you enough time to get from Mayfair to Marylebone, shoot her, and return to your office."

"It would. It would even give me time to get rid of the gun and still have enough left over to buy those all-important ladies' things."

"The door to your flat was unlocked when the body was discovered," said Cavendish. "Jablonska didn't have a key. You still have yours?"

She opened her bag, removed it, and placed it on the table.

"Did this Rigby have a key?" he asked.

"That would seem likely, he being the keeper of the kept," she said.

"Look, Miss Sparks," he said wearily, "we have a murdered woman in your flat who was pregnant and had prior contact with you. We have circumstances suggesting an illicit arrangement between you and the man who took the flat. I put it to you that this woman also had some connection to this Rigby fellow, that she confronted you about it, and that you subsequently murdered her in a fit of jealous rage."

Damn, thought Sparks. That does sound plausible.

"Do you have proof of that?" she asked.

"The night is young," he said. "Linden, you need a break? Go have a cigarette."

The WPC looked back and forth between him and Sparks, then nodded slowly, got up, and left the room. The door closed silently behind her. Cavendish bolted it, then took off his coat and draped it over the back of his chair.

"Now, Miss Sparks," he said, sitting back down, "concealing information from the police during a criminal investigation is a serious matter."

"I'm taking it seriously, Detective Inspector," said Sparks. "And if you let me make some calls, I may be able to help you more than I can at the moment."

"I can take you to my office right now for that," he offered.

"No," she said. "Not like that. I need to be at liberty to make them. Hold off on charging me, and I will be back here in the morning at, say, eleven. We can have an unfettered conversation then."

He got up, picked up the handcuffs, then grabbed Sparks's chair and dragged her over to the wall. He cuffed her left wrist, then secured it to the metal bar. He retrieved his chair and sat in front of her.

"I prefer fettered," he said. "Let's start over. How do you know Helena Jablonska?"

Gwen couldn't sit still in her room after kissing the boys good night. She paced back and forth, making occasional forays across the landing to the guest wing to rap softly on Iris's door, but getting no response.

On her third such trip, she was interrupted by a voice saying, "She hasn't come back. Probably out to the wee hours with that gangster of hers."

She turned to see her father-in-law standing in the doorway of his temporary quarters, leaning on his cane.

"I'm sorry, Harold," she said. "I didn't mean to disturb you. I thought I was being quiet."

"I'm a light sleeper nowadays," he said, shuffling into the hall. "I'm not used to being in this room. Strange. When I was a young man sleeping in a ratty tent in those sweltering Rhodesian nights, nothing could wake me, and God knows there was danger enough prowling about. But now, sleeping here in the lap of luxury, thick carpets on the floors and everyone bending over backwards to smother me in silence, I pop awake at the slightest noise."

He held his arms out suddenly.

"Freedom!" he cried. "Freedom from the Bainbridges!"

He laughed when he saw her stricken expression.

"Yes, my dear daughter-in-law, I heard your supplication," he said. "It's one my younger self frequently made to no avail under the generational yoke of this place. Have you applied to the Courts of Lunacy yet?"

"You'll be notified when I do," she said. "Still planning on opposing my petition?"

"Maybe," he said, leaning with both hands in front of him on the cane. "What do you intend to do if our bonds are severed?"

"Whatever I wish."

"Move out of here?"

"Yes."

"With my grandson?"

"With my son, Harold."

"Will you stay in London, at least?" he asked. "Close by? I'd hate to lose him."

"You were ready to send him off to a boarding school in the north for an eight-year stretch," she pointed out.

"I've come to appreciate the benefits of having family about," he said. "Nearly losing everything gives one perspective. What's important—"

"What's important to you is that I inherited forty percent of Bainbridge, Limited," she said. "A share equal to your own. If—no, when I gain control of it, you will no longer be able to run the place as you like. So what is it that you're really asking me, Harold?"

"I'm asking you to stay in London," he said. "If we were to band together, we could still keep things as they are."

"As you want them to be, you mean."

"No one knows our African holdings better than me," he said.

"Not yet," she said.

"What does that mean?" he asked, his eyes narrowing.

"It means I've gone through every ledger in your office over the last two months," she said. "And I've dined with Lord Morrison, who's rather a dear, and lunched with Sandy Birch and Townsend Phillips. Hilary McIntyre personally gave me a tour of the corporate office and of the Croydon factory."

"You're gathering intelligence from the other board members," he said.

"No, Harold, I'm learning the business as a shareholder should," she replied. "I want to be taken seriously when I start attending board meetings."

"You think you will be taken seriously?"

"I think I already am," she said.

"By which one of them?"

"All of them so far," she said. "And now by you."

"Five minority shareholders with four percent each," he said. "All I need is three to keep control."

"As do I," she said. "And after your misadventure in Mopani, you may find that the others no longer share your confidence in your financial acumen."

"So you're planning a coup d'état?"

"Maybe," she said. "Or maybe you and I can reach an accommodation."

"Maybe you won't be deemed competent," he said.

"And maybe you'll remain an invalid," she replied. "But I prefer to be optimistic about things. It's so much more pleasant in the long run. My goodness, how late it's getting! You should get your rest, Harold. I'm going to leave so I won't disturb you anymore. I'll come by and visit tomorrow night if you like."

"Would you?" he asked, a plaintive note creeping into his voice, his shoulders slumping slightly. "That would be kind of you. Maybe we could discuss some of your ideas. Good night, Gwendolyn."

He turned and went inside his room. A moment later, the light went out.

He needs a sparring partner, she thought. He lights up when he has a challenge.

She risked opening Iris's door to peek in, but the room was empty. It was nearly midnight. Iris had been gone for over three hours. Nearly nine more before The Right Sort opened for business. Possibly without Iris.

She wasn't going to wait until then.

She went to her room and pulled her address book from her bag. She kept the number under "O" for "Old Man."

Don't call him from the house, Iris had said.

Gwen put on her coat and hat, then peeked out her doorway. No one was about. She made her way downstairs. As she reached the entry hall, she saw Percival locking the front door. He looked at her with surprise.

"Mrs. Bainbridge, are you going out?" he asked.

"For a few minutes, Percival," she said. "I was feeling restless. I wanted to get some fresh air."

"One second, ma'am," he said.

He disappeared briefly, then returned, wearing a black overcoat and a derby.

"Percival, I was only going for a brief walk," she protested.

"At midnight, Mrs. Bainbridge," he said. "An hour when even Kensington is less than safe."

"You expect bandits to be lurking in the privet hedges?"

"No, Mrs. Bainbridge," he replied. "I fear the unwanted attentions of drunken gentlemen returning from their evenings out. Unless you are off to some rendezvous, in which case I will discreetly withdraw my company, it is my intention to accompany you on this late-night perambulation."

"I don't want to keep you up unnecessarily, Percival."

"I will sleep much better once I know you have returned safely, Mrs. Bainbridge," he said, opening the door for her. "Shall we?"

"Very well," she said. "Thank you, Percival."

She stepped outside and waited while he locked the door, then began walking. He followed her a few respectful paces behind. She glanced back, then stopped.

"This won't do," she said. "I feel like I'm being followed by a bodyguard. It's disconcerting. Please walk by my side, Percival."

"Of course, Mrs. Bainbridge," he said.

He came up to her and offered his arm. She took it, and they began to walk.

"I don't believe I've ever been escorted by you in this manner," she said.

"I thought it would be best to maintain the illusion," he said.

"What illusion would that be?"

"The illusion of normality," he said. "To all appearances, a man and a woman out on an evening stroll together. Much more ordinary than a woman out alone at this hour."

"You're right as always, Percival," she said. "I should have asked you from the start."

"If I may be bold enough to venture an observation, Mrs. Bainbridge, I have noticed that your recent friendship with Miss Sparks has led to more and more frequent deviation from what one used to term normal behaviour."

"Have you? I'm happy to think that there was a point when you considered my behaviour normal, given that you were the one who pried the knife from my hand two years ago. No, two and a half years now."

"It would have broken my heart to see you like that, had it not already been broken by the news of Mr. Bainbridge's death," he said gently. "I consider it one of the great blessings of my life that I was able to prevent you from doing further harm to yourself."

Her tears came quickly, and his handkerchief was out just as quickly.

"I'm sorry, ma'am," he said. "I didn't mean to cause you any distress."

"No, no," she said, wiping her eyes. "The world is such a cruel place nowadays that the rare moments of kindness catch me completely off guard. Thank you, Percival."

"Think nothing of it, Mrs. Bainbridge," he said. "Now, where are we going?"

"To the telephone boxes by the Kensington High Street station," she said. "I need to make a call. No, two calls."

"We do have a telephone or two in the house, you know," he reminded her.

"I know, Percival," she said. "I can't make these calls from there."

"Might this have something to do with Miss Sparks's sudden departure earlier this evening?"

"It does, but I'd rather not say anything more, and I would be grateful if you kept this nocturnal excursion under your hat."

"The derby of discretion is ever at your service, Mrs. Bainbridge."

There was a row of telephone boxes near the entrance to the Underground. She stepped into the first, pulled out her address book, and copied the number. Then she stepped into the second box and closed the door as Percival stood guard.

She paused to remember Iris's instructions, then put in a coin and dialled.

Any time of day or night, they'll answer, Iris had told her when she gave her the number. *But you must stick to the script.*

"Hello," a man answered.

"Mr. Petheridge, please," she said, her voice quavering.

"I'm sorry, you have the wrong number."

"Isn't this NOble five-seven-two-one?" she asked, reading it from the note she had jotted in her address book.

"I'm afraid it isn't."

"I'm terribly sorry," she said.

She hung up and stepped out.

"Was that it?" asked Percival.

"Not quite," she said, stepping back into the first box.

Precisely five minutes later, the telephone jangled. She answered on the first ring.

"Sparks, why are you calling me at this ungodly hour?" came a gruff voice.

"Actually, it's Mrs. Gwendolyn Bainbridge," she said. "I believe we've met, if you are who you're supposed to be."

There was a moment of silence.

"Mrs. Bainbridge," said the Brigadier. "Do you have any idea how much trouble you're in right now?"

CHAPTER 8

Trouble?" asked Mrs. Bainbridge. "Why am I in trouble?"

"Having my number without authorisation is trouble, Mrs. Bainbridge," said the Brigadier. "Using it is tantamount to an admission of breaking laws that most British citizens aren't even allowed to know about."

"I was given it by Miss Sparks," she said.

"Clearly. You may inform her that she's in hot water as well."

"I doubt that you could put her in any more than she's in already," said Mrs. Bainbridge. "She's been arrested."

"Has she? For what?"

"Suspicion of murder."

"Who did she kill?"

"No one, in my opinion," she replied. "But they found a dead woman in her flat."

"Who? What was she doing there?"

"I don't know."

"And what does any of this have to do with me?"

"Miss Sparks used to work for you," said Mrs. Bainbridge. "She told me to contact you in an emergency."

"Mrs. Bainbridge, she hasn't worked for me for some time," said the Brigadier. "I fail to see how this is any of my concern.

People get murdered every day without British Intelligence being involved."

"Does the name Andrew mean anything to you?" asked Mrs. Bainbridge.

"I know several."

"This Andrew is someone she used to be involved with romantically," said Mrs. Bainbridge. "I think he has something to do with this."

"Why?"

"Because he's been staying at her flat for the past few days," said Mrs. Bainbridge. "Which means he may be the one who killed this woman. Even if Miss Sparks is no longer working for you, I believe this Andrew person still is. Is that sufficient connection to get you involved?"

There was a long pause.

"Are you certain she didn't do it?" he asked.

"Fairly certain."

"That doesn't inspire me," he said. "What do you expect me to do, Mrs. Bainbridge?"

"I'm sure I'm not qualified to tell you, sir."

"You said Sparks told you to call me."

"Yes."

"I should let her rot in jail until trial and have you arrested," he grumbled.

"But you're not going to do either of those things, are you?" she asked, feeling a glimmer of hope for the first time in the conversation.

"Go home, Mrs. Bainbridge," he replied. "Go to work in the morning. Don't call this number again. Ever."

"Thank you, sir," she said.

She hung up and stepped out of the box.

"Home, ma'am?" asked Percival, offering his arm.

"Home, Percival," she replied, taking it.

* * *

It was five thirty in the morning when the call came through to Scotland Yard. A very annoyed night shift detective supervisor named Stone received it from an even more annoyed detective chief superintendent who had in turn been woken up by the latest in a series of telephone calls stretching back into clouds of obscurity that nevertheless carried clout that could not be ignored. Clout that forced Stone to get up from his chair and deliver the order himself.

While he descended the several flights to the basement, Sparks was leaning back in her chair, looking glumly at her left arm, which was still handcuffed to the bar on the wall.

"I would appreciate it if you would switch arms," she said. "This one's gone numb."

"But then I'd have to move my chair all the way to the other side," said Cavendish. "Who is Rigby?"

"I am feeling less cooperative by the moment," said Sparks.

"You haven't been cooperative at all."

"But I was willing to be," she said. "I gave you a chance."

"You're either a murderess or hiding a murderer," he said, leaning forward so that his face was close to hers. "I intend to get it out of you."

"So far, the most frightening thing about you has been your breath," she said, wrinkling her nose in distaste. "It may violate the Geneva Conventions."

"They don't apply," he said. "You're a noncombatant."

"Uncuff me and we'll see about that."

"Are you threatening an officer of the law, Miss Sparks?" scoffed Cavendish. "You've picked up a trick or two from the boyfriend."

"Did Archie threaten you?" asked Sparks. "Every day he does something to make me love him even more."

"I expect he'll bring you flowers every day you're in jail."

"What are you going to charge me with?" asked Sparks. "I haven't given you anything to hold up a murder. Some form of hindering, maybe. I don't know what the common-law term is for it. What's the bail generally for that sort of thing?"

"Don't be so sure," he began, then stopped when he heard a knock on the door.

"What now?" he shouted.

"It's Stone," came a voice.

"Can't it wait?"

"Not one second," said Stone. "I have orders concerning Miss Sparks."

Cavendish and Sparks looked at each other.

"You should probably uncuff me before you open the door," she said. "You don't want to make a bad impression on the boss."

"Shut up," he said, getting to his feet.

"Oh, now he wants me to be quiet," she muttered.

Cavendish opened the door to see Stone standing before it, crooking his finger. Cavendish stepped out into the hallway, which was otherwise deserted, and closed the door behind him. The second he did, Sparks closed her eyes and rested her head against the wall.

"What brings you here?" asked Cavendish.

"You're not going to like it," said Stone. "I don't like it. Has she confessed to murder?"

"Not yet," said Cavendish. "But I've got her on the ropes."

"Have you enough to convict her without a confession?" asked Stone. "Be straight with me, Nyle."

"There's a body in her flat. They were known to each other. They may have both been involved with the same man."

"And?"

"And that's it," he said.

"Not enough," said Stone. "If you had it, I would have fought them tooth and nail."

"Them? Who's them?"

"Men above my rank who report to men whose names I will never know," said Stone. "Our orders are to cut her loose."

"No!"

"It's not up to you, and it's not up to me," said Stone.

"I could keep her on perverting the course of justice," argued Cavendish. "She's hiding evidence. Maybe conspiring with someone."

"Cut her loose, Nyle," said Stone. "I'll buy you a drink when it's over."

"Who is she?" wondered Cavendish, staring at the closed door.

"If you don't know after this much questioning, then you're piss-poor at your job, lad."

"I mean who does she know? Who made the call to the hidden powers?"

"These are fine questions to ask," said Stone. "Unfortunately, I don't have the answers."

"Were you told anything other than to let her go?" asked Cavendish.

"That was the full extent of my orders," said Stone.

"So there's nothing stopping me from continuing the investigation? From having her followed?"

"Not a thing," said Stone. "I will authorise anything you want."

"She's tough," mused Cavendish. "She's been trained to handle interrogation, and she's got friends in high, secret places. She's government. Has to be. Which means maybe the dead woman is, too."

"So you'll have to tread lightly," said Stone.

"Who's on the rota right now who's got top tailing skills?"

"Henderson. Capshaw."

"I want them both."

"They're yours."

* * *

Sparks had drifted off, but snapped awake when the door opened. Cavendish stood for a moment, looking at her.

"Sorry, was I snoring?" she asked, blinking uncertainly.

Then she giggled for a second, startling him.

"What's that all about?" he asked.

"You're not the first man I've ever asked that," she said. "But never under these circumstances."

He shook his head, then stepped forward and uncuffed her.

"Thanks," she said, massaging her arm as it fell limply by her side. "What did I miss?"

"We're done," he said, picking up her bag and handing it to her.

"So soon? What's the hour?"

"Nearly six."

"I don't suppose a cup of tea would be possible?" she asked hopefully.

"There'll be places open," he said. "Come on."

He led her upstairs, then to the door to the courtyard.

"You know your way," he said.

"I've been here before," she replied.

She took a step outside.

"You weren't bad," she said, squinting in the early morning sun. "Another hour, you might have actually got something out of me."

"I might yet," he said. "Get on with you."

She gave him a quick, small wave, then turned and walked through the courtyard and out through the arches to the Victoria Embankment.

She headed to The Right Sort, stopping halfway there for a desperately needed cup of tea and a scone at a shop by Piccadilly Circus. Feeling marginally refreshed, she stepped into a telephone box outside the shop and closed the door.

She didn't need to write anything down. There were several boxes between there and the office with numbers she had memorised.

One was less than five minutes' walk from her current location. She dropped a coin in the slot and dialled the Brigadier.

"Hello," answered a woman.

"Mr. Petheridge, please," said Iris.

The woman hung up.

That's not right, thought Iris.

She tried the number again. It rang several times without an answer.

Which was an answer.

She replaced the handset. Her coin clattered into the change receptacle, and she picked it up automatically.

I've been cut off, she thought. Why?

She debated whether she should call Archie at this hour. The team for the proposition He's Your Boyfriend held sway over the opposition He's a Gangster and It's Seven in the Bloody Morning. She called him.

"Yeah?" he answered groggily after the third ring.

"I'm available for tonight," she said.

"When did you get out?"

"Not long ago."

"They give up, or were strings pulled?"

"A genie granted me a wish, but it may have been the last one. If I need to run and hide . . ."

"Not with me, Sparks."

"You did offer to put me up."

"That was before I got 'auled in for a murder investigation with you in the middle of it," he said. "I can't 'ave them barging into my places of business looking for you. Or pinning anything else on me to make me give you up. It's time to maintain a respectable distance."

"So you're saying tonight is off."

"Tonight's off, tomorrow's off, next week is off, everything's off. Call me when you're a free woman."

He hung up.

We told you so, said the voices of the opposition team.

Shut up, she thought.

Oh, good one, they replied. Enjoy your lonely post-breakup walk to the office.

That wasn't a breakup, she thought.

Was it?

She pondered the question as she walked the rest of the way. It was close to seven when she reached the building. It was empty at that hour. Not even Mr. MacPherson was prowling about. She unlocked the front door, then locked it behind her, glancing out at the street in time to notice a man ducking into the alley next to the shoe shop.

She winced, but wasn't surprised.

She climbed the steps wearily and unlocked the door to her office. The first thing she did was to rummage through her papers, looking for the application form from Jablonska. She couldn't find it.

How long has it been since Tuesday? she thought.

She looked over at her partner's desk. Then, with a pang of guilt, she began going through Gwen's papers.

There! The carbon. Thank God for retentive partners, she thought.

She copied Jablonska's number and address, then put it back in the stack.

Gwen would be up and about by now. Iris called the Bainbridge number. Percival answered.

"Good morning, Percival. It's Iris Sparks."

"Good morning, Miss Sparks. Are you at liberty and in good health?"

"I am both, thank you. May I speak with Mrs. Bainbridge, please?"

"Of course. One moment."

A minute later, Gwen's voice came on the line.

"Iris, thank God you're out," she said. "Where are you?"

"At The Right Sort," said Iris. "Have the police spoken to you?"

"Not yet. Will they?"

"I expect so. Look, could you meet me here? I don't want to talk over the phone."

"On my way in ten minutes. See you in an hour."

Iris hung up. A massive yawn passed through her, and the room swam in its wake.

She wrote, "WAKE ME!" on her notepad, propped it against the telephone, then cradled her head on her arms on her desk and was asleep in seconds.

She woke to see Gwen sitting at her desk, contemplating her.

"What's the hour?" asked Iris.

"Nine fifteen," said Gwen. "I gave you some extra nap time. You looked done in. Besides, I was afraid to shake you under the current circumstances. You might have put me in a hammerlock before you were fully awake."

"Very possible," agreed Iris, covering a yawn with her hand. "Was I snoring? Lord, you're the second person I've asked that this morning."

"No. Tell me what happened after you left with Mike."

"I was interrogated for most of the night by the investigating detective, a nasty piece of work named Cavendish. Then word came down from on high to let me go. My guess was the Brigadier. Did you call him?"

"Yes. Around midnight."

"I thought I said wait until morning."

"I thought I would ignore you," said Gwen. "I don't like it when someone is being tortured all night."

"I was being grilled, not tortured," said Iris.

"I was referring to myself," said Gwen. "I was worried sick about you. I wasn't going to wait any longer."

"It wasn't anything I couldn't handle."

"Then why are you holding your left arm like that?" asked Gwen.

"It will be fine in a day or so," said Iris. "Gwen, I appreciate your worry, but I wanted to find out what they knew, or thought they knew."

"So I jumped the gun."

"Maybe."

"What did you find out? Who was the dead woman?"

"Helena Jablonska."

"No! Oh, the poor woman! And—"

She stopped short, her hands covering her mouth.

"She was going to have a baby, Iris," she whispered in horror.

"She was," said Iris. "Now she's not, and I appear to be their only lead."

"Did you tell them about Andrew?" asked Gwen.

"Not yet," said Iris. "Did you?"

"I haven't talked to the police."

"But did you tell the Brigadier?"

"I had to. He wasn't going to lift a finger otherwise."

"I wonder if that was it."

"What?"

"I tried contacting him when I got out," said Iris. "They wouldn't take my call."

"What does that mean?"

"That I can't count on them for any help this time."

"They got you out. That was help."

"I would have got out regardless," said Iris, massaging her temples. "They got me out sooner. So they wanted me out before I said anything they didn't want said. They should have known I wouldn't give Andrew up without their say-so."

"Then why won't they talk to you now?" asked Gwen. "Either to give you permission to reveal him or, I don't know, suppress the investigation somehow."

"Was there any mention of the murder in the newspapers?"

"Not in the ones we take," said Gwen. "I haven't checked the more lurid dailies."

"They're taking stock," said Iris. "The Brigadier and his bosses. Could Andrew be on the outs with them, too? Whatever he got himself into—Andrew told me he came to me because he needed someone outside the organisation. I should have thrown him out on his ear right then."

"Why didn't you?" asked Gwen.

"I'll have to sort that out after I sort out how not to get charged with murdering my romantic rival," said Iris. "A good topic for my next session with Dr. Milford, assuming I'm free next week."

"While you're at it . . ."

"Yes?"

"That hug with Mike last night," said Gwen. "What was that all about?"

"He was relieved I was alive, so he hugged me. A completely natural response."

"And your response to him? Also completely natural?"

"It felt natural," said Iris wistfully. "It felt like the way the world should have been. The phantom limb of a severed relationship."

"You've certainly been buffeted about by the boys this week," observed Gwen.

"They've all shown up in a short span, haven't they?" said Iris. "Well, there's the first fiancé not accounted for, but he can go hang. But Andrew and Mike and Archie—there should be a collective noun for the lovers gone from one's life, like an exaltation of larks. I know! A remorsefulness of exes!"

"Why are you including Archie in that category?"

"He got brought in last night when they still thought I was the corpus delicti. He wasn't happy about it. I've become a liability."

"He said that? When?"

"When I called him this morning. Imagine that. I'm too dangerous for a gangster."

"I don't know what to say," said Gwen. "On the one hand, dating a gangster, even one as nice as Archie, is never the best idea. On the other hand, he really ought to be standing up for you when the chips are down."

"Altruism and gangstering seldom go hand in hand," said Iris ruefully. "So it looks like it will just be you and me for now."

"Me and you? Me and you for what?"

"For finding out who killed Helena Jablonska."

Gwen stared at her partner, open-mouthed.

"Excuse me, but how did that become our job?" she protested. "The police are looking into it."

"The police are looking into me," said Iris. "I do not intend to let them ruin my life because they're lazy and lack imagination."

"Then give them this Andrew fellow if you think he killed her," said Gwen. "You don't owe him anything."

"But what if he didn't kill her?" asked Iris.

"Then let him convince the police of that."

"But what if this is part of some larger machination? What if he's in danger, and by giving him up, I'm making things worse?"

"I don't know," said Gwen. "This is not my game, and I can't play out all the ways it can go."

"You don't have to. I can do that. All I need you to do is help me."

"I can't," said Gwen, her voice distraught.

"What?"

"I'm sorry, Iris, but there's too much at stake."

"What are you talking about?"

"I'm talking about my son, Iris," said Gwen. "I'm on the verge of getting Ronnie back, and I was warned, quite specifically warned, that if I get caught up in anything like this again, it will be treated as proof of my erratic behaviour. I will lose my case, and I will lose Ronnie. And if I lose him, I lose everything."

"I could lose my freedom, Gwen. Hell, I could lose my life."

"I'm sorry. I can't tell you how sorry I am. I've been thinking about it ever since your Brigadier threatened to have me arrested."

"He did what? Why?"

"For calling him. For having his number."

"That's obscene," said Iris hotly. "You only had it—"

"For emergencies, I know," said Gwen. "That wasn't enough of a reason, apparently."

"Gwen," said Iris, her voice breaking to both of their surprise. "I'm exhausted, I'm being cut off right and left, and—and I need you. I need your brain, your talent for reading people, your ability to tell me when I'm going wrong."

"You're going wrong now," said Gwen. "You're plunking your-self into a situation that's far bigger than you. They can't prove you did this. Give them Andrew, and step back for once."

"I would," said Iris. "Except that one of the possibilities is that I'm being set up to take the fall for Jablonska's death."

"By whom?"

"By Andrew, or by the Brigadier, or by other players I don't even know about," said Iris. "And if I step back and watch it un-fold, what I may end up seeing are the headlights of an onrushing train. I won't do that. I can't."

"I can," said Gwen. "I have to."

"So much for standing up when the chips are down."

"If it was anyone other than Ronnie, I'd be right in the thick of it. You know that."

"Fine," said Iris, getting to her feet. "I'm going back to chez Bainbridge to scrub the smell of copper off my skin, then I'm going to figure out my next step. Mind the shop while I'm gone."

"Iris," began Gwen, but Iris grabbed her hat and bag and walked out the door without saying anything else.

*   *   *

She stormed out of their building, walking so quickly that Henderson barely had time to signal Musgrave, his driver, before he took off after her. She knew he was following her. She didn't care. She wasn't going anywhere that they didn't know about, and she didn't want to trigger their suspicions prematurely.

She needed a plan. Then she'd lose them.

Her energy dissipated in short order, and her pace settled into a steady trudge, which Henderson found as irritating as the initial burst of speed. When she reached Hyde Park, he paused to let Musgrave catch up.

"I think she's going to Kensington," he told him. "Call in, tell them to let Capshaw know. Tell him to take the street back of the house, then you meet me by the Bainbridge place."

Musgrave nodded and drove off to find the nearest call box. Henderson followed Sparks into the park. It was an easy tail. She was wearing a purple, wide-brimmed felt hat with a black ribbon that stood out against the reds and browns of the autumn leaves.

When she emerged from the other end, she validated his hunch, taking the direct route to the Bainbridge house. When she went inside, Henderson took up position across the street, down far enough so that he wasn't directly visible from the house while keeping the front door and driveway in view. When Musgrave pulled up, he slid into the front passenger seat and pulled out a pair of binoculars.

"Didn't see a back drive out," noted Henderson. "Thick hedge all around. She either comes out the front or goes through the hedge, and that cute purple hat won't be so pretty if she does that."

"Got a thermos of coffee," offered Musgrave. "You like it black?"

"I like it any which way, so long as it's now," said Henderson.

Percival was too good a butler to let her see his dismay upon seeing her stagger in, but she sensed it.

"What time would you like to be woken?" he asked immediately.

"Eleven thirty should be fine," she said. "Oh, and do you suppose I could borrow His Lordship's office for a quick call?"

"He hasn't used it since his return," said Percival. "Follow me."

He led her to the office, which she had used as a base of operations for one tumultuous weekend during the summer. He unlocked the door, then closed it behind her.

She picked up the telephone and called Sally, hoping he was between odd jobs. He was.

"Sparks, to what do I owe the pleasure?" he said.

"I need a favour."

"Granted. What is it?"

"Who do you know who I can hide out with for the near future?"

"Me," he said immediately.

"Besides you."

"What's wrong with me?"

"They know you."

"Who is they? What are you hiding from this time?"

"Andrew came back."

"Did he? That's unfortunate."

"It gets worse. A woman was murdered in my flat yesterday. The police think I did it."

There was silence at the other end of the line.

"Sally?" she asked.

"Sorry," he said. "You actually surprised me, and I didn't know that was possible."

"You aren't rescinding the favour, are you?"

"No, I'm trying to figure things out. No help from the old boss or the current boyfriend?"

"I'm afraid not."

"Where are you now?"

"At the Bainbridge house with detectives waiting outside."

"You can ditch them?"

"Probably."

"I'll make some calls. Give me an hour."

"You're the best, Sally."

She hung up, then went upstairs to her room. Millie, one of the maids, was outside her door.

"Oh, Miss Sparks," she exclaimed in surprise. "I thought you'd be at the office. I was about to make up your bed."

"I was about to lie in it," said Iris. "Glad I could save you the bother."

"Then I'll make up Mr. Daile's room," said Millie.

"That's right, he's coming in from Royal Ag this weekend," said Iris. "I'm sorry I'll be missing him."

"Missing him? Weren't you going to the exhibition with him, Mrs. Bainbridge, and the boys?"

"Blast, I forgot about that," said Iris. "Something's come up, and I have to go away for the weekend."

"Anywhere fun?"

"Quite the opposite, I'm afraid."

She looked at the maid thoughtfully.

"Millie," she said. "Would you do me a favour?"

"Yes, Miss Sparks?"

"Would you borrow my hat?"

CHAPTER 9

Parham knocked on the door of Cavendish's office. His subordinate was sitting at his desk, unenthusiastically poking a fork at a plate of powdered eggs. He waved Parham to a chair by Myrick's unoccupied desk.

"You heard," said Cavendish.

"I heard," said Parham.

"You're not surprised, though."

"No."

"You knew it was coming."

"I knew that it was a possibility," said Parham.

"You could have told me."

"No," said Parham. "I couldn't. Not directly."

"Anything you can tell me now?"

"No," said Parham. "Not directly. But I can talk you through it indirectly. What time did the call come through?"

"Stone got it at five thirty this morning."

"Kinsey picked her up around nine thirty last night," said Parham. "Interesting."

"How so?"

"You haven't been in this position before. I have. Stone gets the call from the chief. The chief gets called from the top."

"Right," said Cavendish.

"Whatever department makes the call to us has its own hierarchy," said Parham. "Hand me your ruler."

Puzzled, Cavendish gave it to him. Parham picked up another ruler from Myrick's desk.

"This one is us," he said, holding up Myrick's ruler. "The other one is them, whichever them they are."

He leaned the rulers against each other in an inverted V on the blotter.

"Their top calls our top," he said, pointing to the apex. "The commands trickle down to you." He pointed to the six-inch mark on one ruler, then pointed to the same mark on the other. "To reach the top, the news about Sparks's arrest first has to get to their side and then work its way up."

"All right," said Cavendish. "How does that help me?"

"The gap from the arrest to the call to Stone was a long one," said Parham. "What does that tell you?"

"That there were several calls involved," said Cavendish. "A lot of top brass woken in the middle of the night."

"There shouldn't be that many on their side," said Parham. "The chain of command is compact. I would venture to guess no more than three to four were involved, and they have ways of reaching each other quickly. What does that tell you?"

"I haven't had a wink of sleep since yesterday morning," said Cavendish. "Don't make me do this now."

"Who called them, Nyle?" asked Parham. "Who told them Sparks was arrested for murder?"

"Sparks must have called them when Mike arrested her," said Cavendish.

"Then she would have been out before midnight," said Parham.

"Ah, now I see where you're going with this," said Cavendish. "Someone else made the call, and not right away."

"Exactly," said Parham.

"Sparks didn't want it made right away," said Cavendish. "Bloody hell. She wanted to find out how much we knew. And here I was, thinking I was the one doing the interrogating. So she had someone else waiting to make the call for her. That partner of hers, Mrs. Bainbridge."

"A likely prospect," said Parham.

"What do you know about her?"

"Also intelligent and resourceful," said Parham. "She had as much to do with solving those cases as Sparks did."

"Also connected to the unseen powers?" asked Cavendish. "Anything you're not allowed to tell me about her?"

"She's a civilian," said Parham. "There are no restrictions. Ask away."

Gwen's mind was racing in directions that had nothing to do with matchmaking. Fears of being arrested in front of her family, and not by a gentle ex-boyfriend. Being prosecuted for unspecified crimes in a secret court where the judges wore robes passed down from the Inquisition. Being snatched from the street and bundled into a lorry by men in masks.

Actually, that last had happened to her once before, she thought. Score one for rationally based apprehensions.

She wanted to rush home and talk to Iris. She couldn't believe she had let things end at the point they did. She should have followed her immediately, accosted her on the landing.

Like she had with Mrs. Jablonska, and look what happened to her.

Don't be stupid, Gwen. Mrs. Jablonska's death had nothing to do with you, or The Right Sort.

Except she was killed in Iris's flat.

Why was she in Iris's flat? How did she get in? Did Iris know she was there? Did the mysterious Andrew?

She took out her notebook and tried to put what she knew in order.

The mysterious Andrew had shown up at Iris's apartment on Tuesday.

Mrs. Jablonska came to them on Tuesday.

That couldn't have been a coincidence, she thought. What connected the two?

Mrs. Jablonska was Polish.

Mrs. Jablonska was pregnant.

Women get pregnant because of men.

Andrew was a man.

Andrew was married.

Mrs. Jablonska was killed in a flat where Andrew was staying. Therefore . . .

She stopped. She couldn't make either a logical or an intuitive leap to a conclusion. She didn't have enough information to say Andrew killed her.

Yet married men who hide out in ex-lovers' flats are desperate men, and desperate men commit desperate acts. Like murdering pregnant women who show up unexpectedly from Buckinghamshire or Poland or wherever she was from.

The trouble, Gwen realised, was that she wasn't familiar with this dark world. This was Iris's territory, which she explored during the war while Gwen was safely swathed at the Bainbridge country estate, chasing around a toddler until her breakdown sent her to another strange world. A world without maps.

If only she knew Iris's world better. Then she could . . .

No. She couldn't. Her attorney said she couldn't, and her psychiatrist said she couldn't, and they were both sensible, well-educated men who had her best interests at heart.

So why did she want so badly to go plunging into the darkness with Iris again?

Because Iris was her best friend, maybe her only friend, and Iris said she needed her.

Gwen wasn't used to being needed. Her son should have needed her. He loved her, of course. He missed her when she was away. But he was well taken care of while she was gone as only a child of wealth could be. If she had never come back, he would have been raised and turned into a proper Bainbridge grandee without any assistance from her. He would have been sent off to St. Frideswide's and groomed for the peerage that was his due. He would turn out differently if she succeeded with her petition, of course, but that made her more of a variable in the child-rearing experiment than a requirement.

Her own family didn't need her. She was the second child and the daughter—a burden brought up to be disposed of as success-fully as possible, which she supposed they did.

Ronnie, her husband—he had loved her. He had desired her. He had also liked her, which often was the best part. Had he needed her? Was it the same thing, or part of the others, or was it never really there?

She needed him, she thought. She needed him to get free of her family and be—

Be what?

Were you independent before this all happened?

No. She needed Ronnie. The war needed him more.

The war won. Then it devoured him.

But now Iris said she needed her. She wasn't the only one, Gwen realised. They had teamed up to save Dickie Trower from the gal-lows, and that wouldn't have happened if Gwen hadn't convinced Iris that they should help him. So he had needed her, too.

Now Iris needed her for the same reason, and Gwen had said no.

There she was, criticising Archie for not helping Iris, yet when the time came, Gwen had stayed in her chair.

Bravely done, Gwen.

But what could she do? She had no idea.

Of course, she had no idea what she was doing any of the other times, either, and that had never stopped her from diving headlong into the murky waters.

Maybe that's why she shouldn't be doing it now, she thought. Maybe saying no to an irrational course of action was a step back towards sanity. But that step back towards something was also a step away from something else. Friendship, in this case.

Friendship be damned. Independence was what she wanted, and independence meant she had to make her own choices.

She heard footsteps coming up the stairs. She glanced at her calendar. She had nothing scheduled.

A pair of men in dull brown suits appeared in her doorway.

"Are you Mrs. Gwendolyn Bainbridge?" asked the first, a blond with too much slick to his hair.

"I am," she said. "Do you have an appointment?"

"I don't make appointments," he said, approaching her while pulling out his ident. "Detective Inspector Cavendish, CID. This is Detective Sergeant Myrick."

"Ah, I've been expecting you," she said. "Do take a seat."

Cavendish took the chair directly in front of her desk. Myrick grabbed the one in front of Sparks's and pulled it in line with the gap between the desks.

Cutting off my escape route, she thought.

"You know why we're here," said Cavendish.

"Given that you arrested my partner last night, I assume it has something to do with her," said Mrs. Bainbridge.

"That's correct," said Cavendish. "She came here after we let her go this morning."

"You had her followed."

"We did, so don't play the coy maiden with us."

"That was never part of my repertoire, I assure you," said Mrs. Bainbridge. "What do you want to know?"

"Sparks said you might still have the contact information for Helena Jablonska," said Cavendish.

"I believe I do," she said, picking up the stack of papers to her left.

She rifled through them.

Odd, she thought. They're not in the same order.

Iris.

"Here it is," she said, plucking it out. "Telephone number and address."

"Mind if we keep this?"

"I am here to help," she said.

He folded the paper neatly and placed it inside his coat pocket.

"That's Sparks's desk," he said, pointing to it.

"Yes."

"What time did she get here yesterday?"

"Same time I did. About a quarter to nine."

"When did she leave the office next?"

"We took luncheon together nearby. That was at twelve thirty. We came back a little after one."

"After that?"

"She left the office at some point in the middle of the afternoon."

"Why?"

"She said she had some errands to run."

"What errands?"

"She needed some things."

"What time was that?"

"I don't know exactly. It might have been two thirty or three."

"What kind of things did she need?" asked Cavendish.

"Some—ladies' items."

"What's so pressing about buying those things that she couldn't wait until after work?" asked Cavendish.

"She had an appointment after work."

"What kind of appointment?"

"A medical appointment."

"Right, she mentioned something about that, didn't she?" Cavendish said to Myrick, who nodded. "Said you both went."

"Yes."

"What's the name and address of the doctor?"

"That's a rather personal question, don't you think?"

"Oh, I do," said Cavendish. "So personal, I'm blushing to ask it. But unfortunately, I have to verify every step of Miss Sparks's whereabouts yesterday, so give me his name and address, Mrs. Bainbridge."

"Edwin Milford," she answered reluctantly. "Harley Street."

"Milford, Milford," mused Cavendish. "Rings a bell. Wasn't he the one who testified in the Porter case, Ian?"

Myrick nodded again.

"A trick cyclist, right?" asked Cavendish with a leer. "That's what we called them in the army. Terrence Porter killed two nuns at prayer. Milford said he was as crazy as a bedbug. Jury bought it, and now Porter's living easy in a sanatorium out near Ely. Maybe you know the place, Mrs. Bainbridge."

"I can't say that I do," she said coldly.

"So you and Sparks go to a psychiatrist together," he said. "On Harley Street. Which is practically around the corner from her place, isn't it?"

"It's not far," she conceded.

"Who's crazier, you or her?"

"We compete for the title."

"I take it this isn't some kind of group therapy," he said. "You each have your own little chats."

"'Sessions' would be the correct term."

"Sessions, of course," he said. "How long are these sessions?"

"Forty-five minutes."

"So while you were lying on the couch—"

"It's a chair, and I sit upright."

"So while you were sitting on the chair, pouring your upright heart out to the good doctor, your partner could have nipped out and pumped a couple of bullets into Helena Jablonska, then made it back in time to finish reading whatever magazines they had lying about. Couldn't she?"

"You'll have to ask the receptionist about that," said Mrs. Bainbridge. "I'm sure she would tell you that Iris never left the waiting room."

"But you can't be certain."

"No," she said wearily. "Obviously not."

"Who's the man who paid for her flat?" he asked.

"What?"

"You heard me," he said. "You know her story. The guy before Archie Spelling. What was his name?"

"I don't know his full name," she said.

"But you know part of it?" he asked, pouncing on the response.

And there it is, she thought. I don't want to betray her. But I don't owe him anything.

"She mentioned the name Andrew," she said.

"When was this?"

"Recently."

"She never said his name before?"

"No."

"Why now?"

She was silent.

"Sparks left your office at nine thirty this morning, according to my colleague," said Cavendish. "She went to your place in Kensington. She staying there?"

"Yes."

"I'm guessing she had to buy those ladies' things because she left her place in a hurry and didn't pack what she needed," said Cavendish.

"Perhaps. It's currently a crime scene, so she can't go back to fetch anything."

"When did she come to stay with you?"

"Tuesday night."

"So she left before her flat became a crime scene. She needed the ladies' things before then, too. Why was she in such a rush to move in with you on Tuesday, Mrs. Bainbridge?"

"Because Andrew showed up. Unexpectedly. And she didn't want to be there with him."

The words came out in a burst. And with them, the guilt.

Cavendish nodded slowly.

"All right, we're finally getting somewhere," he said. "This Andrew—is he connected with any branch of British Intelligence?"

"I don't work for British Intelligence," she said.

"But do you know if he does?"

"I should say that it's likely," she said. "But I don't know anything more about him."

"Does Miss Sparks work for them?"

"She works here," said Mrs. Bainbridge. "With me."

"What's Andrew's connection with Helena Jablonska?"

"I wish I knew," she said.

"Who did you call for her after she was arrested?"

"What makes you think I called anyone?" she asked.

"The fact that you answered my question with a question, for starters," he replied. "Who did you call?"

"Someone more frightening than you, Detective Inspector, and that's all I'm willing to say on that topic."

"You have any questions?" Cavendish asked Myrick.

"No," said Myrick.

"So he does speak," said Mrs. Bainbridge.

"He listens more," said Cavendish. "Thank you, Mrs. Bainbridge. We may have more questions. For you and for Miss Sparks. I assume she'll be staying with you."

"I don't know if she'll still be there when I get home," said Mrs. Bainbridge, the sadness creeping into her voice.

"If she leaves, we'll know," said Cavendish, getting to his feet.

A slight smile formed on her lips that disconcerted him.

"What?" he asked.

"I will bet you tuppence that before the day is over, she will have given your men the slip," she said.

"You are bonkers," he said. "We're professionals. We're the best."

"Tuppence says she's better," she said, holding out her hand.

"What the hell," he said, shaking it. "You're on."

Henderson was grabbing a catnap, slumped down in his seat with his hat brim pulled down over his eyes, when Musgrave poked him in the arm.

"What?" he asked, straightening.

"Chauffeur's pulling a car out."

Henderson put his binoculars to his eyes to see a black Daimler backing out of the garage to a point concealed from view in back of the house.

"Start the car up," he said.

A minute later, the Daimler pulled up the driveway, paused at the street, then pulled out, passing them. In the rear, keeping her head down, was a woman.

"Purple hat," said Henderson. "Same one. Follow them."

"Yes, sir," said Musgrave.

They kept a decent distance behind the Daimler, which headed north. The chauffeur took a right at Notting Hill Gate, then an abrupt left on Pembridge.

"They make us?" asked Musgrave, accelerating to make the turn.

"I don't think so," said Henderson. "Wonder how she's got the pull with the Bainbridges to borrow the chauffeur like that?"

The Daimler made a dogleg onto Portobello Road, then pulled over to the kerb by a stall with trays of fresh herbs on display. The chauffeur got out, walked around to the rear passenger door, and opened it. A woman got out, carrying a large, wicker shopping basket. She was wearing a brown cloth coat which, when she turned in their direction, revealed a maid's uniform underneath.

"That's not her," said Henderson with a sinking feeling. "It's the same hat, I'll bet my badge on it. Pull over."

He was out on the street and moving before the car came to a stop, dodging around the carts and stalls set up in front of the shops, ignoring the irritated glances from the people he brushed as he strode between them. He caught up to the woman and grabbed her by the shoulder. She turned around indignantly.

"And who might you be?" she snapped.

"Henderson, CID," he said. "Where'd you get that hat?"

"The hat?" she asked, a look of confusion on her face. "Did my hat do something illegal?"

"You stole it," he said.

"I never did!" she said hotly. "I borrowed it."

"From who?"

"From Miss Sparks," she said. "She wanted me to wear it while I was shopping."

"Why?"

"It was some sort of joke she was playing," said the maid. "She gave me a shilling."

Cursing, Henderson dashed back to the car and jumped in.

"She's done a runner," he said. "Back to the house. She's probably on foot. Step on it."

Musgrave peeled away, heading back to Kensington.

Millie watched them go, then walked calmly back to the Daimler where Nigel, the chauffeur, was waiting. She nodded to him. He went to the rear of the car and opened the boot. From inside Sparks, who was curled in a foetal position, looked up at him.

"The coast is clear, Miss Sparks," said Nigel, holding out a black-gloved hand.

"Thank you, Nigel," said Sparks, taking it.

He assisted her to the kerb, then pulled out her train case and handed it to her.

"Do you want your hat back, Miss Sparks?" asked Millie.

"Not for now," said Sparks. "If you hear I'm in jail, keep it and wear it in good health."

"You'll be calling Mrs. Bainbridge, won't you?" asked Millie anxiously.

"I don't know if that would be a good idea if I'm on the run," said Sparks.

"But she'll be so worried!"

"Not as much as you'd think," said Sparks. "Heigh-ho, off to the chase. Abyssinia!"

She walked south to the Notting Hill Gate station and disappeared into the Underground.

The pub on Danbury Street was called Dagome. It had been taken over from its previous British owners and renamed by a Polish-English couple in the early thirties, and catered to the Polish community that had sprung up when the Church of Our Lady of Częstochowa and St. Casimir took over what had been a failing Gothic-style Protestant church on Devonia Road in The Angel in Islington. Devonia Road had itself been renamed from Devonshire Road, whether by the Poles who came there or by the English in derisive reference, nobody remembered anymore. Either way, the name stuck and was official now.

The pub was distinguishable from other London pubs primarily by its decorations. A fairly good copy of the Black Madonna of Częstochowa by a former art student from Lodz hung behind the bar. Below it, in frames more suitable for medieval icons, were black-and-white photographs of the Four Generals: Anders, Sosnkowski,

Bór-Komorowski, and Sikorski. Between the Mother of Christ and the fathers of the Polish Army in exile, many toasts were generated, which was good for business. Some fights were also generated, which was less good for business, but in that Dagome was not distinguishable from other London pubs.

The petite blonde who came in attracted some attention, but it was Friday evening and a payday, so many of the occupants were already deep into political debate or morose solitude, which meant she attracted less attention than she merited. She glanced around the room and spotted the object of her journey who, fortunately for her, was one of the solitary morose. He was sitting alone at a small table for two in the back corner, nursing a glass of porter, which was down to its last third, in his left hand. His right arm hung limply by his side. She slid onto the chair across from him.

"*Dobry wieczór, Poruczniku* Waleski," said Sparks.

He looked up in irritation, which quickly turned to surprise.

"You've changed your hair," he said.

"Temporarily," she said. "I'm staying with a friend of a friend. She's an actress with a decent wig collection. I've never been a blonde before. How do I look?"

"Like a ghost from my past," he said. "How did you know I was here?"

"I thought about trying the Polish Soldiers' House first, but then I remembered that you took me here when we thought we lost Captain Sutton. We got very drunk that night. You taught me a hymn called '*Bogurodzica*' and made me stand on a table and sing it with you."

"You were terrible."

"There were thirteen stanzas, there was alcohol, and I didn't speak Polish apart from the little I picked up listening to you coach Andrzej. Of course I was terrible."

"Andrew," he said, downing the rest of his porter. "Call him Andrew. The war is over."

"You're empty," she said. "Let me buy you another."

"Are you trying to get me drunk?" he asked suspiciously.

"No, you were drunk when I came in. I'm trying to keep you drunk."

He shrugged in acknowledgment, only one shoulder rising.

"What are you having?" she asked.

"*Piwo z sokiem,*" he said.

"*Piwo z sokiem,*" she repeated carefully. "Good enough?"

"Good enough for the bartender."

She went to the bar. The bartender came over.

"*Piwo z sokiem,*" she said. "Actually, *dwa piwo z sokiem.*"

"That would be '*dwa piwa,*' love," said the bartender. "Plural form."

"*Dziękuję ci,*" said Sparks. "Always glad to improve."

He poured two glasses, then added some dark red syrup from a bottle and stirred it into each.

I hope I didn't just buy myself the Polish equivalent of a Mickey Finn, she thought as she brought them back to Waleski.

"*Na zdrowie,*" she said, holding up her glass.

"*Na zdrowie,*" he echoed, clinking his against it.

She took a sip.

"It's sweet," she said. "What's the red stuff?"

"Raspberry syrup."

"Very refreshing."

"So, do I salute you?" he asked. "What rank are you up to now?"

"I've been out for over a year. Left a lieutenant. I thought you knew that."

"I heard something, I suppose," he said.

"You're out, too."

"Yes."

"Then there is no need for military formalities. We're merely friends, now."

"Are we, Miss Sparks?"

"Well, we at least have a mutual friend," she replied. "In fact, he's back in town."

"Is he?"

"Didn't you know?"

Waleski scowled.

"We haven't kept in touch," he said.

"That surprises me. You kept working with him after the war."

"Until I quit."

"Which wasn't that long ago. Why did you quit, Tadek?"

"Are we allowed to be talking like this?" he asked.

"Probably not," she said. "But who cares?"

"I quit because after risking my life for a free Poland, after losing the use of my right arm fighting with the RAF, and after swallowing my pride and working for the Brigadier even after Churchill sold us out to Stalin at Yalta, I went to a parade in June. Wonderful parade, full of happy, cheering English people, with bands and speeches and fireworks. And whatever English leader was making the biggest speech thanked every country who had joined in the Allied effort to fight for the forces of freedom and all that is good and holy. Every country except Poland, because England does not wish to make Stalin angry. Right then and there, I realised that to England, Poland doesn't exist, the Poles do not exist, *I* do not exist. But according to Poland, I no longer exist, either. They erased me, just like they did to General Anders. Not just Anders—Kopański, Chruściel, Maczek, Malonowski, Masny, and those are generals! Deprived of Polish citizenship because they fought for the Allies, even though they called themselves the Polish Army. And if I go back to where I no longer exist, I am a dead man. So I stay here, where I do not exist, a useless man with a dead arm waiting for the rest of my body to join it."

"I'm sorry, Tadek," she said, placing her hand on his left so she knew he would feel it.

"Why did you come here, Sparks?" he asked, shaking it off angrily.

"Can't a girl visit an old chum from the war?"

"Old chum," he said. "This is the first time I've seen you since that night singing '*Bogurodzica*.' No, I'm wrong. Since a week after that."

"I was reassigned," she said. "Don't you remember?"

"Maybe I remember, maybe I try to forget," he said. "What do you want with me?"

"I'm trying to find him."

"Who?"

"Who do you think, Tadek? Andrzej. Andrew. Do you know where he is?"

"Ask the Brigadier."

"I can't. I'm on the outs. Andrew may be as well. He's in trouble, Tadek, and he got me in trouble, too."

Waleski glanced down at her stomach.

"Not that kind of trouble," she said. "But you're not far off the mark. A woman showed up earlier this week looking for him. Helena Jablonska. Know anything about her?"

He shook his head.

"I'm trying to find people who do," she said.

"Who is she with?" he asked.

"Excellent question. She may have worked with Andrew during the war. Maybe at Blizna, with the *Armia Krajowa*."

"I still don't know her."

"Might not be her real name."

"Describe her."

"Short, brunette, beautiful. She was putting on the pounds when I met her because she was eating for two."

"Ah," he said. "That's the trouble."

"There's more. She's dead."

"That's a great deal of trouble," he said. "Are the police involved?"

"They are," she said. "Andrew and I are currently Numbers One and Two on their list of suspects, and I'm not sure who's ahead at the moment. I need to do some fast digging, Tadek. Tomorrow morning, I am going to take an eight thirty train to Iver in Buckinghamshire, then from there to Grove Park Iver."

"What's there?"

"A Polish resettlement camp. I could use an interpreter with a background in intelligence work."

"Why should I add your troubles to my own?"

"Look around you, Tadek," said Sparks. "It's Friday night. You've got no job, no country, no cause, and if I hadn't shown up, no woman. What else have you got to do?"

"Not get arrested?"

"I'll pay you."

He looked at her, then started to laugh.

"I give up, Sparks," he said. "Which station?"

CHAPTER 10

Cavendish and Myrick came back to the office around three. There was a note on Cavendish's telephone. He picked it up, read it, and muttered a profanity. Myrick looked at him in question.

"I owe that Bainbridge woman tuppence," said Cavendish. "They lost Sparks. Tell you what, Ian. We've been up over twenty-four hours. I'm done in, so are you. Go home, sleep it off, then meet me back here midmorning. We'll drive out to that Polish camp, see what we can find."

Myrick nodded, grabbed his hat and coat, and walked out.

Cavendish walked to Kinsey's office and knocked on the door. Kinsey looked up in surprise and waved him in.

"What's up?" he asked. "You look a wreck."

"I'm knackered," admitted Cavendish. "I'm calling it a day, but I wanted to tell you that what I said last night in Parham's office was nothing personal."

"Of course," said Kinsey. "I would have done exactly the same in your position. How goes the investigation?"

"I'm running into brick walls at every turn, and your ex has been the mason for most of them. I just got back from seeing her psychiatrist."

"Sparks is seeing a psychiatrist," Kinsey said, bemused. "I wonder what finally convinced her to do that."

"You don't sound overly surprised."

"That she needs one? No. That she finally bit the bullet and went is a marvel."

"She goes to the same one Mrs. Bainbridge does."

"Well done, Mrs. Bainbridge. What did the psychiatrist tell you?"

"He invoked privilege and slammed the door in my face, or would have except it was padded and didn't make much of a slam. But his receptionist confirmed that Sparks came with Bainbridge for their appointments and remained the entire time."

"Does that give her an alibi for the time of death?"

"The doc thinks Jablonska was shot sometime between two and five thirty in the afternoon. Sparks and Bainbridge were at the psychiatrist's office from five to six thirty. But Sparks was also away from her office for an hour in the afternoon."

"Doing what?"

"Running errands, she said," said Cavendish. "What do you think the matter is with her, Mike? Psychiatrically speaking?"

"I'd be speaking out of turn," said Kinsey. "Everyone thinks his ex is crazy."

"Think she's capable of killing someone?" asked Cavendish.

"Well . . ." said Kinsey, hesitating.

"What?"

"I could never prove anything," said Kinsey, "but there is an unsolved murder in the Don't Ask files that I thought she might have had a hand in."

"So she did work for Intelligence," said Cavendish.

"I never knew that for a fact," said Kinsey. "But in retrospect, it would have explained much."

"An execution, you think?"

"He was stabbed once through the heart. It was expertly done."

"Different weapon. Ever known her to carry a gun?"

"No," said Kinsey. "Not that she wouldn't. But the thing that strikes me about this case is that Jablonska's death was planned. The about-to-be-deceased opened the door to someone with a gun already out. It wasn't a fight or a spontaneous event."

"You're saying Sparks isn't capable of planning a murder?"

"I'm saying that if she did, she wouldn't be so sloppy as to leave the body in her own flat," said Kinsey.

"So I should drop her as a suspect because she's a more proficient murderer than whoever did this."

"Something like that."

"I'm so tired that that actually makes sense," said Cavendish, yawning. "God help me."

Gwen stopped at a newsstand on her walk home, glancing at the evening papers. She plunked down a penny and picked up the *Evening Standard*. She flipped it open and scanned it as she walked.

She was halfway through Hyde Park when she spotted it, a short single paragraph on the lower right of an inside page. "Murder in Marylebone." She stopped to read it through. Jablonska's name wasn't mentioned, but "A Miss Iris Sparks, a resident of the flat, was taken into custody but released after assisting the police in their enquiries."

Nice way of putting it, thought Gwen. I doubt she assisted them much. At least The Right Sort was left out of the story. All they needed was another scandal.

When she arrived at her street, she saw a car across from the house with two men in the front seat, studiously not looking at her. That wouldn't have been something she would have noticed or considered before Iris became part of her life, Gwen thought as she turned down the driveway. Of course, she had no cause for the police to become involved in her life before she met Iris.

No, that wasn't fair. Of their strange journeys of late, only one was due to Iris and her cloak-and-dagger past. And Iris had taken on The Right Sort as a way of putting her past behind her. As had Gwen.

Gwen paused before the door, looking up at her in-laws' house with the same sense of dread that rushed in every time she returned from work.

One's past doesn't like being put behind one, she thought. There are no dungeons strong enough or deep enough to lock it away and forget it forever. It will find a way to erupt back into the present, scorching everything in its path.

Buck up, old girl. You won't be here for much longer if things go well.

With that happy thought, she went inside. Percival was walking in the hallway and stopped upon seeing her.

"Good evening, Mrs. Bainbridge," he said. "I have something for you."

He reached into his pocket, then held out his hand. Resting on his palm were two pennies.

"From the gentlemen in the car outside," he informed her. "They said you would know who they're from."

"Miss Sparks escaped successfully?"

"Apparently so," said Percival. "I believe the gentlemen are keeping watch to see if she comes back. I think they will be disappointed."

"Did anyone in the household break any laws in helping her? Or shouldn't I be asking that question?"

"I think the latter would be the safer course, ma'am," he said.

"Very good, Percival. Has Mr. Daile arrived?"

"He has, ma'am. I believe you will find him in the playroom with the boys."

"Thank you. I'll drop by, then dress for dinner."

She stopped by the hallway telephone and dialled Sally's number to see if he had any updates on Iris. There was no answer.

Out on the town with his Russian delegation, she guessed.

She went upstairs to the playroom to find Ronnie, John, and John's newly arrived uncle Simon Daile engrossed in a board game. Simon saw her, and got up to greet her with a smile. He was an inch shorter than Gwen, with a medium brown complexion, and spoke English with a Scottish burr learned from the missionaries who taught him in Nyasaland.

"Hello, Simon," she said, kissing him on the cheek. "Easy journey, I hope?"

"The journey by train was easy," he said. "But playing pachisi with these two is exhausting. They have demolished me game after game. I have my suspicions about the dice."

"We keep sending his pieces back!" crowed Ronnie.

"I don't think he's ever played this before," said John.

"Not true," protested Simon. "One of my bunkmates in the Royal Navy had a set, and we would play when we weren't keeping the boilers running. He was from India, and told me that the Emperor Akbar had a giant pachisi board built of great slabs of stone in the courtyard of his palace in Agra, where they would play with sixteen of the most beautiful girls from his harem as living pieces."

"Gosh!" exclaimed the boys, duly impressed.

"You play with the pieces you have," said Gwen sternly. "Let me borrow your uncle for a moment. He will be back to finish the game."

They stepped into the hallway.

"Don't give them ideas about harems," she cautioned him. "Otherwise, they'll be doomed to disappointment later. As will the women they marry."

"An excellent point, Gwendolyn," he said. "I will try not to be such a corrupting influence in the future."

"Now, if you are willing to restrict yourself to one woman in your life, then here's a start," she said, pulling an envelope from her bag and handing it to him.

"You found someone!" he exclaimed, opening it.

"No guarantees, of course."

"No, of course not. Miss Bitsy Sedgewick. Bitsy? That is an actual English name?"

"A nickname. Her full name is Elizabeth."

"Like the queen," he said. "Does the king call her Bitsy in private?"

"I have no idea, although she is tiny."

"What is this Bitsy like?"

"That, Simon, is something you'll have to learn for yourself."

"But you and Miss Sparks think we might suit each other."

"We do," said Gwen.

"What does she know about me?" he asked.

"She knows that you come from Nyasaland, that you served in the Royal Navy, and that you're currently a student at the Royal Agricultural College. She's from Camden Town, but she was a Land Girl during the war, so the two of you can talk shop if you want to."

"That sounds like a dreadful way to begin," he said. "'Hello, my name is Simon. How do you feel about barley blight?'"

"I wouldn't lead with that. Maybe save it for the second date."

"She's not expecting to see me this weekend, is she?"

"Not at all. Write her, set up a time and place. The Bainbridge house will be your base of operations when you come to town, as long as the boys are willing to part with you."

"How is John doing?" he asked softly, the smile replaced by concern.

"He's had a hard time of it, frankly," she replied. "His father isn't well enough to be a proper father. He may never be well enough. It helps John so much to have you visit."

"I understand we have an expedition tomorrow."

"Yes, to see the exhibit at the V and A. The boys are very excited."

"I will be interested to see what Britain can make. And Miss Sparks will be joining us, I hear."

"Unfortunately, she won't," she said. "She's had a change in plans."

"Is something wrong?" he asked, catching something in her voice.

"I'll tell you what I can after the boys have gone to bed later," she said. "Iris and I have had a bit of a falling-out."

"That must be remedied right away," he said.

"Right away was several hours ago, so that won't happen," she said. "Now, go back in there and face the dice. And, Simon?"

"Yes, Gwendolyn?"

"Don't let them win every game," she said. "I don't want them thinking life's that easy."

"Another sound parenting tip," he said, heading back to the playroom. "I have much to learn."

So have I, she thought.

The following morning, a still bewigged but now bespectacled Iris Sparks purchased two round-trip tickets to Iver, then bought a cup of tea from a stall and sipped it, glancing about the station. She wondered if Waleski would keep his promise from the previous night and show up. She wondered if he was sufficiently awake to make his way from The Angel to Paddington in time to catch the eight thirty.

She wondered most of all who he had called from the telephone box outside of Dagome after she left him there, assuring her that he was sober enough to remember everything even though she tried to write it down for him. She watched him speak, softly and urgently, his hand cupped by his mouth so she couldn't read his lips.

She followed him after that, but he simply walked a block to the Polish Soldiers' House on Devonia and went inside.

He probably slept better than I did, she thought. Doris, Sally's actress friend, may have had a store of wigs, but she didn't have a second bed. Iris had to scrunch up on the sofa by the unlit fireplace, her toes poking out from under the inadequate woollen blanket. Doris had got in much later and considerably drunker than Iris had. She had insisted on regaling Iris about her own evening, with stories that she found hilarious even though she couldn't remember their punch lines, the laughter gradually dissolving to tears as she wondered if this was what her life would be like from now on, and how she should have married that boy back in Yorkshire when he had asked her, but it was too late, he had probably moved on to that slut Ruthie, and she would never have treated him like she (meaning herself, she clarified between sobs) would have done, given half the chance.

Iris nodded throughout, resolutely refusing to venture either opinion or consolation, and ended up tucking her in, contemplating stealing the very warm and comfy-looking quilt Doris had reserved for her own use, but ultimately deciding against it in case she needed to continue using the flat as her temporary hideout.

She wondered where Andrew had gone to ground. Could have been anywhere, although if he were staying away from people connected to Intelligence, that would have limited his choices considerably. Limited them to people like her. People who had left the secret wars.

People who had given up. People who had quit.

She wondered if Waleski was outside of the organisation enough for Andrew to turn to him in time of need. Was it Andrew who he'd called from the box outside Dagome? And was Andrew's mistrust in the Home Office because they could no longer be trusted, or because he had turned?

She swirled the dregs of the tea in her cup, trying to read the answers in the leaves. It seemed as good a method as any at the moment.

Then she looked up to see Waleski walking towards her, wearing an RAF flight jacket. He had shaved, and she detected no whiff of *piwo* emanating from his pores.

"You look quite dashing in that," she commented. "Good to see it still fits you so well. Is that the same one you wore when you flew?"

"The one I wore when I flew got two holes in it right about here," he said, pointing to his right shoulder with his left hand. "Then they had to cut it off me when they pulled me out of what was left of the cockpit. I bought this one from a friend who went back to what is left of Poland. If he wore it there, he would be dead inside a week. Shall we go?"

They boarded the middle car. She motioned him to a window seat, figuring he had not done much traveling recently and might enjoy the view.

He didn't say anything until the train had left the station.

"How long will it take?" he asked.

"About forty minutes to Iver," she said, consulting her schedule. "Then it's a longish hike unless we catch the bus."

"Can't we take a taxi?"

"First, I don't know how likely it is there will be taxis there. Second, it's a lovely day for a walk."

"Third, you don't have enough money for a taxi."

"Not after hiring you for the day."

"If I had known I was going to walk so much, I would have charged you more," he said grumpily. "What do you expect to find when we get there?"

"If I knew, I wouldn't need to go."

He stared moodily out the window as the train left the city behind.

"I keep forgetting there are such things as forests and fields," he said. "This is a beautiful country when you leave London."

"I suppose it is. But I like London."

"I remember flying over the countryside in training, thinking,

'Poland has farms. Poland has fields. Poland has forests. Why do they not look the same?' There are different shades of green here. Have you ever seen it from the air?"

"A few times," she said, shaking involuntarily. "Let's not talk about flying."

"What shall we talk about?"

"Anything but flying."

"I remember asking you out once," he said. "You said no. Do you remember that?"

"I do, Tadek," she said.

"You were in love with him."

"I was."

"Even though he was married."

"Yes."

"Even after you thought he was dead."

"Maybe especially then."

"And now?"

"Quite the opposite. But to anticipate your next question, sorry but no. I'm seeing someone."

A brief, sad smile, then he turned back to the window, choosing to look at her faint reflection shimmering over the fields and towns as they passed by.

"Was it because of my arm?" he asked, tapping it with his good hand. "I am finding that women are repulsed by it."

"Those are women unworthy of you," she said. "But in an odd way, yes, it was because of that, although not in the way you think."

"Explain, please."

"When we first met to train Andrew, I was coming off a series of assignments that came after I failed parachute training and couldn't bring myself to repeat it. Every time I met someone who had actually gone into combat, I felt my own cowardice. You were a constant reminder of that, Tadek. You are even now."

"But you became Andrew's woman after he came back."

"You knew about that?"

"As you know, I continued to work with him after one war ended and another began," he said with a one-shouldered shrug.

"He talked about me," she said, more to herself than him. "Of course he did. The Brigadier knew about us. But I never thought it would be a wider topic of conversation."

"It wasn't," said Waleski. "I mentioned your name once when he was back in London, wondering what had become of you."

"What did he tell you?"

"He gave one of those Andrew smiles that takes you into his confidence and said, 'Oh, I've got Sparks stashed away all to myself now.'"

"Rotter," said Sparks.

"He always was," said Waleski. "I'm surprised you didn't see it from the start. What was it about him that made you fall?"

"He was our creation, Tadek," said Sparks. "Yours and mine. We built an Andrzej from an Andrew, and he was going to do what I couldn't bring myself to do. We created someone to die in glory, and I gave myself to him so he could bring my soul along with his."

"And you thought it would die there with him."

"Yes. Like the lovers in Mayerling. Romantic, wasn't it?"

"Pathetic."

"It was certainly that," she agreed.

"Does your new man make you feel something other than pathetic?"

"Excellent question, Tadek. Normally, I scrutinise relationships with my friend Gwen, but she's not here and you are. Are you brave enough to indulge me in forty minutes of girl talk?"

"If I had known I was going to talk so much, I would have charged you more."

"That's what happens when you make a deal with Iris Sparks," she said with a laugh. "Now, let me tell you about my current man."

* * *

Gwen fussed with Ronnie's collar, making sure it was even and symmetrical after she had wrested the sweater over his head. Normally, this was Agnes's job, but Gwen wanted the pleasure of over-mothering her son this morning. When she had his collar perfected, she grabbed his hairbrush.

"Mummy, they're waiting for us," he protested.

"The museum will not move before we get there," she assured him. "There! What a handsome young man you are!"

She put on his jacket, then stepped back and indulged herself in maternal pride for a moment.

"Perfection," she said. "Let's go."

"I wish Iris was coming," he said as she led him downstairs.

"I wish she was, too," said Gwen. "We'll have to do something else with her sometime."

John, Simon, and Agnes were in the front hall when they came down. Simon was wearing the grey demob suit he wore the first time he had walked into The Right Sort and upended their lives.

"We're ready," he said. "How far is it?"

"About a twenty-five-minute walk," said Gwen. "And there will probably be a queue to get in."

"Here we go!" said Agnes, taking the boys' hands.

The boys and their governess walked ahead, chattering away. Simon offered Gwen his arm, which she took.

"I'm not sure who is protecting whom," he said as they drew hostile stares from a family across the street.

"I have been taking self-defence lessons," she said. "Once a week with a very deadly former master sergeant named Macaulay."

"I am impressed," he said. "Is Miss Sparks taking them with you?"

"No. She's much more advanced in that area."

"Somehow, I am not surprised," he said.

He glanced ahead at the boys.

"Have the other children been terrible to him?" he asked. "I've had my share of despicable comments from supposedly mature men at Royal Ag. I imagine children could be far worse in that area."

"It hasn't been easy," she said. "He aches for your visits."

"I'm sorry they can't be more frequent," he said. "May I ask you a question?"

"Of course."

"Why are we bringing Agnes? I should think the two of us would be perfectly adequate for herding two young men through a museum."

He felt her arm tense in his.

"What is the matter?" he asked.

"I'm not permitted to take my son out on my own," she said softly so the others couldn't hear. "I had to beg and cajole to be allowed even this much of an outing."

"For heaven's sake, Gwendolyn. Why?"

"You're family now," she said. "This is as good an opportunity as any to tell you about when I was away."

There was supposed to be a bus that meandered along High Street to Langley Park Road, but whatever schedule it was on was out of phase with Sparks and Waleski's. They gamely trudged along, passing through the small village into an area populated more by cattle than humans. They drew little attention from those humans they did see, Waleski's RAF jacket serving as a passport.

"Bomber Command used to be around here somewhere," he commented. "Then they moved."

"Why?" asked Sparks.

"They were bombed."

"Nowhere to hide in the countryside," said Sparks. "At least London has the Underground."

She looked at her notes.

"It should be coming up on the right fairly soon," she said.

The first sign was the shouts of children. The two paused to peer over the bushes lining the road to see a game of football in progress, boys and girls of many ages dashing at breakneck speed in pursuit of a decrepit ball that barely maintained its shape.

The shouts were in Polish.

"Looks like we've come to the right place," said Sparks, turning to look at Waleski.

He was gazing at the game with a look of longing.

"Did you play?" asked Sparks.

"Of course I played," he said. "I could run forever back then. Now? When I was in the hospital, waiting to see if my arm would ever regain feeling and motion, they tried to get me into a game. 'Come on, Tadek, it will be fun, and the arm won't matter at all.' But the moment I started to run, the damn thing kept flapping about. It was laughable, only no one had the courage to laugh. That was the last time I played football."

"Would you like my advice?" asked Sparks as they resumed walking.

"Advice? What possible advice could you have?"

"If you want to play football, play football," said Sparks. "Next time, strap the arm down first."

"You think this is easy?"

"Not at all, but easy or not, it's possible. There's the entrance up ahead."

They had turned north off the main road, just before a two-story white public house at which they both looked longingly. A sign with a lion painted in red on a field of white dangled from a post.

"Probably worth investigating afterwards, don't you think?" commented Sparks.

"I do."

The resettlement camp was on the grounds of a large manor

house, which loomed with an air of decaying gentility in the distance. The camp consisted of fifty or so Nissen huts laid out in rows
of ten. They very much resembled giant oil barrels sawn lengthwise
neatly down the middle and tilted onto their open faces. Windows
had been punched out on the sides and doorways in the front ends.
At the end of the rows were larger structures: a washhouse with a
queue of men and women waiting patiently holding metal pails containing soap and toothbrushes, towels slung over their shoulders; a
laundry with its own queue, mostly women with wicker baskets of
dirty clothes; and a large assembly hall of some kind with the words
"*Komitet Zarządzający*" painted neatly on one of the doors.

"'Management committee,'" said Waleski. "We should start
there."

They walked towards it, passing by the huts. Each had its own
rectangle of land, Sparks observed, with vegetable gardens and
chicken coops crammed into every available foot of space. Everywhere she glanced, someone was hard at work repairing a doorframe, running electric wires from a dangerous-looking jury-rigged
transformer by the side of the road up light poles and into houses,
or painting the semicircular fronts of the huts to give them a bit of
individuality. The huts were numbered. Some even had mailboxes,
which Sparks found both optimistic and depressing. She couldn't
imagine living here long enough to have a mailing address.

They reached the assembly hall and knocked on the door. It
was opened by a man in his forties, wearing brown wool pants
with suspenders over a collarless white shirt, its sleeves rolled up
to his elbows. He looked back and forth at the two of them suspiciously, then settled his gaze on Waleski.

"*Co chcesz?*" he asked him.

"My name is Mary McTague," said Sparks, producing an identification card in that name. "I'm with the government."

She paused while Waleski translated. The man looked at her
with disdain.

"I have lived in England six years," he said. "I speak English."

"I didn't mean to offend," said Sparks. "I am looking for people who knew Jerzy Jablonski."

"Jerzy Jablonski is dead," he said.

"Yes, I know," she said. "But I thought there might be someone here who also knows Helena Jablonska. Friends or family."

"Helena Jablonska?" he replied. "What has she done?"

"Why do you think she's done anything?"

"Because you are with the government," he said. "And because she is a traitor."

CHAPTER 11

The queue at the Victoria and Albert Museum was worse than they had feared, stretching north from the Exhibition Road entrance and around the corner of the building. Mounted police patrolled its length, allowing the children to come forward and pet their horses, which tolerated the experience. Agnes went up to one of the officers and engaged him in a brief conversation. He glanced over to where the two boys were standing with Gwen and Simon, then said something that made Agnes's shoulders sag slightly. She came back to them with an insincere smile that Gwen knew meant trouble.

"Only forty-five minutes to get in from this point," she chirped. "Aren't we lucky? He said it was quite the scene the other day when the king and queen were here to open the exhibition."

"That must have been exciting," said Gwen. "Remember, boys, anything with a queue is something worth waiting for. Agnes, why don't you pick up a guide from that vendor by the gate, and we'll spend our time figuring which rooms we want to see the most."

"We want to see the toys!" shouted Ronnie as John nodded vehemently in agreement.

"And so you shall," said Gwen. "But no shouting, especially indoors."

Agnes returned with a copy of the guide, which she handed to Gwen. Gwen opened it, and the three adults pored over it like a trio of generals in the War Room.

"Interesting," said Simon. "It's designed to keep you moving in the same direction as everyone else."

"Which means you end up seeing everything," said Gwen.

"But do we want to see everything?" asked Agnes. "More to the point, will the boys be patient enough to see everything?"

"Look at that," said Simon. "The largest room is devoted to women's dresses."

"Oh, I really want to see those," said Agnes eagerly.

"So do I," said Gwen. "But look what's in the room right after them."

"The toys," said Agnes with a sigh.

"That's diabolical," said Gwen. "Any mother bringing a child will be dragged through the fashion exhibit like a water-skier behind a speedboat."

"This is where having an adult male on the expedition becomes invaluable," said Simon.

The two women looked up at him, their faces suddenly hopeful.

"Do you mean to say that you will volunteer to take them on ahead while we linger and admire the pretty dresses?" asked Gwen.

"I do."

"He's very brave, isn't he, Mrs. Bainbridge?" said Agnes with a mischievous twinkle.

"Positively gallant," said Gwen. "We accept your generous offer, Simon. Now, there is a tea lounge before the dresses. That will be our first resting point. Once properly fortified, you continue on, and we shall catch up to you by the restaurant. We'll look for you by Sports and Leisure. That looks large enough to keep a pair of boys interested for a while."

"And me," said Simon.

The forty-five-minute estimate proved accurate. Fortunately, a pair of buskers were on hand to entertain the queued crowd, belting out "Knocked 'em in the Old Kent Road," "Any Old Iron," and "Don't Dilly Dally on the Way," accompanying themselves with ukuleles and a homemade assemblage of pots, rattles, and bells. Gwen found the last song completely inappropriate for their circumstances, but Ronnie and Simon quickly joined in the choruses, jumping up and down in time. By the time they reached the entrance under the giant, three-dimensional mock-up of the multicoloured pennant that was on all the posters for the exhibit, the boys were like a pair of cannonballs begging for the fuses to be lit.

After they passed through the chrome-plated turnstiles into the foyer, they turned right, taking them to an exhibit grandly titled "From War to Peace," with a vaguely Constructivist depiction of a dove flying with the requisite olive branch in its beak over what Gwen supposed was meant to be a factory but which looked more like terraced houses for dogs.

It was dark past the entrance to this section, and Ronnie instinctively took his mother's hand as they went in. To their left was a mural of London during the Blitz, with bombed-out buildings in the foreground, the dome of St. Paul's looming behind, standing damaged but proud. Thin beams of light played across it like searchlights probing for enemies in the painted skies. In front of the mural, amidst piles of rubble artfully strewn about, were a scale mock-up of a barrage balloon and, to the boys' mingled astonishment and delight, a fighter plane crashed at an angle.

"That's a Spitfire," exclaimed John. "A real Spitfire!"

The nose of the plane was connected by a row of painted strings to a group of saucepans. "Once you gave your saucepans for Spitfires," read the copy. "Now the experience gained in aircraft production gives you better and more durable saucepans."

"Well, that makes it all worth it, doesn't it?" muttered a man ahead of them.

He was wearing a demob suit and limped badly, using a cane for support. Gwen wanted to say something to him, but couldn't find the words.

"Was it really like this, Mummy?" asked Ronnie, gripping her hand tightly.

"It was," she said. "But you were safe from it."

Other objects of modern warfare stood side by side with their benign offspring. A tank periscope hovered over a cut- and ground-glass bowl. A commando's waterproof suit hung by a beach bag made from the same fabric. Most tellingly, an aluminium ammunition box for a Hurricane fighter was mounted next to a pram made by the same London manufacturer.

"This must be our version of beating swords into ploughshares," commented Simon while the boys stared goggle-eyed at the flight suits.

"I pray those boys never have to live through anything like this again," said Gwen.

"With these new bombs the Americans have, no one will ever want to start another war," said Simon.

"Do you think so?" asked Gwen.

"I want to believe it," said Simon. "Otherwise, what was the point of it all?"

They passed quickly through the Great Hall, now labelled "Shopwindow Street," a Surrealist's idea of a London shopping district filled with a bewildering variety of commodities, most tagged with the disappointing label "Available Later." At Gwen's insistence, they took a quick detour into a gallery featuring domestic appliances. She looked at cookers that used coal and oil, then more approvingly at the new electric designs.

She suddenly realised she was thinking about having a kitchen of her own.

"I need to learn how to cook," she said in a tone of revelation.

"But you never cook," said Ronnie.

"I should learn," she said. "I'll ask Prudence for some lessons. It's a good thing to know."

"Why do you want to cook?" asked Ronnie.

"What if Prudence is on holiday, and there are hungry boys to feed?" said Gwen. "All right, I've seen enough here. Let's skip the furniture and textiles sections and get to the furnished rooms."

These were in the lower gallery, and were the most commented upon exhibits in the articles she had read. Twenty-four fully equipped rooms, each by a different designer, drawing upon the combined imaginations of furniture makers, potters, engineers shifting their focus from destroying the Axis to improving the lives of ordinary households, and artists of all kinds. Each room was created for an imaginary occupant or family, with a drawing and a quick biographical sketch mounted above the listing of the items displayed and their manufacturers.

Living models, mostly young women, passed through, demonstrating the products. As the Bainbridge party looked at the first, a combined kitchen and dining area, a prim, professional woman in a business suit came in carrying a large ceramic bowl filled with flowers, put it in the stainless steel sink, and pretended to fill it with water before placing it on the centre of a circular table made from birch and beech.

"It says this is for a family," Agnes read to Ronnie and John. "The dad is a young architect who paints in his spare time. The mum is keen on amateur theatrics. And they have a son! See him in the picture? He's playing with a toy plane."

"So she's the mummy?" asked Ronnie, pointing to the model.

"She's pretending to be the mummy," explained Agnes.

"Which fits in with the theatrics," said Gwen.

"It's like a zoo, but with people in it," said John.

The model, overhearing that, gave him a quick appreciative smile, then exited the room.

"She didn't really put water in the flowers," said Ronnie.

"It's all right," said Simon. "They're made of plastic. They'll be fine."

The party drifted ahead of Gwen, who found herself fascinated by the rooms and the imaginary lives that belonged to them. The next was a kitchenette for a small flat. She looked at the sketch copy. "The Occupant: Single woman; dietitian at a hospital; excellent cook." The illustration was of a blond woman wearing a short-sleeved white blouse and a plaid skirt, sitting on a curved, wooden high-backed chair. She had her hands in a bowl on her lap, but Gwen couldn't quite figure out what she was doing. Shelling peas, perhaps? Her eyes were closed, her expression downcast, her thoughts somewhere else.

How would they describe my exhibit room? she wondered. "The Occupant: Widowed, lunatic mother of small boy. Enjoys playing the piano and interfering in other people's lives." With padding on the walls from a former wartime manufacturer of life jackets.

"That's the one *The Times* referred to as a spinster," commented a woman standing next to her reading the description. "I'm glad the exhibit just calls her a 'single woman.' Maybe there's some hope for romance for her after all."

"I'm glad they didn't use 'bachelorette,'" said Gwen. "I've never liked that word. It makes us the inferior to the male."

"A bachelorette in a kitchenette," said the other woman. "I agree. That would have been too much."

"She looks sad," said Gwen. "Or possibly tired. It must have been a long day at the hospital."

"Poor thing," agreed the woman as she glanced at Gwen. Then she looked at her more closely. "Hold on, I think I know you. Aren't you Thurmond Brewster's sister?"

"I am," replied Gwen. "Gwendolyn Brewster. Mrs. Ronald Bainbridge now."

"Of course," said the woman with a warm smile. "I remember when you first started showing up. You were probably sixteen or so, but already stunning. We all thought you would become one of the great beauties of the day with a few years of seasoning. I must say that turned out to be an accurate prediction."

"You're very kind," said Gwen. "How do you know Thurmond?"

"Oh, goodness, I didn't introduce myself, did I? Penelope Carrington, but call me Penny, please. I was a friend of Trelinda Sanders. She dated Thurmond for a while, but they didn't take."

"I remember Trelinda," said Gwen. "I liked her. I was glad they broke up. I thought she could do much better than my brother."

"That's cruel but true," said Penny with a quick, sharp laugh.

"Whatever happened to her?"

"Unfortunately, she got caught in the Blitz," said Penny. "Rumour had it she was in the midst of a rendezvous, but no one ever knew for certain. I hope it was true. You certainly did well, marrying Lord Bainbridge's son. What's he like?"

"I lost him," said Gwen. "Two years ago."

Penny closed her eyes for a moment, then looked at Gwen sympathetically.

"I offer my condolences," she said. "I won't go on. I lost my husband to the war, too. The expressions of sympathy do wear one down after a while."

"They do," agreed Gwen wholeheartedly. "No one really understands that."

"Except the other widows," said Penny. "Well, if you don't mind, how about we explore the rest of these little rooms?"

Dr. Milford's advice floated into Gwen's head. *Contact old friends, make new ones.* And Iris was gone.

"I'm with a group ahead," said Gwen. "But we planned to meet up at the tea lounge, so I would be glad of your company until then. And call me Gwen, please."

* * *

"A traitor? How is she a traitor?" asked Sparks.

"Ask the *Armia Krajowa*," said the man. "If you can find any still living."

"Any of them around here?" she asked.

"Maybe."

"Can you tell me anything specific?"

"No."

"What about her family? Or Jerzy's? Would they know anything?"

"His wife lives here. Widow, I mean."

"That's a start," said Sparks. "What's her name?"

"Urszula. Urszula Jablonska. Number twenty-seven."

"Thank you," said Sparks. "You've been very—"

He closed the door.

"That went well," said Waleski. "So glad I made this trip."

"Let's find Number twenty-seven," said Sparks.

They walked down the ends of the rows, checking the hut numbers.

"You didn't know there was a wife, did you?" asked Waleski.

"No," she said. "What strikes me is that Helena Jablonska gave this settlement as her address, but no hut number."

"Maybe she wasn't living here."

"Maybe not. Although our new friend seemed to know who she was."

"And didn't like her," said Waleski. "Perhaps for good reason."

"If she was regarded as a traitor by the Polish community here, then any number of people could have killed her," said Sparks. "That might move me down the list considerably."

"And Andrew."

"And Andrew. There's Number twenty-seven. Let's hope she's in."

A small boy opened the door and looked up at them. Mostly at Waleski, whose jacket he regarded with awe.

"*Tak?*" he said.

"*Poszukujemy Urszuli Jabłońskiej,*" said Waleski. "*Czy ona jest w domu?*"

"*Tak,*" said the boy. He turned to yell into the recesses of the hut. "*Urszula! Pilot i pani są tu, aby się z tobą zobaczyć!*"

A woman emerged through a door in the wall that divided the interior of the hut into two living quarters. She was a slender woman in her early thirties, with sandy hair gathered in a bun under a tied red cloth. She wore no makeup, and her face was drawn and tired.

"Good morning, Mrs. Jablonska," said Sparks. "My name is Mary McTague. I'm with the government. Do you speak English?"

"I do," said the woman. "What do you want?"

"May we speak privately?" asked Sparks. "I'm afraid I have some bad news."

Mrs. Jablonska flinched slightly, but brought them inside and through the door to the rear living quarters.

There wasn't much in the way of decoration. A single, bare light bulb was suspended by a cord from the ceiling with a thin chain dangling from it. There was a pair of mattresses on the floor in one corner and a dresser by the wall. A small table with a single chair was by a solitary window to the left. There was a dank smell to it all, emanating through the floorboards.

Mrs. Jablonska sat in the chair and looked at them expectantly.

"What is it?" she asked.

"Do you know a Helena Jablonska?" asked Sparks.

"I know a woman called that."

"Unfortunately, I have to inform you that she is dead."

Mrs. Jablonska slowly shifted her gaze from Sparks to Waleski, who nodded in affirmation.

"I understand," said Mrs. Jablonska. "So?"

"She died under violent circumstances," said Sparks. "We are looking into it."

"You are police?"

"Not exactly," said Sparks.

"Ah," said Mrs. Jablonska. "You are with government. With—"
She motioned helplessly, then looked at Waleski.

"*Agencja wywiadu?*" she asked.

"'Intelligence agency,'" he translated.

"We need to know what she was doing here," said Sparks, ignoring the question. "What can you tell us about her?"

"Not much," said Mrs. Jablonska. "Jerzy did not—Jerzy was my husband. He died last year."

"We know," said Sparks. "I'm sorry."

"He and I fled Poland early, before things became terrible," she said. "He left behind entire family. His sister had gone to Grodno to work for a cousin's family. That was before I met him. Then Soviets invaded, and we did not hear from her. We thought she was dead."

"Grodno is in eastern Poland," muttered Waleski in response to a questioning glance from Sparks. "Or what used to be eastern Poland."

"Did you hear from her after you fled?" asked Sparks.

"No," said Mrs. Jablonska. "But someone from Jerzy's family said she come back home after invasion."

"Where is home?"

"Mielec."

That's where Helena said she was from, thought Sparks.

"Did they say what she was doing there?" she asked.

"No, only that she was home and still alive."

Mrs. Jablonska closed her eyes and smiled for a moment.

"Jerzy was so happy when he heard that," she said. "He thought he had lost her. When the war ended, he wrote to her. He was ill. He couldn't travel. He wanted to see her before—before he couldn't."

"Did she write back?"

"We received a letter," she said. "It confused him. He was already fading, but the letter—he kept saying, she called me Jerzy, she called me Jerzy."

"Why was that confusing?"

"Because in family, they called him Jurek," she explained. "Is—*przezwisko*?"

"Um, like friendly name," said Waleski.

"Nickname?" suggested Sparks.

"Nickname, yes."

"So she was more formal in her letter," said Sparks. "Was that unusual?"

"It bothered him," she said.

"Do you still have that letter?"

"No," she said. "He got angry and tore it up. His mind was not good. And then he died a month later. I wrote to tell her, but I heard nothing from her. Until she showed up here."

"She came here? To you?"

"Yes. She said she had to get out of Poland, and there was no one else she knew."

"When was this?"

"Maybe two weeks ago."

"She stayed here? In this room?"

"Yes. For a few days."

"Are any of her belongings still here?"

"No," said Mrs. Jablonska. "She did not have much. All she had was in one suitcase, and she took that with her when she left."

"Why did she leave?"

"There was trouble with some of the others here," said Mrs. Jablonska. "Even if there had not been, I would have made her leave."

"Why?" asked Sparks.

"Because she was lying to me."

"About what?"

"She was not Helena Jablonska."

"How did you know that?"

She got up, opened a drawer, and took out a small bundle of photographs. She untied the string securing them, then removed one and brought it over to the desk where the light was better. She beckoned to Sparks and Waleski, who peered at it over her shoulders.

It was a formal portrait of an extended family at a wedding. The bride and groom were at the centre, looking rapturous, and a score of members of the wedding party fanned out on either side of them. It was taken on the front steps of a brick church with copper sheeting on the roof.

"This was wedding of Jerzy's cousin Sygmunt," she said, pointing to the groom. "Jerzy was sixteen then. That is him."

She pointed to one of the young men to the right of the groom, a strongly built, black-haired adolescent grinning broadly.

"Very handsome," commented Sparks.

"He was," said Mrs. Jablonska sadly. "Over here, this was Helena."

The girl she was pointing at looked maybe ten or eleven, in what Sparks guessed was traditional dress, with an embroidered vest over a white blouse and flowers and ribbons in her hair. She was pouting.

"What year was this taken?" asked Sparks.

"1930. She left for Grodno when she was fifteen."

"It's hard to tell with children's faces what they will look like when they grow up," said Sparks, looking at it closely.

"Have you met this woman who says she was Helena?" asked Mrs. Jablonska.

"I've seen a recent photograph," said Sparks. "Taken at the morgue."

"Morgue?" asked Mrs. Jablonska, glancing at Waleski.

"*Kostnicy*," he said.

She looked at them, her expression hard.

"Good," she said. "Then you can see. She is not girl in this picture."

"Maybe not," said Sparks. "Why did the man at the committee office think she was a traitor?"

"Someone else here recognised her from Mielec, started to scream at her about being traitor. I did not hear about it until after I came home from factory. By that time, she and her suitcase were gone."

"Who was it?" asked Sparks. "Who was the person who screamed at her?"

"His name is Karol Celinski."

"Did you learn why he called her that?"

"No," she said. "I did not care. She was gone. Somehow, I knew she would not be coming back."

"Do you know where I can find this Celinski?"

Mrs. Jablonska looked at her wristwatch.

"Yes," she said. "There is only one place he will be right now. You may want to get there quickly if you want him to speak to you."

"I think I've just figured out where that is," said Sparks.

"'A bedroom in a detached town house,'" read Gwen. "'Young doctor, newly in practice; studies social conditions. His wife; likes outdoor sports and photography.' I like them."

"Which one do you think will have an affair first?" asked Penny.

"Already? They've only just moved in."

"He'll be out studying social conditions and meet some sweet earnest thing," said Penny. "She will find a more rugged man, a tennis instructor or a wilderness photographer."

"God, now that I think of it, you may be right," said Gwen. "And their furniture is so drab. I thought we would be getting beyond Utility designs."

"They're all meant for export, anyway," said Penny. "Did you read Raymond Mortimer's review about them in *The New Statesman*? He wrote, 'They may be good enough for foreigners; they are certainly not bad enough for the English.'"

"Too true."

"Look at this one," said Penny, moving to a bed-sitting room. "'Single woman; aged thirty-five; journalist; now in the Civil Service; widely travelled.'"

"What happened to the journalist job?" asked Gwen, feeling indignant over the fate of this imaginary female.

"The men came back," said Penny. "At least she got to see the world."

"Now she is forever doomed to this gloomy walnut prison."

"But over here is a bed-sitting room with a single man. 'Sportsman and sports commentator at Broadcasting House.' Shall we introduce them? They have so much in common."

"No," said Gwen. "We should fix him up with the dietician. They'd be a much better match. He wouldn't be happy with a woman still capable of expressing an opinion at thirty-five. And he could stand to lose a few pounds. Look at him!"

"You sound very certain about that," said Penny.

"Matchmaking is something I do professionally," said Gwen.

"How do you mean?"

"I run an agency. The Right Sort Marriage Bureau in Mayfair."

"No!" exclaimed Penny. "You mean you actually do that for a living?"

"It's not much of a living yet," Gwen confessed. "We've only been in business for half a year. But it's growing steadily."

"But this is fascinating," said Penny. "How do the rest of the Brewsters and Bainbridges feel about a woman toiling in the mines of romance?"

"The Bainbridges have come around," said Gwen. "Thurmond—well, he has no tolerance for anything I do, while Mum—frankly, she's never said anything about it."

"Which says everything," said Penny with a sigh.

"Probably."

"Maybe I should take a flyer on it," said Penny thoughtfully. "Do you accept thirty-five-year-olds who are still capable of expressing an opinion?"

"Oh dear," said Gwen, blushing. "I didn't mean anything personal by that."

"Oh, tush, dear," said Penny with a laugh. "I'm having you on." She glanced dramatically in both directions, then leaned over.

"I'm really thirty-six," she whispered in Gwen's ear. "Don't tell a soul."

Gwen laughed. It was an unforced, wholehearted laugh from deep inside, and it loosened tensions she didn't realise she was feeling.

"Here's a nice one," she said as they stopped in front of one labelled "The living room in a large town house." A writing desk, radio cabinet, and matching bookcases made of mahogany and rosewood lined the wall.

"B. Cohen and Sons," commented Penny. "I think we have a few pieces of theirs. Those floor tiles are decent. I like the salmon and white, but that wallpaper is hideous. I take it this room is meant for a more upscale sort?"

"'The Family: Barrister-at-Law,'" read Gwen. "'Collects books. His wife; gives musical parties.'"

"And they never speak to each other except in public," added Penny, bitterness creeping into her tone. "I know so many couples exactly like that. I suppose you manage to keep incompatible clients apart."

"We try," said Gwen. "Nothing is certain, but—"

"Mummy!" cried Ronnie, running up. "Come and see the radios! Please?"

"And who is this handsome young man?" asked Penny, squatting to look at him eye to eye.

"Ronnie, this is my new friend, Mrs. Penelope Carrington," said Gwen. "Penny, this is my son, Ronnie."

"How do you do, Mrs. Carrington?" said Ronnie, holding out his hand. "I am Ronald Bainbridge, Junior."

"So delighted to make your acquaintance, Master Bainbridge," said Penny, shaking it gently. "You are clearly a superior young man. Do you plan to go into the army like your father, or the navy like your uncle?"

"I'm going to be an explorer and a cowboy," said Ronnie.

"Well, aren't you the adventurous one?" said Penny. "I approve. Those are much better choices."

"I'm afraid I'll have to skip the rest of the rooms," said Gwen reluctantly. "I have been summoned."

"I'll come along," said Penny. "I want to see what the new televisions look like."

Ronnie grabbed his mother's hand and pulled her along despite her protests. They quickly arrived at the radio display, which was at the corner past the end of the furnished rooms.

"I found her," said Ronnie as they came up to the rest of the party.

"Well done, Ronnie," said Agnes.

"Hello, everyone," said Gwen. "I hope you weren't waiting for me too long. Let me introduce Mrs. Penelope Carrington. Mrs. Carrington, this is our friend Mr. Simon Daile; his nephew John; and our governess, Miss Agnes Yearwood."

"How do you do?" said Simon, stepping forward to shake her hand.

There was a moment's hesitation, then she shook his, smiling brightly.

"A pleasure, Mr. Daile," she said, pronouncing his name carefully.

"And this is John," said Ronnie, bringing him forward.

"Hello, John," she said more easily as the child stepped up for his handshake.

After the introductions were completed, she drifted back to Gwen and murmured, "Well, aren't you the adventurous one?"

"I'm sure I don't know what you're talking about," said Gwen as the group passed displays of dress fabrics and entered the tea lounge.

"And I'm sure you do."

"Simon is a friend, nothing more."

"Do the Bainbridges know about this—friend?" asked Penny.

"They should," said Gwen. "He's staying with us for the weekend."

"Very progressive of you," said Penny. "Is that a regular occurrence?"

"John lives with us," said Gwen. "Simon is at Royal Ag. He visits when he can."

"Everything you've told me about your life intrigues me more and more," said Penny. "I think I'm going to want to cultivate you. Shall we have some tea?"

Sparks spotted the Wolseley as it turned off the main road towards the encampment. It was heading straight for them as they walked on the side of the road towards the Red Lion.

"Put your arm around me," she muttered to Waleski.

"I can't," he said. "You're on the wrong side."

She slipped her left hand into his right, then casually draped his arm over her shoulders, clasping it with her right hand as she leaned into him, gazing at him adoringly as she slipped her free arm around him. She felt his body stiffen at the unexpected contact.

"Standard police vehicle," she said as it drove past them. "And I bet I know who's in it. Yes, they're turning in to the camp. We won't have much time at the Red Lion, I'm afraid."

"Are they looking for you?"

"No, they wouldn't know I'm here. I expect they're looking into Helena Jablonska like us, only we made better time. Let's find this Celinski fellow."

The Red Lion was a parish-owned alehouse that looked like it had stood on that spot for a few centuries. When they entered, they saw its denizens divided into two distinct groups, conversing in two distinct languages. The Poles were gathered in the corner, presided over by a large, boisterous man who was holding forth with a story that even Sparks could tell his audience had heard many times before. Several of them glanced over at the newcomers entering, their expressions turning to respect as they noted Waleski's jacket.

"I wonder if the noisy one is our man," said Sparks. "I'll get a couple of pints and meet you there."

"No," said Waleski. "I am buying."

"This is my operation."

"I should buy," he insisted. "If I don't, they will know I am not a true Polish gentleman."

"Very well."

The bartender drew two pints and passed them over. They each picked one up and went over to the Polish group, who quieted as they did so.

"Hello," said Sparks. "I'm looking for Karol Celinski. Do any of you know him?"

"*Co ona chce?*" the large man asked Waleski.

"He wants to know what you are doing here," translated Waleski.

"I'm with the government," said Sparks, producing the Mc-Tague identification card. "We are investigating the death of someone you may know."

She waited for Waleski to translate.

"Who?" asked the man.

"Helena Jablonska," said Sparks.

"*Ona jest zdrajcą!*" he roared.

"She is a traitor," said Waleski.

"I thought that might be it," said Sparks. "Are you Karol Celinski? Could you tell me why she is a traitor?"

The man's expression grew belligerent. His reply was spat out angrily. Waleski listened patiently, then turned back to Sparks.

"He wants to know why he should help the British government lady when the British government has sold out his country to the Russians," he said, keeping his tones bland.

"I understand your anger," said Sparks. "As it happens, I agree with you, but I am not with that part of the government. I believe that our Polish friends were treated despicably. If I were in charge, I would have made different choices. All I am trying to do is find out more about what happened to the—*zdrajcą*."

Celinski looked around the group, then directly at Sparks for the first time. As he spoke, Waleski smiled slightly.

"He says you need to prove you believe in Polish friendship. He heard you pronounce *zdrajcą* correctly, and wonders if you truly know our people. He will tell you what you need to know if you do two things."

"What two things?" asked Sparks.

"Make a toast, then sing," said Waleski. "In Polish."

"*Na zdrowie*," she said, raising her glass to the table.

"*Na zdrowie*," they echoed.

"Tell them I don't remember all of it," she said to Waleski. "Here goes nothing." She took a deep breath. "*Bogurodzica dziewica, Bogiem sławiena Maryja! U twego syna Gospodzina Matko zwolena . . .*"

Simon and the boys, energy renewed by tea and buns from a fancified Gypsy caravan in front of murals of circus fairgrounds and commedia dell'arte characters, set off in search of childhood delights. Gwen, Agnes, and Penny stepped into the women's fashions exhibit and halted, their eyes overwhelmed by everything they saw. Their noses as well, as the air in this space had been perfumed to enhance the feminine experience.

The main display was a giant tiered carousel slowly revolving, with gorgeously dressed mannequins on each level posed next to gaudy, jewel-encrusted birds. It was like a giant wedding cake draped in tulle.

"I want all of those," said Gwen as she was drawn hypnotically towards it. "I want them immediately. Have them boxed and delivered to my home straightaway. The rest of you will have to fend for yourselves."

"But none of them are out yet," complained Agnes. "When do we get to wear them? When we're too old to attract anyone? Our boys have been to France and Italy now. How are we supposed to compete with those French girls? They don't play fair—they're already French!"

"I wouldn't mind some more colour," commented Penny. "And better fabrics. If I wanted that much nylon, I would have become a parachutist."

"Those Stiebel evening dresses are stunning," said Gwen. "I just wish we were showing our shoulders again."

More mannequins lined the walls, posing by white wicker chairs on which they'd never sit. A wall of shoes caught the ladies' attention.

"Look, they're transparent," exclaimed Agnes, pointing to a pair of high heels. "Made of some kind of plastic."

"Frankly, I wouldn't be caught dead in those," said Penny. "And those calfskin wedges are hideous, don't you think?"

"Wedges for a woman my height are a liability no matter what they're made of," said Gwen.

"I know that well," said Penny with a laugh. "I used to be the tall girl in our set. Then along came you. We should put together a ladies' volleyball team."

"We would be formidable," agreed Gwen.

After not enough time, they reluctantly moved on, passing through the toy section without stopping. Gwen anticipated getting a full report from the boys later.

The men's clothing caught their interest. A deconstructed evening wear set, complete with top hat, gloves, and cane, was suspended in midair inside a case as if Jack Buchanan had recently evaporated, leaving only his clothes behind. Coats and waterproofs still carrying traces of military design stood guard across the way.

"We should catch up to Simon and the boys," said Gwen. "We don't want to abuse his generosity."

"I have to run myself," said Penny. "It was great fun seeing this with you. Much better than being alone. We should continue this. Are you free for lunch tomorrow?"

"I am," said Gwen. "I would love to."

"I'll make reservations somewhere and call you later," said Penny. "Let me get your number."

Gwen pulled out her notebook and jotted it down, then tore off the page and handed it to her.

"Excellent," said Penny. "I look forward to it. I loved meeting your son. Miss Yearwood, good day to you."

"Good day, ma'am," said Agnes.

They continued to their rendezvous point. Simon was gazing at a two-man folding boat.

"Look at that," he said as they came up. "It fits in two bags you can carry onto the train. Invented by a man named Hirschfeld who came here from Germany before the war."

"Have you lost the boys?" asked Agnes.

"I sent them scouting for free tables," he said. "They greatly enjoyed the toys. I took notes for future Christmas and birthday presents."

As they approached the restaurant entrance, Ronnie and John dashed out, the first with a look of glee, the second with amazement.

"You'll never guess who's here!" said Ronnie.

"Then you had better tell me," said Gwen.

"Sally! And he has Russians with him!"

"He's the biggest man I have ever seen," gasped John.

Ronnie grabbed his mother's hand and pulled her into the restaurant where Sally indeed was to be found, grinning at her from a table filled with a group of seven men, three of whom were in uniform. They all stood as she approached.

"This is a surprise," she said. "Or did you hear we would be here today?"

"I may have been tipped off," he confessed. "But this was actually a scheduled activity. Gentlemen, if you truly wish to see a marvel made by Britain, then here she is. May I introduce Mrs. Gwendolyn Bainbridge, co-founder and proprietor of The Right Sort Marriage Bureau, in case any of you wish to pick up a British bride as a souvenir. Mrs. Bainbridge, this is Major Sergei Federov, Captain Boris Ivanovich . . ."

By the time the five in the Bainbridge party had been introduced to all seven Russians, ten minutes had passed, and both Gwen and Agnes were trying to surreptitiously wipe the backs of their hands after having them kissed seven times each. Simon secured a table, and Agnes took the boys to get washed up.

"Sally, may I steal you away for a moment?" asked Gwen.

"You would be doing me a favour," he said.

They stepped outside the entryway.

"Has she called?" Gwen asked immediately.

"Not since yesterday," he replied.

"Will she?"

"Maybe. We don't have a set time."

Gwen pulled out her notebook and wrote down a number.

"This is one of the telephone boxes in front of Kensington High Street station," she said, tearing it off and handing it to him. "I'll be there at nine tonight. I will wait five minutes, then leave. If she can't call me then, tell her I'll be there again at noon tomorrow, then at nine again in the evening."

"Look at you with your spycraft," said Sally, pocketing the number. "I'm impressed. Shall I tell her anything else?"

"Tell her the future is made of plastic and aluminium."

"That would sound like a password if I hadn't just seen it on display," he said.

"Oh, and tell your new friends that hand-kissing went out here decades ago," she added.

"I've kissed your hand," he reminded her.

"You're theatrical," she said. "You do it right."

Celinski let Sparks off the hook after three stanzas, to her great relief, directing Waleski to sing a few more. He patted the bench next to him when the pilot had finished, and enough space was made for her to wedge herself in, Waleski standing at her shoulder.

"Tell me why Helena Jablonska is a traitor," she asked.

Celinski spoke, his tone vehement, his expression furious. Waleski kept his tones even and neutral as he translated.

"In 1941, a miracle happened for us. Hitler attacked the Soviets, and suddenly Poland had value to Stalin. Sikorski and Maisky signed an amnesty agreement, and a new Polish Army was born.

"That's when Helena Jablonska returned to Mielec. I was there, already working for the *Armia Krajowa*, as were others. Her family was gone by then, so she stayed with an old woman she knew as a child. Only one who knew her from before, she said."

"Was that true?" asked Sparks.

"The woman was old, half-blind. She said it was Helena, so we assumed it was. She was a pretty thing. Smart. She wanted to fight the Nazis like we did. She joined us. She turned out to be good. Much information came from her, and the Germans never suspected.

"Some were sent to Blizna, including her. I went along, worked on a farm outside town. Many stolen things ended up buried under bales of hay in the barn. Some made their way onto a British plane that landed on a muddy airfield at Wał Ruda. When the plane got stuck, people of the *Armia Krajowa* came from everywhere in the middle of the night to lay planks and build a runway. I remember Helena there, scooping up mud with her bare hands, working as hard as anyone."

He stopped to drink from his glass.

"But she was watching everyone. I noticed that," he said. "Watching, memorising each face."

"How do you know that's what she was doing?" asked Sparks.

"Because after the war ended, when the Lublin Committee was in charge with the Soviets pulling their strings, people began to disappear. One by one, those who had been in the *Armia Krajowa*, especially those who had helped make that wooden runway, vanished. There were rumours of trials in the middle of the night, followed by immediate executions. A child who hid in an attic saw his parents taken away by the NKVD. The men who took them were in a truck. In the front seat, smoking a cigarette and watching them, was Helena Jablonska. As they drove his parents away, the child heard her speaking and laughing with the soldiers."

He shook his head in anger and despair.

"She wasn't speaking Polish," he said.

"You escaped," Sparks pointed out.

"I ran," he said. "Before they came for me. I ran a long way. I had help, joined family here."

"Did anyone else here recognise her?"

"I am only one here from Mielec who knew her," he said. "If that was even her. Urszula thinks she was not Helena Jablonska at all."

"Who do you think she was?" asked Sparks.

"*Wcielony diabeł,*" he said.

Waleski, taken aback, didn't translate immediately.

"What did he say?" asked Sparks.

"The devil incarnate," said Waleski.

A small boy rushed into the alehouse and made a beeline for Celinski.

"*Nadchodzi policja!*" he cried.

"You've been very helpful," Sparks said, getting to her feet. "I will mention that in my report."

"You don't want to speak to police?" asked another man there.

"I've already spoken to them," said Sparks. "They'll probably want to ask you the same questions."

"Should I tell them you were here?" asked Celinski through Waleski.

"I'm sure they know," she said. "Tell them we're going to take the train from Iver if they want to catch up with us. Shall we go, Captain Waleski?"

"Yes, ma'am," he said.

They walked out to the street in front. A bus was coming towards them.

"So it does exist," said Sparks, flagging it down.

They boarded it quickly. She paid their fares and the driver put it in gear, heading east. Sparks glanced out the window to see the Wolseley pulling up to the Red Lion.

"You told our new friends we were taking the train from Iver," said Waleski.

"I did," said Sparks.

"Iver is in the other direction."

"It is. We'll take the train from Langley instead. No reason to let the police track us down yet."

"Ha! You are good at this," he said. "I'm surprised you ever left. Why did you quit?"

"You quit because England betrayed your country," she said. "I quit because she betrayed herself."

"In what way?"

"Can't tell you, Tadek. I'm sorry. And sorry about the arm earlier. I know you don't like people touching it."

"I think I am willing to make an exception for you, Sparks," he said, putting his good arm around her shoulders.

"Please, Tadek," she said, gently removing it.

"I am not as brave as you think," he said, looking away from her. "I fled Poland to Romania with the remainder of our air force to keep our planes out of German hands. From there by fishing boat across the Black Sea to Turkey, then by whatever transport we could get to Basra, then Karachi. Then a very long boat ride to South Africa, where we trained at Camp Haydock in the desert with snakes and spiders all around. And finally to England. Half of us went down when their transport ship took a torpedo. All that time and distance so I could get in the cockpit of a Hurricane and go shoot down the Luftwaffe."

"Sounds plenty brave to me," she said.

"We gathered together before our first mission and sang '*Bogurodzica*,'" he said. "Do you know the story of that hymn?"

"No."

"It is the oldest hymn in Poland. They say Saint Adalbert himself wrote it, and that Polish soldiers sang it before going into battle against the Teutonic Knights."

"Sounds very appropriate."

"I got in my plane, full of hope and prayer and duty, and flew into the sky," he said. "Then we were surprised by German fighters and I went down without ever firing a single round. I was lucky to make it home and land with only one arm. That was the end of my career as a pilot. One failed mission. I used to joke I would give my right arm to fly again, only I had none to give. So not so brave after all."

"You were," she said. "You got in a plane and flew into battle, which makes you a hero in my book. And that's what I told her."

"Told who?"

"That pretty young lady at our table," she said, reaching into her bag and pulling out a napkin and handing it to him. "She couldn't take her eyes off you. Here's her name and address. Write to her and see what happens. Make sure you wear that jacket."

"When did you find the time to do this?" he asked.

"When you took over the singing," she said. "I'm a professional matchmaker, remember? I normally charge five pounds for this service, so consider that a bonus for all the walking and the girl talk."

CHAPTER 12

The train from Langley pulled into Paddington Station in late afternoon. Sparks and Waleski got off and walked in silence until they reached their separation point, then turned towards each other.

"The ale wasn't bad," said Sparks.

"It was weak and watery," said Waleski.

"All right, it was weak and watery," said Sparks. "The company, however, was excellent. It was good catching up with you again, Tadek. Nice to see an old friend."

"Are we friends, Sparks?" he asked. "Will we see each other again?"

"I hope so. If I can make it through next week without getting killed or arrested, then we should have a drink or three to celebrate, this time without an agenda. You can tell me how the date went, and I'll teach you a nice English hymn with lots of verses. May I ask you something before we part?"

"What?"

"Who did you call last night?"

"What are you talking about?"

"Last night. The telephone box outside Dagome after I left."

"You followed me," he said, looking at her mournfully.

"I didn't follow you," said Sparks. "I waited outside to see what you would do. You came out and made a drunken beeline for the telephone box. After that, I did follow you until you got home, but it was only for a block so that barely counts. Who did you call, Tadek? Was it Andrew?"

"You ask me to help you, then you don't trust me."

"I didn't know if I could trust you last night," she said.

"But you trust me now."

"If I didn't, I wouldn't be telling you that I followed you," she said. "Look, Tadek, if you are in contact with Andrew, tell him I need to speak with him. Tell him if he's innocent, then I'm on his side."

"What if he isn't innocent?"

Sparks shrugged.

"We wander blindly through one massive grey area after another in our particular world," she said. "I need to speak with him either way. I'll call you at the telephone box outside of Dagome at eight tomorrow morning."

"You have that number?"

"I went back after you went home last night and got it. I've got telephone boxes all over the city tucked away in my little black book."

"Yet you say you're not in intelligence work anymore."

"One never knows when they'll come in handy. So if you are in contact with Andrew, and if he's willing to see me, tell him I'll be in front of the music shop at five o'clock tomorrow."

"Which music shop?"

"He'll know."

"All right," said Waleski. "One more thing."

"Yes?"

"You shouldn't date gangsters," he said. "That is my girl talk opinion."

"You're probably right," agreed Sparks. "Goodbye, Tadek."

"Goodbye, Sparks."

He turned and left. She watched him for a moment, then walked the other way.

Alone again, she thought. Both of us. Funny, all that time we spent together training Andrew, and we almost never spent any time on our own together. Apart from that night in Dagome.

She wished now that she had said yes when he had asked her out back then.

Then you would have had another ex to add to your collection, whispered the voices of the opposition team.

"Still here, are you?" she muttered. "Fine. Put your fractious minds to the task at hand."

A woman passing by shot her a startled glance.

Oh good, I'm talking to them out loud now, she thought. Fine, ladies. What have we learned today about Helena Jablonska? Who may not have been the real Helena Jablonska, but either way seems to have been working for the Soviets. Which was all well and good when they were on our side, but not so much currently.

The information came as no surprise. Jablonska was too accomplished to be an ordinary village girl who joined the underground. She had to have had training.

Was she a Polish Communist or a Soviet masquerading as a Pole? A female, Russian equivalent of an Andrzej?

No wonder he fell for her. He was a narcissist and she was his mirror image.

Would she have matched them if they had wandered separately into The Right Sort and she knew nothing else about them? Shared interests: Deception and amorality. Shared dislikes: Societal convention. And Nazis.

Honestly, she could think of worse matches.

Enough, Sparks, enough. Concentrate on the new information. Jablonska was a Soviet spy who had come to England in search of Andrew. What was her real interest in him? Sparks didn't think for a moment that it was love, or a quest for paternity. If it was for compromising him, then how did that get her killed?

The most likely explanation was that it was done by Andrew himself. He had the Browning, she remembered vividly. If Jablonska had compromised him, he would have been doubly at risk, both from the Soviets and his own masters. So it might have been a desperate attempt to get out of the jam before the Brigadier and company learned about it.

Only now they knew, thanks to Gwen. No, they probably would have tumbled to Jablonska's murder without help. A foreign body found in the flat of a former operative who was the former lover of a current operative. Alarms would have gone off.

What was happening right now in the secret War Room? she wondered. Were the bloodhounds on the scent? Had they caught Andrew yet? Would they turn him over to Cavendish if they did? Or would they quietly lock him away in one of their oubliettes? Or close ranks and hush it up, as they had once done for her?

But this was different, she thought. She killed Carlos because he attacked her. Helena Jablonska was gunned down in cold blood. The Brigadier wouldn't countenance that from one of his people.

Or would he? If he would, then he might not blink an eye at the prospect of throwing someone else to the lions. Especially if that someone else had walked away from the secret wars.

This is not my game, Gwen had said, *and I can't play out all the ways it can go.*

I can, thought Iris. And I'm not liking most of them.

I need to talk this out with someone.

I need Gwen.

Cavendish returned to his office an hour after Sparks returned to Paddington Station. He saw Parham's door was open, although his secretary wasn't in. He walked past her desk and knocked. Parham looked up from a report he was reading and waved him in.

"Didn't know you were working today," said Cavendish, taking a seat.

"Mullings wanted to go to his niece's birthday party, so we switched shifts. Where are you coming in from?"

"Iver. Checking out Helena Jablonska's last known address. It's a Polish camp."

"Any luck?"

"Not much," he said. "Everyone was annoyed that they were being asked questions about her again."

"Again?" asked Parham. "Why were they being asked again?"

"Someone else was poking around before we got there," said Cavendish. "A blond woman. Called herself McTague, said she was with the government, and was smart enough to bring an interpreter with her, which I wish I had done."

"From one of the Intelligence branches, you think?"

"Sure sounded like it, although she never actually said so," said Cavendish. "The name ring any bells with you?"

"I'm afraid not. Did you find anything useful?"

"Jablonska wasn't too popular in that quarter. One of the refugees accused her of working for the Russkies, so she packed and left."

"Anyone know where she went?"

"No," said Cavendish. "Which means there's a gap in the narrative. She leaves there Wednesday before last, then shows up at The Right Sort on Tuesday, and ends up taking two slugs on Thursday. Where's she staying? She didn't have any money when we found her. A hotel is out of the question."

"If our Intelligence people are looking into her, then she may have been working for the other side," said Parham. "She could have been in a safe house somewhere."

"Do we have an idea of where that would be? Do we have any information on Russian safe houses?"

"I'll make some calls," said Parham. "But I can't promise you any results before Monday. Go home. Take tomorrow off."

"Big of you, giving me a Sunday," said Cavendish.

"I've never seen so many model airplanes," cried Ronnie at dinner. "Thunderbolts and Meteors and Barracudas and Fairey Battles!"

"Fairey Battles?" Lady Bainbridge laughed. "That's a name for a plane?"

"It's a light bomber," John explained with an expression so serious that Gwen wanted to hug him. "With a pilot, a bombardier, and a tail gunner."

"How do you know all this?" asked Simon.

"I love airplanes," said John. "There were some Fairey Battles flying out of Nyasaland, fighting the Italians in East Africa. We went to look at them at the airstrip. They had South African crews. Most of them wouldn't talk to us, but one pilot was nice and let us get a closer look."

"Why wouldn't they talk to you?" asked Ronnie.

"Because they were South Africans," said John.

"I don't understand," said Ronnie.

"We'll explain it when you're a little older," said Simon.

"What else did you like?" asked Lady Bainbridge, changing the subject.

"The bicycle!" the boys said in unison.

"I liked that, too," said Gwen. "It had a rounded, shiny aluminium frame with an electrical motor of some sort. It looked like something you could ride on Mars."

"There was a miniature train you could sit on!" said Ronnie.

"And a model of a destroyer like Uncle Simon was on," said John.

"Yes, but more hopefully, there was a model of the tractor that I am learning to drive at school," said Simon, ruffling the boy's hair affectionately.

"You know, we should bring the boys out to visit you there," said Gwen.

"Could we?" asked John to Lady Bainbridge.

"We don't have the petrol rations for that," she replied. "But I suppose we could take the train together for a weekend."

"That would be lovely," said Ronnie.

"Now, on to more important matters," said Lady Bainbridge. "Tell me about the frocks."

"Oh, there were so many," said Gwen. "Peter Russell had some stunning designs. There was a lilac evening gown with silver lace and an embroidered bolero that I wanted to wear on the spot. Molyneux had one in yellow moiré that was gorgeous, although Penny thought it wouldn't be a good colour for me with my blond hair."

"Penny? Who is that?" asked Lady Bainbridge.

"Mummy's new friend," said Ronnie. "She was on the queue to get in right behind us."

"Was she? I didn't realise that," said Gwen. "Anyhow, she's one of Thurmond's old set. I didn't know her then, as far as I can remember, although she looked familiar. Funny how an eight years' age difference was an eternity back when I was sixteen, and it doesn't mean anything now."

"Penny what?" asked Lady Bainbridge.

"Carrington. She was a friend of one of Thurmond's many girlfriends. We started talking at the museum and we hit it off. We're having lunch tomorrow after church if you can spare me."

"That would be fine," said Lady Bainbridge. "We'll be coming back here so the boys can spend some more time with Simon."

"There is a pachisi board that is crying out for my revenge," he growled with a fearsome glance that set the boys to giggling.

"I will be back in time to say goodbye," promised Gwen.

"I'm glad you were able to go with the boys today," said Lady

Bainbridge. "I remember all the times I took my Ronnie there when he was that age."

Ronnie and John immediately asked to hear about that.

How strange it was to have the two boys want to hear about him, Gwen thought, as Lady Bainbridge regaled them with a tale of youthful mischief that Gwen had heard many times before. Ronnie wanting a story about the father he barely remembered, John about the brother he never knew. And Simon, thrust into a family that wasn't really his, listening politely and laughing at the right moments.

Her thoughts drifted back to the museum. Ronnie had presented himself so properly on being introduced to Penny. Gwen was very pleased with his behaviour in public, and reminded herself to thank Agnes for that. She had often been envious of the amount of time their governess had spent raising her son when Gwen couldn't, but so many of their set did it that way without the excuse of forced confinement.

She wondered how Penny managed. She realised that Penny hadn't mentioned if she had any children or not. She'd have to ask her.

Sally sat at his desk in his flat, wrestling for the eleventh time with the scene where Muriel confronts Bill about his affair. He was in mid-thought, his pen ready to stab at the decreasing blank space on the page beneath the angrily crossed-out sections, when the telephone rang. He grabbed at it irritably.

"Go away unless you can fix the opening of the second act," he said.

"Are you still starting it with Muriel telling Bill she knows?" asked Sparks.

"I am," said Sally. "Yet again. It still drags. It's angry, but it drags. It's drangry. I need it to move. I need it to seize the audience by their throats so they can't breathe. No, so they dare not breathe for fear of missing a single syllable."

"Less anger, more tension," suggested Sparks. "Let the audience figure out she knows before Bill does, so they'll be wondering what she's going to do to him, and when she's going to do it."

"Slow asphyxiation rather than a quick chop to the throat," mused Sally. "I'll give it a try. Thanks, Sparks. How was your day?"

"I took a trip to the country," said Sparks. "Inhaled fresh air, drank weak ale, and confirmed a suspicion."

"Sounds productive. I have the night off from shepherding my Russian wolfhounds, so I'm squeezing the Muse for whatever few drops of inspiration she deigns to drizzle on me. Oh, and I have a message for you."

"For me? From whom?"

"I ran into Gwen and party at the V and A. She wants you to call her."

"I can't call her. They may be tapping the phones there."

"Our Gwendolyn has anticipated that possibility, and will be waiting in a telephone box at nine tonight."

"She will?" exclaimed Sparks. "How marvellous! Was this your idea?"

"You'll be shocked to know it was hers. Consorting with ex-operatives like ourselves has rubbed off on her."

"Lie down with dogs," agreed Sparks. "Good. Let me have that number."

Agnes came in to collect the boys as dinner concluded.

"Shall we have sherry?" suggested Lady Bainbridge as if it were a novel idea to her.

"By all means," said Simon, rising to assist her with her chair.

Percival, who didn't need much in the way of clairvoyance to anticipate this particular finish to the evening, had decanter and glasses ready when they came into the library. He poured three and served them.

"To your success and survival of a museum visit with two young boys," said Lady Bainbridge.

"To the future of Britain and all she can make," replied Simon.

They drank.

"Mrs. Bainbridge, a Mrs. Penelope Carrington called," said Percival. "She didn't want to disturb you at dinner. She said that she had made a reservation at Veeraswamy for twelve thirty tomorrow afternoon."

"Thank you, Percival," said Gwen.

He bowed, then left them to their sherry.

"I hope you get over to see the exhibition, Carolyne," said Gwen.

"I'll wait until the fuss dies down," said Lady Bainbridge. "I detest crowds. But I'm glad you were able to go."

"I found myself very moved by it," said Gwen. "To see all the ordinary and commonplace things again, teakettles and suitcases and vacuum cleaners and such. Even with all the puffery about the designs of the future. It gives one hope that there will be a future, and that it will be ordinary again and what a relief that will be."

"I, for one, hope that the new ordinary will be an improvement over the old ordinary," said Simon.

"It always is," said Lady Bainbridge. "That is the tragedy of growing old."

"You're not old, Carolyne," protested Gwen.

"I've lost a son," Lady Bainbridge replied. "Nothing makes you feel older than that."

No one said anything. Nor did they say anything when she refilled her glass.

Gwen stood and walked over to one of the bookcases, running her eyes across the shelves.

"What are you looking for?" asked Lady Bainbridge.

"*Burke's Peerage*," said Gwen. "I thought I'd look up Penny, see if anything jogs my memory."

"You could call your brother."

"I wouldn't want to bother Thor over anything so trivial," said Gwen.

"Thor?" said Simon.

"Sorry. Thurmond. Thor was a family nickname. The name Thurmond had something to do with Thor, which got him very excited when he first found out about it. Ah, here we are."

She flipped through the pages until she came to "Carrington."

"Curious," she said. "Penny's not in there. Let me try *Landed Gentry*. No, she's not in there, either. Not as a Carrington, not as married to a Carrington. Of course, not everyone is in *Burke's*."

"Everyone who is anyone would certainly be in there," said Lady Bainbridge with a sniff.

"I am not in there, and I assure you that I am someone," said Simon.

"You know what I mean, Simon," said Lady Bainbridge. "Someone of our—background."

"I hope you will add John to your family entry someday," he said, rising. "Speaking of which, I promised to read *Treasure Island* with him before he turned in. I must say good night to you, ladies."

"Good night, Simon," said Lady Bainbridge, her voice slurring slightly.

"I'll walk out with you," said Gwen. "Carolyne, should I ring for Percival?"

"I will ring for him myself when I'm ready," said Lady Carolyne. "I'm going to read for a while."

Gwen and Simon walked into the hallway and closed the library door behind them.

"I'm sorry," said Gwen. "I think she's trying in her own way, but she isn't even aware of how offensive she's being half the time."

"And half the time, she is aware of it," said Simon. "It's frustrating. She's been very generous to John and me in many ways, but the air of superiority, the noblesse oblige—it becomes very grating."

"You've only been here for a day and a half," said Gwen. "Try living with it."

He took her hand in his, then held them up so they were side by side, her pale complexion setting off his brown one. Or was it the other way around?

"You still don't know what it's like," he said. "Good night, Gwendolyn. I'm off to search for buried treasure with John."

"Give him a kiss from me," she said. "Good night, Simon."

She watched as he climbed the stairs, then glanced at the grandfather clock in the hall. It was eight thirty.

She needed to be at the telephone box on Kensington High Street before nine. Percival would be in attendance on Lady Bainbridge, Simon was with John, and Nigel had the night off, which meant that she had no options for male company for the walk. On the other hand, evening was not the same as midnight in Kensington, so she thought she could risk it safely.

Maybe she could come out of the house acting suspiciously enough for the detectives monitoring the house to follow her. That would give her protection, except that the whole point of the telephone box was to avoid them.

Anyhow, they were watching the house for Iris. She was willing to bet their orders didn't extend to following her.

She put on her coat and hat, grabbed her bag, and slipped quietly out the front door. Suppressing a mischievous impulse to wave at the watchers, she walked briskly south.

As she approached the intersection, she heard a car start up somewhere behind her.

Are they going to follow me after all? she wondered. How do you lose a police car when you are on foot?

She contemplated dashing through the yards and hedges, but

decided against anything that precipitous. Instead, she merely turned left at the intersection and kept walking, listening for what they would do.

The car came to the intersection and turned right. She risked a quick glance over her shoulder to see its taillights receding into the distance.

False alarm, not their car, she thought. Good. Not every car in London is filled with menacing stalkers, although it certainly felt like that lately.

It was a fifteen-minute walk to the Underground station on Kensington High Street. She was ten minutes early, so she walked around the block once to kill some time, hoping no constables would mistake her conduct for something less acceptable. None did, fortunately. In fact, she saw none about.

She tried not to look at her watch as she approached the telephone boxes. She stopped as she saw a man in the one she had selected, happily gabbing away. She hadn't thought about that. What if Iris called, and couldn't get through because some random Londoner who had every right to use a public telephone was monopolising the very one she needed? She should have given Sally two numbers to pass on.

She had much to learn about spying, she thought.

She couldn't very well ask the man to leave, given the perfectly empty set of telephone boxes next to him. If only there was some way of luring him out.

Well, of course, there was, she thought, her heart sinking.

Iris had better call on time.

Gwen strolled casually over by the entrance to the Underground, turned towards the telephone box so the man could see her, and smiled.

He paused for a moment, looking at her. She let the smile widen, cocked her head slightly, and arched one eyebrow.

He raised his own eyebrows in reply, and she gave an almost

imperceptible nod. He said something quick and final into the telephone, then hung up.

Success, she thought. At least as far as that step went. The next few would be tricky.

She approached him slowly as he came out of the box, waiting for him to make his move.

"Now, I know this is South Kensington," he said. "Respectable part of town from all reports."

"I've heard that, too," she said.

"And knowing that, I was on the horn to a china of mine with a plan to find a less respectable part of town," he continued.

"Why would you want to do that?" she said.

"Because life is short and Saturday nights should not be thrown away lightly."

"Very true. What would you say are the attractions of that less respectable part of town?"

"Nothing that could match what I'm seeing right now," he said. "The question is how can a prize piece of nice like yourself be out and about on your own?"

"Because life is short and Saturday nights should not be thrown away lightly," she replied.

"Well, then," he said, grinning. "The name's Billy Young, though the lads call me Brig."

"Brig?"

"Short for Brigham. You know, like the—"

The telephone rang. Before he could react, she slipped past him into the box.

"Sorry, it's for me," she said. "Nice to meet you, Billy. Say hello to your china."

She closed the door as he gaped at her in dismay. She picked up the handset.

"Hello," she said.

"Is that you?" came Iris's voice.

"It's me," she replied as Billy tapped on the door. "One moment."

She opened it a crack.

"I do apologise, Billy," she said. "Give me your number and I'll call you next Saturday night."

"You won't," he said.

"Probably not," she admitted. "Go away now."

She closed the door. He stormed away, turning once to glare at her and mutter something she couldn't hear and chose not to interpret.

"What was that all about?" asked Iris.

"Something I will atone for in church tomorrow," said Gwen. "Are you all right?"

"Still at large, and I haven't seen my face on any wanted posters yet."

"You sound frightened," said Gwen.

"I am a bit," Iris confessed. "Being on the run is unnerving, even though I know I'm innocent. I don't have a base where I can collect my thoughts. My new temporary roommate is noisy, needy, and increasingly resentful."

"See what happens when you walk out on me?"

"Please, darling. I've had enough dealing with the exes on the male end of the spectrum."

"Sorry," said Gwen. "I know how worried you must be. You left your Allingham book behind. That's a bad sign."

"It is, isn't it?" agreed Iris. "*Wanted: Someone Innocent.* I couldn't lug that around. It's too apropos for my current situation."

"Have you made any progress?"

"Everything I learn spawns more possibilities, most of them bad."

"Well, I may have something to add to that stew," said Gwen.

"Wait. Are you back to helping me now?"

"God help me, I am," said Gwen. "You said you needed my

ability to tell you when you're going wrong. I am offering it now. Don't tell anyone."

"We see Dr. Milford again on Thursday."

"Especially not him."

"Gwendolyn Bainbridge lying to her therapist? I'm shocked. So, where have I taken a wrong turn?"

"With all of your rushing around to find out about Helena Jablonska, you've forgot something important."

"What?"

"The first time you were followed," said Gwen. "Tuesday morning. That wasn't Helena Jablonska then."

There was silence, then a long breath drawn in and let go.

"Absolutely right," said Iris. "Jablonska was a professional. The first woman was not in her league and not the same woman at all. And I have no idea who she was or what she has to do with any of this."

"Here's the thing," said Gwen. "I think she's following me now."

CHAPTER 13

W hat makes you think that?" asked Iris.

"At the V and A today, a woman struck up a conversation with me," said Gwen. "She said she recognised me from years ago, and that she was one of my brother's acquaintances. We ended up strolling through the exhibition together, chatting away while the boys went ahead with Simon. She was rather fun, in fact. Smart and witty, well-read—"

"Should I be jealous?" asked Iris.

"Under normal circumstances, possibly."

"What set off the clangers?"

"Small things," said Gwen. "When we first caught up to the boys and Simon, I introduced them, of course."

"And?"

"And she reacted to Simon, then made some comment to me after about how adventurous I was."

"Because he's black."

"That certainly seemed to be the reason."

"Honestly, Gwen, that reaction would not distinguish her from most people in your set. It's despicable, but I don't see how it's suspicious."

"Normally, I would agree with you," said Gwen. "But at dinner tonight, when I brought her up, Ronnie mentioned that she was on the queue right behind us. Iris, Simon and I were on that queue together for forty-five minutes, trying to keep the boys entertained. She had ample time to observe and know that we were all in the same party, yet she reacted to Simon as if she were seeing him for the first time."

"Interesting," said Iris. "So if she were pretending to be one of your exalted class, she would have to adopt that attitude to sell the act. Ugly, but clever. What else?"

"When she met Ronnie, she asked him if he wanted to be in the army like his father or in the navy like his uncle."

"So?"

"I never said my husband was in the army or that my brother was in the navy."

"If she ran in your circles, she could have heard that elsewhere."

"Yes, but she addressed me by my maiden name, as if she didn't know I had married Ronnie. She asked me what he was like. Yet she already knew he was in the army. She had researched me, Iris."

"Where could she have found that information?"

"In *Burke's Peerage,* of course," said Gwen. "A reference work on the aristocracy, which, by the way, does not contain her. Neither does *Landed Gentry.*"

"I'm not in *Burke's.* Either of them."

"Look," said Gwen in exasperation. "When this is over, we will start our own reference work containing people we like based only on merit."

"I'm not sure I would qualify for that one, either," said Iris. "What name was she using?"

"Penelope Carrington, and I couldn't find anyone of that name in the telephone directory. She asked me to call her Penny. And I asked her to call me Gwen."

"What did she look like?"

"Tall brunette," said Gwen. "Almost as tall as me, in fact. Admitted to thirty-six, so possibly older."

"The woman Tuesday morning was a tall brunette," said Iris. "Was she wearing a burgundy coat and a red felt fedora with yellow feathers?"

"No."

"That would have been too easy," said Iris.

"Nevertheless, let's say she's the same woman," said Gwen. "I assume she's coming after me to find out where you are."

"That's my thought as well," said Iris. "The question is who does she work for? Us or the Russians?"

"Russians?" exclaimed Gwen. "When did Russians come in to all of this?"

"Jablonska was working for them, or so everyone at the Polish camp she gave as an address seems to think."

"Penny didn't have a trace of an accent," said Gwen. "Her tones were as upper-crust as one could possibly want."

"Well, lor' love a duck, missus," said Iris. "I would expect nothing less of a Soviet plant, although her tailing skills leave much to be desired. Let's categorise our possibilities. One: Say she's on our side. Maybe the Soviets concocted some plan to have Jablonska use me to find Andrew, but our side got wind of it and Bad Penny turned up, hoping I'd lead her to Jablonska."

"Then why would she show up again now?"

"Haven't worked that out yet. Possibility two: She's Soviet, still looking for Jablonska."

"Why would a Soviet spy be looking for another Soviet spy?"

"Maybe to establish contact. Maybe Penny was the spy in place first, and Jablonska was supposed to convey some message or order to her. Or, and this is an intriguing one, maybe Jablonska was defecting and Penny was looking for her! Although that still doesn't explain why Penny is bothering you about all of this."

"Iris, Jablonska's name wasn't in any of the papers," said Gwen. "It could be that the Soviets don't know she's dead yet."

"Was my name in the papers?"

"Yes. Assisting Scotland Yard in their enquiries."

"I'd like to assist DI Cavendish with a swift kick down a steep flight of stairs," said Iris. "Did this Penny give you her number?"

"No, come to think of it," said Gwen in chagrin. "And I gave her mine. I'm a terrible spy."

"No, you're doing quite well for a beginner," said Iris. "How do you like it so far?"

"It has its thrilling side, to be sure, but I prefer matchmaking."

"Honestly, so do I," said Iris. "I'm realising that more and more."

"Then you had better come back to it."

"I'm working on that, darling. So, if she calls you back—"

"But she did call. This evening. We're having lunch tomorrow at Veeraswamy. I'd cancel, but I can't reach her. And it would be gauche, don't you think? After all, this is only speculation. She may be exactly who she says she is."

"Yet your instincts say otherwise," said Iris.

"Yes."

"So do mine. This is what I recommend. Go ahead and meet her for lunch. Let her take the lead in the conversation and see what she wants from you. What time is the reservation?"

"Twelve thirty."

"Then I'll call you at three to debrief you."

"Here?"

"Might as well. I don't think we're so deeply immersed that we need to have a moving series of locations."

"Very well," said Gwen. "Are you coming in to the office on Monday?"

"I can't think that far ahead," said Iris. "You can do without me if I don't?"

"Of course. But I am not letting you use any of this as an excuse to dodge our theatre date with Sally on Tuesday night."

"What if I'm in jail?"

"I'll bail you out."

Iris gave a quick, short bark of laughter.

"All right, then," she said. "Good luck with tomorrow. Don't try to do too much, or you'll tip her off. And, Gwen?"

"Yes?"

"Thank you."

"Of course," said Gwen. "Be careful, Iris."

"It's far too late for that advice, darling," said Iris. "But I'll try for once. Good night."

Gwen heard the click as Iris hung up. She hung up her phone and opened the door, glancing around to make sure Billy wasn't still hanging about.

He wasn't, but there was an older gentleman in his fifties standing by the kerb. He had a brown goatee, and was wearing a thin, grey overcoat over a charcoal grey two-piece suit. And he was looking directly at her.

"Mrs. Bainbridge, a word with you if I may," he said as she stepped out of the box.

"I'm sorry, I don't know you," she replied.

"No, you don't," he said. "And before this afternoon, we did not know you, either, which I find very interesting."

His accent, thought Gwen, fear gathering in her chest. He's Russian.

"Who is this 'we'?" she asked, glancing around for any police who might happen to be near. She saw none.

"This afternoon, I received a call from a member of our visiting cultural committee," he said. "They were being escorted through a tasteless exhibition marking the return to decadence by British manufacturers. Their guide was a very tall Englishman who spoke fluent Russian. Now, any Englishman who speaks fluent Russian we must assume is working for British Intelligence, wouldn't you agree?"

"I'm sorry, but I really must be going," said Gwen.

"Not until you hear me out," he said, holding up his hand. "So, this guide brings them to lunch where he chances to meet what was described to me as, it turns out quite accurately, a very beautiful English lady. The guide and the very beautiful English lady step away for a moment to have a private conversation, during which she writes something down on a piece of paper and gives it to him."

"What of it?" asked Gwen.

"It could have been anything," said the man. "An arrangement for a rendezvous of a romantic nature, perhaps. Nevertheless, you may see how curiosity was, shall we say, piqued. A telephone call is made, and an investigation is made into the circumstances of the very beautiful English lady. I am assigned that investigation. I begin by going to the offices of The Right Sort Marriage Bureau. It is closed."

"We aren't open on the weekends," said Gwen. "But if you'd like to make an appointment, I could give you one of our cards."

"I am not in the market for a bride," he said with a slight smile. "What intrigued me about your agency was the sign outside. 'Miss Iris Sparks and Mrs. Gwendolyn Bainbridge, Proprietors.' Miss Iris Sparks, as it happens, is a name not unknown to us, which I find very interesting indeed. In fact, we would like very much to speak with Miss Sparks, but she is nowhere to be found. So I took it upon myself to keep surveillance on the very beautiful English lady, which I must say has not been the worst assignment I have ever had. And what do I see but you emerging from your very large house at night. Alone. How scandalous! Well, I think, maybe it was a romantic rendezvous with the tall man after all. But I follow you, and see you commandeer this telephone box for the purpose of a lengthy conversation. This is strange behaviour for someone who clearly can afford a telephone in her very large house."

"Sometimes a woman wants to be alone," said Gwen. "In fact, now is one of those times."

"I will be happy to leave you alone, Mrs. Bainbridge, once you have told me the whereabouts of Miss Sparks."

"I am afraid I don't know the answer to that."

"I am sorry, but I cannot accept that answer," he said, making a gesture with his right hand.

From behind him, she saw a dark green Vauxhall saloon pull up to the kerb. The man motioned to the car.

"Get in," he said.

"I think not," she replied.

He pulled back his coat to reveal an automatic in his waistband.

"I wasn't offering you a choice, Mrs. Bainbridge."

"Ah, there you are, dearest," said Sally from behind him.

The man turned. Sally was standing by the rear of the Vauxhall, casually holding a long, black umbrella by his side.

"I hope you haven't been waiting long," Sally continued. "The train was beastly crowded. I thought it would never get here."

"It seemed like an eternity," said Gwen. "But I'm awfully glad to see you."

"So who's this chap?" asked Sally. "Do I have a romantic rival?"

"You know you're the only man for me," she said. "However, he wants me to get in that car with him."

"Does he?" said Sally. "That doesn't sound like a good idea at all."

He jabbed down and to his right with the umbrella. There was a loud report, then the Vauxhall slowly settled down as air hissed out of the rear tyre.

"Oh dear," said Sally. "You seem to have had a puncture. Fortunately, I see you have a spare."

He took two quick steps forward and jabbed again. This time the front tyre fell victim to what was clearly no ordinary umbrella.

"The question is, do you have two?" he asked.

The man in the overcoat looked up at him.

"They told me you were tall," he said. "They did not exaggerate."

"I'm glad to hear it," said Sally. "I detest exaggeration in all its forms, especially when it comes to my own form."

"However, I have in my waistband something that can bring down even a tall man," he said.

"So you do," said Sally. "All I have is this rather sharp umbrella. But it does have the advantage of already being deployed, unlike your superior weapon. So, tovarich, if you make the slightest move towards your waistband, I will puncture you far worse than I did your tyres. *Vy ponimayete?*"

The man looked back and forth between Gwen and Sally, then stood aside so that Sally could pass.

"Perhaps I will make an appointment at your office," he said to Gwen as Sally came up beside her.

"Please do," said Gwen. "Monday through Friday, normal business hours. Call first. And no weapons, please. They do set such a negative tone when one is seeking love, Cupid's arrows notwithstanding. Now if you don't mind, I have a romantic rendezvous with this gentleman. We're keeping it secret, so please don't tell anyone. Nice to meet you—Oh, you haven't told me your name, have you?"

"No," said the man. "And I don't think I will."

"Well, nice to meet you anyway," said Gwen. "Shall we go, darling?"

"Let's," said Sally, offering his arm.

She took it and they strolled away.

"This is where we turn our backs on the man with the gun and hope for the best," she said softly.

"It is," said Sally. "Ten more steps to the corner, then we turn.

And here's the corner, and here's the turn. Huzzah, we lived. Hold up a second."

He peeked around the corner. The Russian wasn't following them. Sally returned to Gwen, who was starting to shake.

"I will be walking you back home, if you don't mind," he said.

"I very much don't mind," she said, taking his arm again. "Thank God you got there in time."

"I was there before you were."

"What made you decide to do that?"

"I didn't like the idea of you being out at that phone box on your own, given everything that's been going on, so I decided to keep watch to make sure you were safe. As it turned out, you weren't."

"I'm no good at this, Sally," she said.

"On the contrary, you amaze me at every turn," said Sally. "What would you have done if I hadn't shown up?"

"I hadn't settled on anything specific," said Gwen. "There was a side of me that wanted to get in the car and find out what he knew, there was a side that was figuring out if I could disarm or disable him, and there was the majority vote that wanted to scream at the top of my lungs."

"Each had its merits," said Sally.

"The side where you showed up and saved me was better than all of them," said Gwen. "Where did you get that umbrella?"

"I know a chap," he said, holding it up so the sharp steel tip gleamed in the lamplight. "It comes in handy in certain situations. It can even shelter one from oncoming storms. Now tell me what this was all about."

"He wanted to know where Iris was."

"How did he get on to you?"

"Because I passed you a note this afternoon."

He stopped, shaking his head in anger.

"It's my fault," he said. "I put you in danger."

"You protected me, Sally," said Gwen. "I put myself in this

situation. I shouldn't have asked you to contact Iris for me when there was a roomful of Russians watching you."

"And I should have thought better of it. Well, water under the bridge now. Did you speak to Sparks?"

"Yes."

"Fill me in. Tell me everything."

By the time she was done, they were at the Bainbridge house. This time, she waved to the detectives watching it. They didn't wave back.

"Would you like to come in for a nightcap?" she asked. "I have it on good authority that the bar is still open."

"Under normal circumstances, a thousand times yes," he said. "But the present ones would require you to explain more than you should to your household, and not necessarily be believed. I have saved you from abduction by Communists and brought you safely to your doorstep. I call that a good night's work."

"Do you have any way of telling Iris what happened?" asked Gwen.

"I'll figure out something," he said, taking her hand and kissing it.

"As I said, you do it right," said Gwen, smiling. "Good night, Sally. Thank you. For everything."

She went inside. He waited until he heard her lock the door, then walked back down the driveway and turned north. As he passed by the parked car, the two detectives watching gave him a pair of thumbs-up. He saluted them with two fingers to his brow and kept walking.

Sparks was brushing her hair, which had spent far too much time stuffed under a wig for the past day and a half and was now resisting her attempts to wrestle it into submission. The knock at the door to Doris's flat was unexpected. So much so that she followed her instinct to take her knife from her bag and flip it open before she went to answer it.

"Hello?" she said, keeping out of the direct line of the doorway.

"Open up, Sparks," came Sally's voice. "Or I'll blow the door down. Or maybe up."

"Are you alone?"

"Sadly, yes. Are you decent?"

"They tell me I'm damned good," she said, opening the door. "Do come in."

He entered, his eyes scanning the room for the piece of furniture that would best accommodate him. She pointed to the couch, then sat on the ancient armchair across from it, her legs curled underneath her.

"Doris not about?" he asked as he sat.

"She had a date after her show," said Sparks. "We have the place to ourselves."

"There was a time when that would have been an exciting prospect," he said. "When we were young and too clever for our own good."

"What's going on, Sally?"

"Gwen was accosted tonight by an unnamed Russian."

"No! Is she all right?" exclaimed Sparks.

"She's unharmed," said Sally.

"When was this?"

"Immediately after hanging up the phone with you. He approached her with a gun in his waist and a car waiting. He was asking about you."

"How on earth did she—" Sparks began.

Then she saw the umbrella clenched in his hand, its blade visible.

"Were there any casualties?" she asked.

"Two tyres," he replied. "Yes, I have nothing better to do on a Saturday evening than to stand at the ready while an amateur jumps into a professional's fight."

"Where is she now?"

"I walked her home. It's still being monitored by your watchers from Scotland Yard, so she's safe."

"So you came here to tell me."

"I came here because I am furious with you," he said sharply. "How dare you involve her in this insanity?"

"I didn't think—"

"Didn't think what? That she would be in any danger? How exactly did this mad adventure begin?"

"Its roots started deep in the war—" she began.

"No, you don't do that," he interrupted. "No dramatic recitations, Sparks. That's my department. This started with a woman getting murdered in your flat, then Russian spies show up, yet you failed to perceive the possibility that Gwen could be in danger."

"I didn't kill Jablonska," said Sparks. "I didn't make any of this happen. Do you think I wanted to be in this fix, much less rope Gwen into it? Or you, for that matter?"

"I can take care of myself," said Sally. "Gwen can't. Do you know she was actually considering taking the Russkie on herself before I leapt into the fray?"

"She's had some training now."

"Ten lessons with Gerry Macaulay, as good as he is, is not enough to prepare her to take on an experienced operative."

"Did she tell you combat was her first choice?"

"No, as a matter of fact, she didn't," he said.

"What was?"

"Screaming."

"Much better idea," commented Sparks. "Still, all in all, I'm glad you were there."

"So am I."

"Did you at least get a kiss out of it?"

"That's not how I want to be kissed, Sparks," he said, flopping full-length onto the couch, his feet projecting over one arm. "Not out of gratitude, not to pay a debt."

"That's too bad," said Sparks. "I was about to kiss you right now in some combination of the two."

"Don't start," he said, waving the umbrella menacingly at her. "I don't like having my emotions toyed with."

"You wrote an entire play for me at Cambridge just so you could kiss me in the third act."

"I was nineteen. I know better now."

"I wish I did. That's terribly sad for both of us, isn't it?"

"You're not trying to get me in bed this late in the game, are you, Sparks?"

"Technically, you're already in it," Sparks pointed out. "That's where I've been sleeping since I came here."

"What are we going to do about Gwen, Sparks?" asked Sally. "We have to keep her safe."

"Best way is to figure out who killed Helena Jablonska and why," said Sparks. "I'm trying to fit the new Russian piece into the puzzle. Did Gwen bring you up to speed?"

"Yes. How does their desire to find you change things?"

"It's odd that Gwen would be sought out by two different people in the same day," said Sparks. "Especially since the approaches were so different. Bad Penny used subtlety, while Evil Ivan was the epitome of blunt force. I don't think they're on the same side in this."

"Why?"

"Because if they were, then Ivan should have let Penny complete her play without interfering. If it worked, fine. If it didn't, then he could bring out the rack and thumbscrews."

"So if she's not working for the Russians—"

"Then she must be working for us."

"You should talk to her," urged Sally.

"No."

"Why not?"

"Because I'm not working for us," said Sparks. "Are you?"

"What?"

"Are you back on board? Reporting on the sightseers?"

"It's nothing like that," said Sally.

"But it's something like something, isn't it?" Sparks persisted. "A crisp word in your ear? Nothing official, just keep your eyes and ears open, old boy, and let us know if anything juicy pops up?"

"There may have been a favour asked," he admitted. "Nothing permanent. I still plan to be England's third or fourth most successful playwright some day."

"Which is more than I plan to do," said Sparks. "All I want is to bring lonely people together for the lifetime of love that has been denied me. I don't want death and subterfuge dogging my footsteps everywhere I go. I want to show up at the office at nine o'clock Monday morning and find that Gwen has beaten me there yet again to regale me with Little Ronnie's latest. And when the workday is done, I want to go back to my own flat and curl up in my own bed with a good book or a bad man."

"You want to do that, you'll have to solve the murder by tomorrow night," he said. "Well, if you won't speak to Bad Penny, maybe you should talk to Evil Ivan. That at least would take the pressure off Gwen."

"How am I supposed to get in contact with the Soviets?" she asked. "My only contacts were from working for the Brigadier, and I've been cut off from whatever connections I had there. There's no one I can call. I've been banished. Shunned. Exiled. Napkin!"

"Napkin?" asked Sally as she picked up her bag from the floor and opened it.

"Where is it, where is it?" she muttered as she shuffled its contents.

She upended it onto the floor, makeup, lipsticks, and weapons clattering about. Sally reached down with his umbrella and hooked the metal knuckles on its tip, then raised them to his eye level.

"The most frightening thing about these is that you had them before you started dating a gangster," he said, contemplating them.

"Here it is," she said, triumphantly holding up a napkin folded into quarters.

"That is definitely a napkin," observed Sally. "I know we're trying to clean up a mess, but it's larger than any one napkin can handle. How does that help?"

She unfolded it and showed it to him again.

"There's a number on it," he said, squinting at it.

"A telephone number," she replied.

"Whose?"

"The late Helena Jablonska's," she said. "She gave it to me when we had tea. Let's see if anyone else is at home."

CHAPTER 14

Sally stood a few feet away, keeping watch on the street as Sparks stepped inside a telephone box and pulled the door shut. She summoned up her two encounters with Helena Jablonska, concentrating on the tones of her voice, the cadences of her speech.

Would she have spoken Polish or Russian? Sparks wondered. If Polish, then Sparks was out of luck. With Russian, however, she might get away with a brief conversation, although Jablonska might have spoken Russian with a Polish accent, and Sparks wasn't sure she knew what that sounded like.

Still, she was testing a hypothesis as much as anything. She decided on Russian.

She deposited a coin, then dialled the number. It rang several times without an answer. She was about to abandon the attempt when someone picked up.

"Yes?" came a man's voice.

English, thought Sparks.

She made a split-second decision.

"*Eto ya*," she said in what she hoped was a reasonable facsimile of Jablonska's voice.

"Who is this?"

"*Eto ya, Yelena. Ya nakhozhus' v bede.*"

There was a long pause.

"No, I don't think so," said the man. "Good try."

"All right, it's Iris Sparks," she said quickly before he could hang up.

There was an even longer pause.

"What do you want, Miss Sparks?" asked the man.

"The question is what do you want with me?" asked Sparks.

"You called me. I don't know who you are."

"I think you do," said Sparks. "I think you've been trying to find me."

"Why would I want to do that?"

"Because you want to know what happened to Helena Jablonska."

"I don't know anyone by that name."

"Yet she gave me this number a few days ago, then you answered when I called it."

"If you say so."

"Are you the man who tried to abduct my friend earlier tonight?"

"I don't know anything about that."

"Fine, you're a switchboard operator," said Sparks. "Tell the man who is looking for me that I will meet him by the *Agriculture* statue at the Queen Victoria Memorial at ten tomorrow morning. Tell him to quote me something from *The Three Sisters*."

"In English or Russian?"

"I'm insulted. Russian, of course."

"How will he know you?"

"If he's looking for me, he'll know me," said Sparks.

"One condition," said the man.

"Yes?"

"The large gentleman must not be there."

Sparks glanced over at Sally, who at that moment was glowering at a drunk who had paused in his homeward meander to become instantly enamoured of her.

"All right," she said. "He won't be."

He hung up.

Sparks stepped out. The drunk, who had finally taken in the full stature of Sally, staggered away, heartbroken. Sally turned his attentions back to Sparks.

"Well?" he asked.

"Ten o'clock tomorrow morning at the Queen Victoria Memorial."

"Right. I'll be there early."

"Not this time, Sally," said Sparks. "They specifically said that the large gentleman must not be there."

"How do we know they meant me?" asked Sally.

"Sally, you can't be on this date."

"I was for Gwen."

"Which is why they know who you are and what you look like," said Sparks.

"They could be dangerous."

"So am I, remember? Anyhow, that's why I picked a spot by Buckingham Palace. Where in London could I be safer?"

"The palace was bombed nine times during the war," said Sally.

"The war is over."

"That war is over. There's a new one in town, and you may be charging into the thick of it."

"I am going in as a peacemaker," said Sparks.

"But he'll be armed."

"That's all right," said Sparks. "So will I."

A minute before eight on Sunday morning, after another restless night, Sparks stepped into a different telephone box in a different neighbourhood, dropped in a coin, and dialled the number for the box outside of Dagome. Waleski answered on the third ring.

"Yes?"

"It's Sparks. Did you contact Andrew?"

"No, I didn't," he replied.

"So much for that," she said. "I guess I'll—"

"You don't understand," he said. "He was supposed to call me. I'm sorry, you were right. He had contacted me earlier this week. We had an arranged schedule for calls. Last night was one of them. He didn't call, and I haven't been able to reach him."

"Where was he staying?"

"I don't know, different places. But he had been scrupulous about making the schedule."

"Was he the one you called after I left Dagome?"

"Yes. Or rather, I made a call to a contact to tell him there was an emergency."

"Meaning me."

"Yes."

"So he knew we were going to Iver yesterday."

"He did."

"You would think he'd want to know what we found out," said Sparks.

"You would think so," replied Waleski. "I think he's in trouble."

"He was in trouble before," said Sparks. "Ever since Jablonska was killed three days ago."

"This is different," said Waleski.

"Tadek, did he tell you anything when he first contacted you? About what was going on?"

"No, just that he needed my help with a place to stay and as a contact for others. I sent him to someone who sent him somewhere else so I wouldn't know the location. I'm sorry I couldn't tell you before."

"Did he tell you who he was running from?"

"Yes," said Waleski.

"Who?"

"Everyone."

At eight thirty, Mrs. Michael Kinsey, née Beryl Stansfield, hastily cleared the breakfast dishes, leaving them to soak in the sink while she and Michael were at church. She was about to rush upstairs to fix her makeup when the front doorbell rang, which irritated her no end.

She untied her apron and threw it on the kitchen table, then walked through the house to the front door, hoping it wasn't some proselytiser from one of those oddball religious organisations come to bother her on the Sabbath. But when she opened the door, it turned out to be someone far more irritating standing there.

"Good morning, Beryl," said Sparks. "Is Mike about?"

"That's Mr. Kinsey to you," snapped Mrs. Kinsey.

"Very well, if you prefer," said Sparks. "Is Mr. Kinsey about, Mrs. Kinsey?"

"What do you want with him?"

"Nothing that's yours," said Sparks. "I need to ask him about a police matter."

"Here? Now? When good Christian women should be preparing for church?"

"I'm not much of a Christian nowadays," said Sparks. "But I am striving for goodness in my own peculiar fashion. Is he about?"

"I don't think—" began Mrs. Kinsey.

"Beryl?" her husband interrupted her as he came down the stairs, knotting his tie. "Is there someone at the door?"

He came up behind her with a smile, then froze as he saw their visitor.

"Sparks," he said, the smile fading immediately. "What in heaven's name are you doing here?"

"I need a favour, Detective Sergeant," said Sparks.

"Now? We're about to leave for church."

"I won't be stopping you for long," said Sparks. "Do you happen to have the home telephone number for Cavendish? He's not at work, he's not in the directory, and Scotland Yard felt they shouldn't give it to me for some reason when I called there."

"Maybe because he doesn't want suspects ringing him at home on a Sunday."

"She's a suspect?" exclaimed Mrs. Kinsey in mixed horror and delight. "What did she do?"

"Nothing this time," said Sparks. "Unfortunately, I'm at a point in my life where I arouse more suspicions than desires. Mike, this is terribly awkward, but I'm in a rush. Things are up in the air, and I could bog up the works very easily. Mrs. Kinsey, I am going to ask you to give us a minute alone. This is a confidential matter."

"I will do no such thing," declared Mrs. Kinsey.

"Beryl, you need a minute to get yourself ready, don't you?" said Kinsey.

"Michael Kinsey, are you sending me away while you talk to this, this, well, I don't even know a proper word for her."

"There are no proper words," said Sparks. "But there isn't much even I can do in a minute's time, so go make yourself pretty for God while I have a word with your husband."

Mrs. Kinsey looked back and forth at her husband and his ex. Then, with an exhalation of disgust, she turned and went upstairs. Kinsey stepped into the doorway.

"In a minute's time, you could wreck a marriage," he said. "Say what you have to say, then leave."

"Anthony Rigby's real name is Andrew Sutton," she said. "He's gone missing. He may be in trouble, or he may be the man who killed Helena Jablonska."

"How do you know him?"

"From during the war," she said. "Then from after."

"How long?"

"Two years or so since he came back. I broke it off in June."

"Is he with some branch of Intelligence?"

"I can't tell you."

"Were you?"

"I can't tell you," she repeated, her voice breaking. "Andrew was long after you and I broke up, Mike."

"Did you love him?" Kinsey found himself asking before he could stop himself.

"No," she said. "I don't think I did."

"Then why for God's sake were you with him, Sparks?"

"Because I hated myself," she said. "Being with Andrew was some ghastly combination of penance and comfort. I hated myself for what I did to you. For letting them let me do it. It was the worst decision I have ever made in my life because it hurt you so much. I wanted you to know that, Mike. You deserved better. I hope you got it with Beryl."

"Sparks," he said, taking a step forward.

She recoiled.

"Minute's up," she said, skittering down the front steps. "Tell Cavendish. And tell him I bet him tuppence I find Sutton first."

She turned and practically ran away, slowing as she reached the corner. He watched her until she vanished from sight.

Beryl came up by him, tying a scarf around her head.

"She's gone?" she asked.

"Yes."

"Good. Ready?"

"One more minute," he said. "I have to make a call."

He went inside to the telephone, pulled out his book, then dialled Cavendish's number.

"Nyle, it's Mike Kinsey."

"What in the blazes do you want?" asked Cavendish, sounding tired and surly.

"Iris Sparks showed up at my house just now."

"She did? What did she want?"

"To give you a name and a message."

"Wait, let me grab a pencil. All right, go."

"Anthony Rigby's real name is Andrew Sutton. Probably British Intelligence, although she wouldn't confirm it directly."

"And the message?"

"Tuppence says she finds him before you do."

"Another bet from a lady marriage broker. She still there?"

"Gone. Not three minutes ago."

"Right. Thanks for the call."

"You don't need help?"

"I'll call Ian," said Cavendish. "Go to church, Mike. Pray I win the bet."

Cavendish disconnected, then called Myrick.

"Ian, it's me," he said, pulling on his pants with his free hand. "Got a lead from Iris Sparks. No, from her, not on her. I'll tell you at the office. Yeah, so much for getting Sunday off."

He hung up.

How did you let that girl get away, Kinsey? he wondered as he threw on the rest of his clothes.

Myrick came in minutes after Cavendish reached the office.

"Doing the Lord's work in our own special way, are we?" he asked.

"Sorry to pull you away from services," said Cavendish.

"They can spare a lost soul or two. What's the lead?"

"Sparks dropped in on Kinsey, told him the mystery man is named Andrew Sutton."

"Common first name, common last name," said Myrick. "How many have you found so far?"

"Eleven in the London directories," said Cavendish.

"You want to divide and conquer?" asked Myrick.

"Hell, no," said Cavendish. "We're going after a potential murderer who may be with some branch of Intelligence, which means he may be very good at killing people. We'll take the list on together, and we are going to be very, very careful."

"Have you considered the possibility that she gave Kinsey a false name to throw us off the scent?"

"I have," said Cavendish. "I don't think that's what she's doing."

"Why not?"

"I spent a night interrogating her. She wouldn't crack. If she's giving this up for free now, it's because she thinks she could get herself killed tracking Sutton down."

"What makes you think she's tracking him down?"

"She bet me tuppence she'd find him first," said Cavendish. "We'll start with the one farthest north, and work our way down."

"Where's that?"

"Highgate. Let's get cracking."

Sparks walked along the Mall towards Buckingham Palace. She was wearing a pink cardigan sweater over a floral print dress, looking like a young woman either coming from or going to church, which was unlikely in her actual life but allowed her to blend in with the crowd well enough. Even though it was Sunday morning, the area was busy, mostly with soldiers and sailors gawking at the sights, the luckier ones with sleepy but adoring London ladies clinging to their arms.

She strolled around the memorial, pausing to take in the details of the various statues, panels, and reliefs. She paid particular attention to the four bronze statues flanking the two entrances to the central monument. Which has the better view? she wondered. *Peace* and *Progress* get to look down the Mall, while *Agriculture* and *Manufacture* get to watch the palace. The never-ending, always varying passage of humanity versus the abiding stolidity of the royal family, interrupted by the regular entertainment of the changing of the guard. And why do *Peace* and *Agriculture* have lions by their sides? Lions had little to do with either peace or agriculture.

She guessed the designers must have really liked lions.

She gave a polite nod to the queen as she passed, then continued on to *Agriculture*. She sat on the low marble wall behind it that separated the steps from the ornamental pool, drawing her knees up and wrapping her arms around them, watching the people go by. A pair of soldiers, American boys who couldn't have been more than twenty, approached her hopefully.

"Excuse us, miss," said one of them. "We just came back from Germany, and we were wondering if you could show us around."

"Sorry, lads," she said with a warm smile. "I'm waiting for someone. Thanks for what you did, and I'm glad you survived it."

They smiled back and continued on, zeroing in on a pair of girls who were staring at the nude young man representing *Progress* and giggling.

Good luck to all of you, thought Sparks.

An older man in a thin, grey coat over a brown suit with a dark green chequered vest wandered up the steps by her, then stopped, gazing up at the statue *Winged Victory* as it shone in the midmorning sun. Apparently lost in thought, he muttered something softly to himself.

In Russian.

"'In this town, to know three languages is an unnecessary luxury,'" she translated, glancing at him.

He nodded. She jumped down from the wall, came up, and kissed him on the cheek.

"Hello, Uncle," she said. "It's so good to see you again. Shall we stroll about and look at the gardens?"

"Please," he said, offering his arm.

She took it, and they walked down the steps and crossed over to the flower gardens that abutted St. James's Park. The roses this late in the season were fading, but the buddleia in the park beyond were in full bloom, their soft, lavender spikes pointing in every direction.

"Nice choice of quotes," she said as they walked.

"Thank you," he replied. "I must ask. Of all the statues here, why did you choose *Agriculture*?"

"She carries a sickle," said Sparks. "I thought it would make you feel at home."

"Humph. Thank you for not bringing your friend," he said. "We have no more money to waste on fixing tyres."

"Your fault for underestimating the ladies of The Right Sort Marriage Bureau."

"I will not make that mistake again. So, what is that a front for?"

"It's not a front. It's what we do. Come by and I will show you around all two of our offices."

"But you do work for the British government."

"Not generally, and only for affairs of the heart. What should I call you, Uncle? If you don't have a preference, it's going to be Vanya."

"My name is Ivan."

Sparks broke into laughter, which she quickly suppressed before she drew anyone's attention.

"What is so amusing?" asked Ivan.

"Private joke between me and the tall man," she said. "You wouldn't find it funny. Well, here we are, together at last. What do you want from me?"

"There is no point in pretending that I don't know Helena Jablonska," he said.

"None."

"We have not heard from her in several days," he said. "Then you called."

"And you knew my name," said Sparks. "I haven't worked in

Intelligence in—well, I can't be specific as to the date, but long enough ago that I should have been of no interest to you now. Yet you knew my name."

"We did."

"Which suggests that you sent Jablonska to me with an eye towards tracking down—well, I should let you tell me who."

"Major Andrew Sutton," said Ivan. "Of MI6. But we did not send her to you. Major Sutton gave her your name as a way of contacting him which would not be observed by British Intelligence. On Thursday morning, you telephoned her with an address. She left to meet him there. That is when we lost contact."

"You didn't have someone follow her?"

"It was too risky," he said. "He might have had people watching her for a tail."

"When did she leave?"

"In the morning. Right after your call. That was the last time I spoke with her."

"I'd say the next time will be in Heaven, except we're both atheists," said Sparks. "She was killed sometime on Thursday afternoon."

Ivan was silent for a moment. Then he quickly touched his thumb and two fingers to his forehead.

"Any more than that, I could be transported," he said.

"I'm sorry," said Sparks.

"We didn't know if she had been arrested, killed, or simply run away with Major Sutton to some seaside hotel," he said. "Did he kill her?"

"I don't know," she said. "Maybe. Maybe it was someone else. Who's the tall brunette woman looking for me? Is she one of yours?"

"I don't know who you are talking about," said Ivan.

"Maybe I believe you, maybe I don't," said Sparks.

"Unfortunately, it is hard to trust anyone in these matters," he said.

"Very true," she said. "There is, however, one thing I want you to be very clear about."

"Yes?"

"Mrs. Bainbridge is not part of this. You've spoken to me. Now, you leave her alone. Do you agree?"

Ivan looked at her, weighing her words.

"Because you willingly came to me, Mrs. Bainbridge will be left alone," he said carefully. "But now you must tell me where to find Major Sutton."

"I've been trying to find him myself since Scotland Yard let me go Friday morning," said Sparks.

"And have you?"

"Not yet."

"What will you do when you find him? Turn him over to the police, or help him escape?"

"I haven't quite made my mind up on that score," said Sparks. "Obviously, neither of those options would involve you."

"Not necessarily," said Ivan. "If he wishes to escape in an easterly direction, we may be in a position to render him some assistance."

"Even if it turns out he killed Jablonska?"

Ivan shrugged.

"My, my, they certainly breed them cold in Russia," said Sparks. "All right, I'll pass that offer along. Does he contact you at the same number?"

"It will be answered for the next twenty-four hours," said Ivan.

"Do you trust me to give it to him?"

"I don't trust you at all," said Ivan. "How do I know you didn't kill her?"

"You don't," said Sparks. "Even the police haven't ruled me out. That's why I'm trying to solve it. And I don't want you having anyone following me and queering the pitch. If you try, I will lose them."

"Jablonska followed you."

"She was very good," said Sparks. "Yet she still got herself killed."

"Are you making threats now?"

"No, Ivan. But I am not about to let myself be tailed success-fully twice in one week. Shall we play a game?"

"What kind of game?" asked Ivan.

"Let's see how many of our people each of us can spot," said Sparks.

"Very well. You go first."

"All right, let's see," she said. "There's the woman in the light blue jacket taking a picture of Queen Victoria. I imagine she has a few shots of me by now."

"She does."

"I hope she got my good side. There's the man in the tweed jacket relighting his pipe. He's trying too hard to blend in."

"I will let him know. Thank you."

"And the young man in the brown cap sitting on that bench, ig-noring the pretty girl trying to catch his eye. That's it. Your turn."

"You missed one."

"No, I didn't. Your turn."

"Very well. The two gentlemen walking through the Australia Gate."

"You know, I was wondering about them myself," said Sparks. "I thought they were yours for a second, but there is something excessively English about them."

"Are you saying they're not with you?"

"They may be with some branch of British Intelligence, but I didn't bring them. My guess is that they've been following you."

"Quite possible," said Ivan. "Maybe I'll have some fun losing them. All right, Miss Sparks, I give up. Who else is on your side?"

"I brought no one, Ivan," she said. "I'm a lone wolf, although I like to think all those handsome men in the red jackets and the bearskin hats would leap to my aid if you got too fresh."

"Are those hats really made of bearskin?" he asked, glancing at the palace guard.

"All the way from Canada," she said. "'One of the sergeants looks after their socks.'"

"Excuse me? Socks?"

"That's from a children's poem by our Mr. Milne," she said. "My father used to read it to me when I was little. Not on the same exalted level as your Mr. Chekhov, but it pops into my brain whenever I come here. And now I must leave you, Uncle Ivan. 'The game's afoot,' to quote another of our greatest writers."

"It has been a distinct pleasure to meet you, Miss Sparks," he said. "I hope you clear yourself. If you are able, tell me how things turn out in the end."

"I will," she promised. "And I do know that you have a fourth person watching, and that he'll be the one trying to follow me. Don't be too hard on him when he fails."

She stood on her toes and kissed him on the cheek, then walked away. He watched her as she crossed through to the Canada Gate and disappeared into Green Park.

The two men by the Australia Gate also watched her walk away.

"Was that Iris Sparks talking to Burlakov?" said one.

"It was," said the other grimly.

"I thought she left the shop."

"She did. Over a year ago."

"Then why is she chatting with him?"

"I don't know, but that's going to cause a stir. You go after her. I'll stay with him. Check in with the boss when you get the chance."

The first man set off after Sparks.

Ivan watched him go, smiling as his own man arrived at the gate nearly at the same moment. The Russian politely gestured to the Englishman to proceed first. The Englishman tipped his hat and entered.

Ivan noted his remaining pursuer, now watching the palace guard in an effort to appear as if he wasn't watching Ivan.

Maybe I should let him keep tailing me, thought Ivan. Take the longest, most boring, innocent stroll a man could take in London.

He decided instead to lose him. Just for fun.

The Russian emerged from Green Park first, across from the RAF Club on Piccadilly. He looked up and down the street in frustration, then behind him just in case. A minute later, the Englishman strolled up and repeated the Russian's actions, then looked at the Russian in mute question.

The Russian shrugged. The Englishman sighed, then tipped his hat. The Russian nodded, then the two of them walked away in opposite directions.

CHAPTER 15

S parks watched her two followers separate and walk away from within the safety of the RAF Club, peeking through the muslin curtains. She became aware of a grey-haired man staring at her from behind the front desk.

"Oh, hello," she said, turning to smile at him. "I'm early for a lunch date. I was looking to see if he was coming."

"Who are you expecting, miss?" asked the man.

"Arnold Wentworth? That's Captain Arnold Wentworth, he's with Bomber Command, we only met last week, but it feels like we've known each other forever," she said breathlessly.

"Wentworth, Wentworth," he said, running his finger down a ledger. "I don't see any luncheon reservations under that name."

"Are you sure?" she asked. "He said to meet him at the RAF Club for the eleven o'clock seating."

"No, there is no Wentworth here," he said. "In fact, I don't know of any Captain Wentworth who is a member of this club."

"But he said," she began, her lip quivering in dismay. "You don't think— Oh, golly, could he have been having me on?"

"Now, now, don't get upset," said the man reassuringly. "He probably neglected to make the reservation for some reason. I doubt that he would be so unmannerly as to forget a lovely girl like you."

"But if he didn't make a reservation—"

"I am pencilling in the two of you for the eleven o'clock seating right now," said the man, writing in the ledger.

"But what if he's not a member? What if he was only trying to take advantage?"

"Young lady, if he shows up with anything remotely resembling wings on his uniform, I promise that the two of you will have lunch."

"You are so terribly kind," said Sparks, sniffling and pulling a handkerchief from her bag. "Would it be all right if I sat here and waited for him?"

"Perfectly all right," said the man.

She composed herself and took up position in a comfortable armchair by the window, watching the gallants of the air come in with wives or WAAFs, wondering how many of them were having a morning after a night before. It was as good a place as any to kill time before heading to Veeraswamy.

The first address Cavendish and Myrick checked out was on Bishopswood Road in Highgate. This turned out to be a street of large brick Victorian houses, separated by gardens, walls, and snobbery. The one they found was looking rather the worse for wear, with ivy running rampant over brickwork badly in need of pointing. It was situated across from a vast playing field for a school distantly visible on the other side.

There were no cars in front of the house or visible in the driveway. No lights were on.

"Think he's at church?" asked Myrick.

"Would you go to church if you were a killer on the run?" returned Cavendish.

"No," said Myrick. "But you have to admit, it's the last place we'd look."

They got out of their car, walked up to the front door, and rang the bell. There was no response.

"Shall we try the neighbours?" suggested Myrick.

They trooped over to the next house. This time, the bell was answered. A housekeeper, a woman in her late forties, opened the door. Her eyes narrowed when she saw their idents.

"Sorry to bother you, madam," said Cavendish. "We're looking for Mr. Sutton next door."

"He's not here," said the woman.

"And he's not at home," said Cavendish. "Do you know if he's been about?"

"I haven't seen him in months," she said. "He travels."

"Do you know why?"

"Something for the army," she said. "I don't know much about it."

"Thanks," said Cavendish. "Good day, ma'am."

She closed the door.

"What do you think?" asked Myrick. "Poke around inside?"

"Not yet," said Cavendish. "Travelling army man would be a good fit with Intelligence work, but we've got a long list to get through. We'll come back to this one."

The Brigadier returned from services to a telephone ringing inside his house. He unlocked the door and walked briskly to his office to answer it.

"Sir, it's Rutledge at MI5," came a man's voice.

"Yes?"

"As you know, we've been keeping tabs on Ivan Burlakov. Something came up."

"What?"

"He had a meeting with Iris Sparks this morning."

"What? Where?"

"At the Queen Victoria Memorial at ten o'clock. They walked around the gardens and spoke for perhaps ten minutes. Then she left through Green Park. One of our men followed her."

"Let me guess. He lost her."

"I'm afraid he did. Sir, we were given to understand that Miss Sparks resigned from your section last year. Is there some extra-curricular operation going on we don't know about?"

"Iris Sparks is not, I repeat, not working for any branch of military intelligence," said the Brigadier, choosing his words carefully. "She is not part of any operation under my command."

"You understand our concerns," said Rutledge.

"Of course."

"Our inclination is to pursue this matter rather vehemently."

"Hold off a day," said the Brigadier.

"But, sir—"

"I said she wasn't working for us," said the Brigadier. "But I don't doubt for an instant her loyalty to the Crown. Miss Sparks has her own way of doing things. If she met with Burlakov that publicly, it's because she wanted us to know about it."

"Why wouldn't she just tell us?"

"She doesn't trust us," said the Brigadier. "Not without reason. Give her a day, Rutledge, then check back with me."

"Yes, sir."

The Brigadier hung up, then sat, drumming his fingers on his desk.

Sparks, he thought. What have you got yourself mixed up with now?

Nigel parked the Daimler in the driveway, then got out and held the door. Lady Bainbridge and Gwen emerged first, followed by the two boys, dressed in the same suits they had worn to the museum the day before.

Simon, who attended services at the Free Presbyterian Church of Scotland, had already returned and was waiting for them at the front door. The boys flew toward him, yelling, "Pachisi!" He stopped them with a stern look and a raised finger.

"Lunch first," he said. "We do not go to battle on an empty stomach. Go wash up, laddies."

They stormed up the stairs.

"I have a lunch date myself," Gwen said to Simon. "What time do you anticipate leaving today?"

"Four o'clock," he replied. "Carolyne has been kind enough to have Nigel drive me to the station."

"Then I will be back in time to say goodbye," she said. "Good luck with the game."

"Will you be needing the car, Mrs. Bainbridge?" called Nigel.

"No, thank you, Nigel," she replied. "The restaurant is only five minutes from The Right Sort. Save the petrol, I'm fine with the walk."

"Very good, ma'am," he said.

She went inside, freshened up her makeup, then left, giving a wave to the current shift of detectives watching. One of them waved back this time. His partner gave him a dirty look.

Walking gave her time to think about how she was going to handle the conversation with Penny. Let her take the lead, Iris had said. But Gwen thought she shouldn't give too much away. She was trying to find out what Penny wanted, not give her what she needed.

Good lord, it was very much like a first date, thought Gwen.

She wondered if she was being followed again. Could she lose a professional tail? She had no doubt that Iris could. Was this another clandestine skill she was going to have to learn from her? The martial arts course was easy enough for a woman who had grown up with training in dance and deportment, but spycraft was very different, and she doubted she would be able to spot someone who really knew what they were about.

Even Sally, for all of his size, could be stealthy when he wanted to. She had had no inkling as to his presence last night until he magically appeared to rescue her.

He could have kissed her last night. She knew he wanted to.

Why didn't he?

Had she wanted him to?

Gwen had been kissed exactly twice in the two and a half years since Ronnie was killed. Once against her will, the other—well, the other was complicated, a moment heightened by the events surrounding her first foray into murder investigation.

Des. A dockside carpenter whom she had met under false pretences using a fake name. That single kiss with him had reverberated through her in ways she never imagined possible, because she never imagined that there could ever be anyone else. She had told him that she couldn't consider beginning a new relationship until she had reclaimed her son. Now there was a glimpse of light at the end of that long, long tunnel. Once she emerged fully back into the world, should she call him? She felt she owed him that much at least.

She had not seen Des since that day. Hadn't called, hadn't written, hadn't asked Archie, who knew everything about everyone in the East End, if he had heard anything about him. He didn't interrupt her dreams on a regular basis. And, when it came right down to it, the differences in their situations were too extreme for her to think there was any real possibility there.

It was the murder that had flung them briefly together, just like the war had done for so many others. The war that she never experienced directly until it took away the love of her life. Once, back in 1941, she had run into a friend from her Swiss finishing-school days, now a Wren who was passing through on a week's leave before shipping out to the Pacific as a radio operator.

"It's amazing, Gwen," she confessed as they had tea in a small shop next to the train station. "I've been with men I never would

have dreamed of considering before the war. We've all been thrown into the scrum, and who knows if we'll ever see each other again? If we'll even be alive six months from now? I wouldn't want to end up with any of them, but at least if I die, I'll die with a smile on my face."

Maybe Des was Gwen's wartime romance, collapsed into the few days of her first murder investigation.

Her first murder investigation. Now here she was on yet another, blithely walking to have Indian food with a possible operative from who knows which side, her senses tingling and her mind racing as they did last night, when Sally had saved her and taken her home, then only kissed her hand.

She would have kissed him last night had he asked, she decided. Why hadn't he? He had been approaching steadily on her periphery for months. He had fallen for her, she knew that.

Maybe he recognised that she was still in the throes of recent imperilment and refused to take advantage of her susceptibility. Like a gentleman not pressing his luck with a girl who had too much to drink.

In which comparison, Gwen thought uncomfortably, I am the drunk girl. Addicted to danger.

Like Iris.

Iris sneaked a peek at her watch, then gave a loud, forlorn sigh. The man at the front desk looked at her sympathetically. She stood and walked over to him.

"It looks like I am the victim of some duff gen," she said.

"If this is how he treats women, you're well rid of him," he replied.

"You're right," she said. "Live and learn. Thank you for being so sweet. And I don't even know your name!"

"Thomas Craddock, at your service."

"A pleasure, Mr. Craddock," said Sparks. "I'm Mary McTague."

"Hold on one moment, Miss McTague," he said.

He stepped into the office, then returned with something wrapped in a napkin.

"I can't make up for an entire luncheon," he said, pressing it into her hand. "But the kitchen always sends me a couple of scones to get me through. I have always found comfort in scones. Have one with my compliments."

"Oh, Mr. Craddock, thank you," she said. "If nothing else, I have met one real gentleman today. Good day to you."

"Good day, Miss McTague. May there be better ones in your future."

She exited the RAF Club and turned left on Piccadilly, greedily devouring the scone. She hadn't realised how hungry she was. She'd have to grab something from a stall and hope for the best.

She finished it, brushed the crumbs from her mouth, then stepped into an alley, reaching into her bag.

When she emerged from the other end, she was a blonde again.

Penny waved to Gwen from the entrance to the restaurant when she saw her.

"Perfect timing," she said. "How were services? Did the boys sit through them?"

"Some squirming is inevitable," said Gwen. "But they both fear God, and they fear my mother-in-law even more. In fact, I think even God may fear her."

"She sounds formidable," said Penny. "I want to hear all about her, and your son, and especially you. Shall we go up?"

"After you."

From across Regent Street, Iris watched them go in. Veeraswamy was one storey up, with windows overlooking the street. She couldn't risk going in and either startling Gwen or being recognised by Penny, but the restaurant was at an inconvenient location for decent surveillance, situated to the right of where Swallow Street came through a short tunnel in the middle of Victory House, the massive, colonnaded building that ran along the outside of the curve. Given the geometry of the geography, she couldn't venture too far from the restaurant entrance without losing sight of it.

She wondered how long their lunch would be. The street was filled with people window-shopping, even with the shops closed. Some of the larger department stores had taken serious bomb damage that was only just beginning to be repaired. More hopefully, some stores were setting up displays of new items in their front windows, and the clumps of window-shoppers provided useful cover. She passed some time watching salesclerks from Maxwell Croft drape furs on white mannequins in the window of their new shop, wondering if she'd ever own one in her life.

Gwen probably had several.

She hadn't told Gwen she was going to tail Penny from the restaurant. She hadn't come to that decision until after she had learned about Gwen's encounter with Ivan, and there was no safe way for her to contact her after that. In any event, Gwen would have enough on her plate without worrying about what Iris was going to do.

Speaking of plates, she was still hungry, the scone notwithstanding. She glanced at her watch, then walked towards Piccadilly Circus where there was a fish and chip van parked.

"Good afternoon, ladies," said the maître d' as they came in. "Welcome to Veeraswamy. Do you have a reservation?"

"For two, under Mrs. Penelope Carrington," said Penny.

"Of course," he said, checking his list, then picking up two menus. "Come this way."

He was elegantly dressed in a black three-piece suit and a wing-collar shirt, with a green bow tie that matched his turban. He brought them into the dining room, set up so that the rows of tables faced out to the windows. Waitresses in colourful saris and turbaned waiters wearing white kurtas belted over white pants passed swiftly through the room. The chairs had carved, green wooden backs with oval rattan panels and red-striped legs. Each table was covered with a tablecloth embroidered with lotus flowers, on which rested a lamp with a shade that echoed the shape of a Hindu temple.

The maître d' held their chairs for them, then handed them their menus.

"Cocktails first?" he asked.

"Oh, goody, yes," said Penny. "I'll have a White Lady."

"A Bamboo cocktail for me, please," said Gwen.

"I will put your orders in at the bar," he said. "Govinda is your waiter. He will come by shortly."

He left them to peruse their menus.

"Now we play guess which item isn't available," said Penny. "They have pigeon, rabbit, lamb, and vegetable curry listed, but I would be very surprised if there is lamb to be had."

"Especially this time of year," agreed Gwen. "That's the good thing about pigeons. They breed like—well, like rabbits."

"That they do," said Penny with a laugh.

Gwen watched Penny's face over the top of her menu, trying not to be obvious about it. Nothing about her demeanour at their first encounter had set off Gwen's alarms. If it weren't for Penny's knowledge of Ronnie's background, Gwen might never have suspected her. Now, however, she was on full alert, waiting for any giveaway that would indicate fabrication.

"I'm leaning towards the mulligatawny soup to start," Penny said. "Never know how much chicken there'll be in it, but all one can do is hope for the best."

"I'll do the same," said Gwen. "I haven't had it in ages."

"Have you been here before?"

"Before the war a few times," Gwen replied. "My husband and I used to challenge each other over spicy foods."

"He sounds like he was fun," said Penny.

"He was."

"Anyone since?"

"I'm working my way up to it," said Gwen. "Slowly. And you?"

"Frankly, I'm having difficulty understanding why I should trouble myself with men at all," said Penny. "They're such bothersome creatures when you come right down to it."

"They have their good points."

"Some do," acknowledged Penny. "But if a woman can manage without one, go ahead, I say. That's why I was so intrigued about this business venture of yours. How long have you been at it?"

"Since March."

"How big a firm?"

"Not big at all. It was only the two of us in a tiny office at first, but we expanded recently into the medium-sized office next door and hired a secretary-receptionist."

"And— Oh, here's our drinks."

A White Lady and a Bamboo cocktail were placed before them.

"What may I bring you, ladies?" asked Govinda. "I regret to inform you that there is no lamb today, either the curry or the braised."

"You go first," said Penny.

"I'll start with the mulligatawny soup," said Gwen. "Then the rabbit curry, and the coupe Canterbury for dessert."

"The same," said Penny.

"Very good, ladies," said Govinda.

He collected their menus and left to place their orders.

"Great minds, it seems," commented Penny. "Let's see. It's Sunday, so to absent friends."

"To absent friends," echoed Gwen.

They drank.

"So who did you start this marriage bureau with?" asked Penny.

"A female friend," said Gwen.

"Even better," said Penny. "Who?"

"Her name is Iris Sparks. Do you know her?"

"I can't say that I do," said Penny. "What's she like? Another widow with time on her hands?"

"She's never married," said Gwen.

"Really? How does she qualify for matchmaking?"

"She has a nose for it," said Gwen. "We both do. We complement each other."

"But all of those poor, hopeful, single men wandering in—how does she manage to focus on business?"

"We don't date the clientele," said Gwen. "We were quite firm about that when we started the business."

"You mean if some particularly handsome young stalwart walks through the door, you won't sample his wares? Not even for the purpose of assessing him for others?"

"It will take more than a pretty face in a nice suit to win me over," said Gwen.

"I might settle for that," said Penny. "For a fling, at least. Ah, here comes the soup."

They tentatively tasted the mulligatawny.

"There might be some chicken in there somewhere," said Penny dubiously.

"I think they waved a chicken over the pot, then sent it back to the farm to live a full life," said Gwen. "They didn't stint on the curry, at least."

"Is Miss Sparks seeing anyone outside the office?" asked Penny.

There it is, thought Gwen.

"I think she's in between men at the moment," she said.

"Oh? Who was the last?"

"You wouldn't believe me," said Gwen.

"Try me."

"A spiv."

"No! Really? An actual spiv?"

"Broad ties, chalk stripes, and all," said Gwen.

"Is it safe to break up with someone like that?" asked Penny. "I'd think cement overshoes would be a possibility."

"You've been watching too many gangster movies," said Gwen. "He's rather a decent fellow outside of his professional activities."

"You met him?"

"Oh, yes."

"I'm empty," said Penny, looking mournfully at her glass. "Garçon? Another round, please."

Gwen was still working on her cocktail. Nevertheless, another one was placed in front of her.

It's a first date, and she's trying to get me drunk, she thought.

Fortunately, the rabbit curry arrived moments later, along with rice, chutney, and a small wicker basket of popadams. Gwen paced her cocktail consumption, although her palate, unaccustomed to curry, quickly demanded cooling down.

"How did you spend the war?" asked Penny as she dug in.

"We rode out the Phoney War in town," said Gwen. "Once Ronnie shipped out, we left for my father-in-law's estate. I had the baby, so I was exempted from signing up, although we took in a number of children from the city and I helped out with the school that was set up for them."

"And Miss Sparks?"

"Something clerical for the army," said Gwen. "She's a fierce typist when she gets up a head of steam."

Penny's eyes narrowed slightly for an instant.

She doesn't believe me about that, thought Gwen. And that she should even need to know if I'm telling the truth is interesting.

"I've been trying to place where we first might have seen each other," said Gwen. "You mentioned it was when I was sixteen, which would put it around 1934 or so."

"My dear, you must never be specific about dates," said Penny. "Otherwise people will know your true age."

"I'll lie about it when the time comes," said Gwen. "But do you remember where it was?"

"Let me think," said Penny as she spread some chutney on a popadam. "It was probably at someone's coming-out party. Maybe Mercy Cartland's daughter?"

"I remember that one," said Gwen.

"I think Mercy had her eye on your brother as a match for the girl," said Penny. "But Thor was with Trelinda, so no go."

"Were you already married then?"

"I was," said Penny.

"What did Mr. Carrington do?"

"He was already in the army," said Penny. "Second son and all that. In the middle of the war, he jumped out of a plane behind enemy lines, and that was the end."

She was telling the truth about that part, thought Gwen. She doesn't sound like a Russian spy.

Then what was she? A British spy? Or was she actually what she said she was?

Govinda cleared the plates, then returned with two coupe Canterburys, which turned out to be coupe bowls filled with lemon custard layered with apple slices and sprinkled with cardamom and cinnamon. Gwen's palate, still reeling from the curry assault, sent its thanks for the cool relief.

The conversation continued, Penny peppering Gwen with questions about The Right Sort, about Little Ronnie, about her mother-in-law, sprinkling in more questions about Iris. Finally, the meal was over and Govinda took away their empty bowls.

"One last drink?" asked Penny

"I have to get back home, unfortunately," said Gwen. "We're seeing Simon off."

"Ah, yes. You haven't explained that interesting connection."

"There's not much to explain. Lord Bainbridge knew the family from his business in East Africa. John lost his parents, so he became a ward of the family. His uncle Simon is in town visiting."

"That's very generous of you," commented Penny. "I apologise for my remarks yesterday. They were uncalled for."

"You are completely forgiven," said Gwen. "This was fun. We must do it again. Let me get your number. I'll ring you up this time."

"By all means," said Penny, opening her bag and fetching a pencil and a piece of paper.

"I'm not always there to answer," she said as she scribbled down a number and handed it to Gwen. "But keep trying, and we'll connect sooner or later."

They paid the bill and descended the stairs to Regent Street.

There were tables set up outside the Soldiers', Sailors' & Airmen's Families Association, which was headquartered across the street. Volunteers were selling various patriotic and military flags to raise funds for the group. Iris was examining a Royal Air Force pennant when she saw Gwen and Penny emerge. She placed it neatly back on the table with an apologetic smile to the volunteers, then casually drifted down to the Ford automobile showroom at Number 88. It was closed, but the large stone arch over the glass storefront gave her both cover and an opportunity to watch the reflection of the two women as they passed by. Then she followed them, keeping other pedestrians between them.

"Which way are you going?" asked Gwen.

"Piccadilly Circus. You?"

"Back to Kensington. But I'll walk with you to the station."

"Gladly," said Penny. "I do want to pay your office a visit and see what it's like. Maybe I'll weaken and fill out an application for the job of wife."

"Please do," said Gwen.

She was doing everything she could not to glance behind her. She had noticed a petite blonde with her back to them as they came out.

You may be the mistress of disguise in your world, Iris Sparks, thought Gwen, but I was with you when you bought that dress.

CHAPTER 16

I ris, accustomed to lengthening her stride when walking with Gwen, was feeling good and stretched out by the time the two women ahead of her reached Piccadilly Circus. She paused as they shook hands, then held for a beat more as Gwen turned right on Piccadilly and Penny crossed towards the Underground entrance on Coventry. Iris crossed from the other corner of Regent Street.

When Penny reached the entrance, however, she didn't go down the steps. Instead, she looked back towards Piccadilly. Iris retreated out of her line of sight to Shaftesbury Avenue. In the distance, she could see her partner's head towering above most of the crowd, disappearing into the distance.

She stepped back to see Penny continuing down Coventry Street.

Did you tell Gwen you were taking the Underground, then change your mind? Iris wondered as she followed her. Or were you never planning to take it at all?

Penny's pace increased now that she was no longer chatting with Gwen, and Iris was feeling the impact of what was for her a quick march. Her quarry turned right when she reached Leicester Square, passing through it and continuing south.

She can't go in this direction much longer, thought Iris. Or she'll wind up in the Thames. And I'm beginning to wish she would.

Ten minutes later, the Thames was looking like a very real possibility. Instead, Penny came to the Victoria Embankment station and went in.

Aha, thought Iris, trotting quickly to catch up.

She went inside and down the steps, spotting the tall brunette ahead of her. She followed Penny through the maze of the station, wondering which of the many trains available she was going to take. Penny didn't stop to purchase any tickets, which caused Iris some consternation. She hoped it wouldn't be a long trip, having already depleted much of her immediate funds on the joint expedition with Tadek the day before.

To her financial relief, Penny's destination was the northbound Number 35 tram. A thruppence Iris could afford. She bought a ticket, then got in the queue four people behind Penny. When the tram pulled up, Iris sat across the aisle and two seats back from her.

The crowd of passengers began to thin when it reached Bloomsbury. Penny stayed in her seat as it continued north. Iris took her bus and tram map from her bag and unfolded it as quietly as she could, checking the route. It ran through Holborn, Islington, and Holloway, then terminated at Highgate.

Where are we going, Penny? she thought. Are we meeting a contact to report on Gwen? Or are we merely visiting Mum and helping her with the gardening?

Gwen walked west on Piccadilly for three blocks, her compact in her hand. She didn't see Penny trailing her. She had no idea if anyone else out of the hundreds of people out on a Sunday afternoon was.

It was a quarter to two. Iris was to call her at three, but if she was now on Penny's trail, it seemed unlikely that she would keep to that schedule. Still, Gwen had promised to be there, and as a novice operative, she felt that she should make every effort.

There had been less prying into Iris's life from Penny during lunch than Gwen had expected. Nothing about where she lived, where she might be on the weekend, or any real information that could help an enemy find or learn more about her.

Yet there was something wrong about her luncheon companion, though Gwen couldn't put a finger on what it was. She certainly seemed familiar with Gwen's world, which would have required a great deal of research to pull off. She knew Mercy Cartland's name, although Mercy was a well-known figure in aristocratic circles. She knew Thor—

She had called him Thor.

Before her mind had fully grasped the implications of that thought, her hand jerked up in the air. A taxi pulled up. She got in.

"Where to, miss?" asked the driver.

"Kensington, please," she said.

It's one thing to know what one can find about me in *Burke's* or in the newspapers, she thought. It's another thing entirely to know my brother's nickname or who he was dating in 1934. That can only come from experiencing my world at the time it happened. Penny might be an operative for somebody, but she was also there.

There was one person she could call who might know who she was.

Unfortunately, it was her brother.

The taxi took fifteen minutes to get her home. She paid the driver and walked quickly into the house, failing to notice or return the tentative waves of the two detectives watching.

She went into the library, which was unoccupied, and rang for Percival. He appeared moments later.

"Yes, Mrs. Bainbridge," he said.

"Percival, I need to make a call to my brother in Tewkesbury. Would you arrange it, please?"

"Your brother, Mrs. Bainbridge? Is everything all right?"

"I don't know, Percival, which is why I need to speak to him."

"Very well. Would you prefer to take the call in His Lordship's office instead of the house telephone?"

"I would like that very much, Percival."

"Very good, madam. I will return when it's ready."

"Thank you, Percival."

He left. She immediately went to the bookcase where the *Burke's Peerage* was located and pulled it out. Simon poked his head into the room as she did.

"I thought I heard you come in," he said. "How was your lunch?"

"The food was good, but the company was confounding," she said.

"How so?"

"I may have eaten lunch with a spy."

"Isn't that an everyday occurrence with you and Miss Sparks?" he asked.

"You know about that?"

"I guessed," he said with a shrug. "Given the acquaintances of hers whom I have met, she had to be either a spy or a gangster, and she wouldn't need to be working with you if she were a gangster."

"Well, it wasn't Iris I was lunching with."

"No, it was the lady you met at the museum. You believe her to be a spy now?"

"I think she might be, but I may also be completely wrong about the situation. I'm sorry, I shouldn't be bothering you about this. How was the game?"

"Vengeance was mine," he said with a grin. "Enough for the boys to demand that I return for a rematch."

"Which you will, of course."

"Of course. And I have the added incentive of my first meeting with my future bride."

"No jumping the gun, Simon," Gwen admonished him. "There is enough pressure on a first date without that."

"I come from a country where arranged marriages still occur," he said. "I like your method much better. Don't worry, I won't propose right away. Has that actually happened with any of the couples you've brought together?"

"It did once," remembered Gwen. "The very first marriage to come out of The Right Sort. We thought, 'Well, that was easy.' But it was beginner's luck, I think."

"I believe that the two of you were meant to do this," said Simon. "I anticipate great things to come from this first date. And I won't mention anything about barley blight, I promise."

Percival appeared at the door.

"Your call is ready, Mrs. Bainbridge," he said.

"Thank you, Percival," she replied.

She gave Simon a quick kiss on the cheek, then went to Lord Bainbridge's office.

Deep breath, no arguments, and don't rise to the bait, she thought as she came in.

The receiver lay next to a brass-plated telephone on a small cabinet, waiting for her. She took a deep breath, exhaled slowly, then picked it up.

"Thurmond? Are you there?" she asked.

"I'm here, Sprout," said her brother. "Which one of us is dying?"

The tram pulled in to Highgate, its brakes squealing. Iris glanced at her watch. She wasn't going to be able to make her call with Gwen at this rate. It all depended on Penny. If she were going to an address close by, Iris might still be able to find a telephone box in time.

The remaining passengers got off the tram and dispersed. Penny walked briskly up Highgate Hill.

Great, thought Iris, as she doubled her pace to keep up. We've come to the long march portion of the tailing. If she keeps up this speed, I'll be too worn out for any proper spying.

She tried to think of anything in the vicinity that had clandestine connections. Caen Wood Towers, perhaps. The RAF Intelligence School was there, nestled inside a massive nineteenth-century brick mansion ostensibly used as a convalescent hospital. Iris had attended some training sessions there during the war, teaching basic German to airmen who might have to use it in extreme circumstances.

If Penny was working for our side, that would be an interesting destination, she thought.

At this point, however, she would have settled for the secret headquarters of the Fourth Reich, as long as it meant she could stop walking and catch a breather.

"Why would either of us be dying, Thurmond?" asked Gwen.

"I'm trying to come up with a reason why you would call," said Thurmond in his lazy, irritating drawl. "It would have to be bad news of the utmost importance for us to break our mutually agreed-upon lack of communication. I know Mother is well since I have already spoken to her today, so that leaves you and me as candidates for the Pearly Gates. I hope it's you."

"I won't bother with pleasantries," said Gwen. "You've never been good with them."

"The point of your call, little sister? You're wasting my leisure hours, and the small amount of curiosity I have is dwindling rapidly."

"Trelinda Sanders."

There was a moment of silence.

"'Thou hast committed Fornication,'" he said moodily, "'but that was in another country, and besides, the wench is dead.' Why in God's name are you bringing her up?"

"I'm trying to locate someone who was a friend of hers back when you were dating."

"You consider this urgent?"

"I'm calling you, aren't I?"

"You are. Urgent gossip. Interesting concept. Very well. Which friend?"

"Someone named Penelope or Penny. Last name may have been Carrington, or it may not."

"No such name is coming up in my memories," he said. "Sorry, Sprout. Will that be all?"

"Penny might not have been her real name. She would be your age, maybe a year or so older. She's brunette, thin, tall, practically my height."

"Oh, you should have said so at the start," he said. "Poppy, not Penny. Towering, gawky girl, snippy sense of humour."

"Could be. Know her last name?"

"Jenkins," he said. "Although she got married to someone after that whose name I can't recall. Never met the chap, but I remember the invite to the wedding."

"You didn't go?"

"Trelinda and I had parted ways by then," he said. "I couldn't be bothered with celebrating the bliss of her friends."

"All right, thanks," she said.

"That's it?"

"I don't have time for more right now," she said. "If you would like to talk at length, try calling me. Evenings, please. Unlike you, I have a job. If you agree to be agreeable, you could chat with the nephew you haven't laid eyes on since he was one."

"He had nothing interesting to say then," said Thurmond. "But I expect he's expanded his vocabulary. Maybe I will. Goodbye, Sprout."

"Goodbye, Thurmond."

She hung up, then opened up *Burke's* to the J's.

Highgate Hill turned into Hampstead Lane, and Penny kept on walking. She passed by shops and houses, playing fields and the occasional church, giving none of them a second glance. Finally, Caen Wood Towers appeared on her left.

I'll bet that's it, thought Iris, relieved that the hike was coming to an end.

But Penny continued on past the entrance, taking instead the next right.

Bishopswood Road, observed Iris, going past it in case Penny was looking back. Then she doubled back and cautiously peered around the brick column at the corner of the wall shielding the first house on the street. The houses were all on the left side, the right being taken up by athletic fields for a nearby school.

About a third of the way down, Penny turned in to a driveway. Iris marked the house, then walked down the street, looking straight ahead. She passed the house in time to get a glimpse of the front door closing.

The place needed fixing up, she thought, but a fair amount of square footage. She quelled a brief pang of envy, comparing it to the small one-bedroom flat that contained the entirety of her existence. Which she couldn't even live in at the moment, thanks to a Russian or Polish operative who had so inconsiderately got herself killed there.

A group of boys was playing rugby in the field. She walked across the road and leaned on the fence, her head at a slight angle so she could monitor the house.

Are you staying in, Miss Penny, or are you going out? she wondered.

Either way, I'm giving you ten minutes. Then I'm coming in.

Gwen stared at the page in shock and horror, then grabbed the telephone directory from the cabinet under the telephone. She found the number and address she wanted and scribbled them into her notebook.

Cavendish, she thought. I have to tell Cavendish.

She looked for his number, but he wasn't listed.

Damn, she thought. If only there was—

Wait, there is.

She jumped up and ran to the front door, then outside.

Henderson and Musgrave were on Bainbridge duty.

"Wonder how much longer we have to keep this up," said Musgrave.

"Until we catch the shooter, or track down where Sparks has been hiding herself, we stay right here," said Henderson.

"Waste of time, if you ask me," said Musgrave. "If she's smart enough to lose us, she wouldn't be stupid enough to come back here."

"Everyone gets stupid enough eventually," said Henderson. "That's when we show up and point it out to them."

"I'm sure Sparks will be grateful for the lesson," said Musgrave. "Hey, there's the blond goddess."

"She's in a hurry," observed Henderson. "Where's she off to?"

"Looks like she's coming our way."

Mrs. Bainbridge walked up to their car, tapped on the window by Henderson, and motioned for him to roll it down. The two detectives looked at each other in bewilderment. Musgrave shrugged. Henderson rolled down the window.

"You want to speak to us, Mrs. Bainbridge?" he asked.

"You work with Detective Inspector Cavendish, do you not?" she asked.

"We do."

"I need to talk to him. Right away."

"You can talk to me," said Henderson.

"You're looking for my partner, correct?"

"Yes."

"I think I know where she is. You need to get someone there immediately. Come inside, you can use our telephone."

"We're not supposed to be leaving this spot until our relief shows up," said Henderson.

"But I told you, you need to send a car there. Maybe several."

"Why?"

"Because I think she's in danger," said Mrs. Bainbridge.

Iris was about to search for a way to sneak into the house when the front door opened and Penny emerged. She had changed into more casual clothing and was carrying a wicker shopping basket. Iris turned back to the game as Penny headed back towards Hampstead Lane.

They had passed a greengrocer a quarter of a mile back, Iris recalled. That meant ten minutes there, another ten back, plus however long it took her to shop. That gave Iris maybe twenty to thirty minutes to poke around inside. She watched Penny until she turned the corner, then crossed over and went up the driveway to the front door.

She listened for a moment. Nothing. She glanced in the front window, then walked around to the rear. There were some haphazard attempts at vegetable gardens and a small patch of grass that had not been kept up. A fountain with a small bronze statue of a nymph supplicating the heavens stood near the back wall. The water was off, apart from a muddy inch or two in the basin. A door in the rear of the house led to a kitchen, and a breakfast alcove overlooked the gardens through a wide window.

No servants, no cook, no children. No sign of any activity.

This must be a safe house, she thought. Penny's using it for her base of operation. But what is the operation?

She pulled on a pair of black leather gloves, then tested the kitchen door. It was unlocked. She opened it quietly and slipped inside.

The kitchen was a large one, designed for a house meant to support a large family and a commensurate number of staff. She opened the refrigerator. It was sparsely stocked, not unusual for these times. There were dishes in the drying rack by the sink. A lunch plate, two cups and saucers, a tumbler, some utensils.

You ate lunch with Gwen, she thought. Are you so large and voracious a creature that you needed another one the moment you came home?

Or was there someone else here?

She walked past a dining room. The table and chairs were draped with cloths, and the dust on the sideboards was thick.

No formal dinner parties recently, she thought. You eat all of your meals at the breakfast table, watching the weeds take over.

She continued on to the living room, which was dominated by an old Broadwood grand piano. The furniture dated from the twenties if she was any judge. The curtains were drawn and the lights were out.

No photographs, she noticed. Not on the walls, not on the mantelpiece, not on the coffee table. What was it Archie had said? *You undercover types don't leave pictures lying about.*

She quickly opened the cabinets, finding only old magazines in one and liquor bottles in the other. The latter, at least, had seen recent usage, given their lack of dust and the faint smells of the contents emanating from the stoppers of the ones in front.

Penny likes her brandy, she thought.

She walked into the entry hall. There was a small table by the wall, but no letters with anyone's name to help her. Of course, it was Sunday, so there would be no post.

She looked at her watch. Ten minutes gone by, and there were still many rooms to search. She'd have to move quickly.

Start with the bedrooms, she thought. Then see if there is anything being used as an office.

She headed up the stairs. The first three bedrooms she tried were empty, the linens stripped from the beds, most of the furniture draped as the dining room had been. Then she came to a room that was locked.

I like locked rooms, she thought happily as she retrieved her lockpicks from her bag.

"What kind of danger?" asked Henderson.

"There was a woman who was following her last Tuesday," said Mrs. Bainbridge. "The same woman, at least I think it's the same woman, showed up at the V and A yesterday and struck up a conversation with me."

"Oh, you saw *Britain Can Make It*?" asked Henderson. "How was it? I might take the wife."

"Very interesting, and you should, but that's not the point," said Mrs. Bainbridge. "She was using a false name."

"And you think she's dangerous because of that?"

"Well, at lunch today—"

"Lunch with who?"

"This woman."

"You had lunch with her?"

"Yes."

"If you thought she was dangerous, why did you have lunch with her?"

"She invited me," said Mrs. Bainbridge. "Will you please stop interrupting? She was calling herself Penny Carrington, but she wasn't in *Burke's* under that name, are you familiar with *Burke's*, by the way?"

"Oh, yeah," said Henderson. "The lads and I spend all our free time thumbing through it at the Yard. So she wasn't a blue blood. So what?"

"She knew me," said Mrs. Bainbridge. "She didn't just pretend to know me, she knew me, she knew my people. So I did some quick investigating. Her real name was Poppy Jenkins."

"Mrs. Bainbridge, I haven't heard anything here that would be of any interest to the police," said Henderson. "People lie about their names for all kinds of reasons."

"But—"

"And I haven't heard anything that constitutes a crime. We have a job to do at the moment—"

"Sitting in a car is a job?"

"It's our job right now."

"But I need you to call Cavendish."

"To do that, I would have to leave the car."

Mrs. Bainbridge stared at him in disbelief.

"What would it take to get you out of this car?" she asked slowly.

"An actual crime," he replied.

"Very well," she said.

She leaned into the car window and very calmly, very deliberately slapped his face.

"Mrs. Bainbridge, what do you think you're doing?" he asked.

"I've just assaulted a policeman," she asked. "Is that enough?"

"Step away from the car, Mrs. Bainbridge," he said. "I don't want to—"

She slapped him again, harder this time, then stepped back, holding her arms out in front of her.

"Handcuffs, please," she said.

It took another precious minute for Iris to pick the lock. She opened the door quietly, her free hand inside her bag, gripping the handle of her knife.

This was clearly the master bedroom. Unlike the other rooms she had checked, it was still very much in use. The bed had a shiny brass Art Deco frame, the headpiece a three-arched triptych with a stag and a doe leaping towards each other on the curved bars connecting the top to the bottom.

The bars had been put to a more functional use. A man lay on the bed, handcuffed to them. He was gagged and blindfolded, his feet tied.

She sat next to him. He lifted his head up and turned towards her, struggling.

"It's me, Andrew," she said, removing the blindfold. "Don't squirm about."

He stared at her in relief as she removed the gag.

"Sparks," he said hoarsely. "You've got to get out of here. Now."

"Not until I know what's going on," she said, sliding forward to inspect the handcuffs.

"No time," he said. "Get out, call the police."

"I might be able to pick these," she said, reaching into her bag. "That woman. Penny, or whatever she calls herself. Which side is she on? Which side are you on, for that matter?"

"It's not about that, Sparks," he said. "She's not on anyone's side."

"I used to be on yours once, isn't that right, Andrew?" said Penny, watching from the doorway, a gun in her hand. "Hello, Miss Sparks. How nice to see a plan actually work."

Welrod bolt-action .32 calibre, Iris thought automatically. Two to three seconds to reload. If I can survive the first bullet . . .

"Hello, Penny," she said. "Are you going to tell me what this is all about?"

"Why don't you tell her, Andrew?" said Penny.

"Her name isn't Penny, Sparks," said Andrew, sagging back against the pillow. "It's Poppy. She's my wife."

"Oh," said Iris. "I see. Some massive apologies are in order, aren't they?"

The two detectives stepped out of the car and looked at Mrs. Bainbridge. She returned their looks defiantly.

"You're the one who's bonkers, right?" asked Henderson.

"The preferred term is 'lunatic,' thank you," she replied. "Yes,

I'm a dangerous, insane woman, but I know where Iris Sparks is going and I know that the person you are looking for will be there when she gets there, so how about it, boys? Give the crazy lady a ride, turn on the sirens, and you might get a promotion out of it. But call Cavendish first. It's twenty minutes to Highgate from here, and someone has to get there immediately. You may use our telephone."

She turned and walked towards the house. The detectives hesitated. She looked back at them.

"I am capable of much worse things!" she shouted.

They gave up and followed her in.

"They're with me, Percival," she said as the butler came up to enquire. "I need Lord Bainbridge's telephone again."

"Yes, Mrs. Bainbridge," he said, leading the way.

"Who's in Highgate?" asked Henderson.

"Poppy Jenkins."

"Now you're going to tell me she was in *Burke's* under that name."

"She was, but she got married," said Mrs. Bainbridge. "She's Poppy Sutton now."

"Throw your bag over here," said Poppy.

Iris tossed her bag in that direction. It landed on the floor with a solid clunk.

"My, my," said Poppy. "I'll bet you have all kinds of interesting items in there. I have a few in mine, too."

She reached into her bag and pulled out a pair of handcuffs.

"How many of those do you own?" asked Iris.

"I always keep an extra for unexpected guests," said Poppy. "Especially the more dangerous ones."

"Look, this doesn't have to go any further," said Iris. "I have no interest in your husband."

"Yet you live in a flat in Marylebone that he pays for," said Poppy.

"You've got it wrong," said Iris. "The flat is paid for by Anthony Rigby."

"Really? What's he like?"

"Sweet, generous, not overdemanding," said Iris. "It's a good combination for a girl who's down on her luck."

"Is that what you are?" asked Poppy. "Then why follow me all the way from Veeraswamy?"

"I wanted to know why you were looking for me," said Iris. "Then I found this man like this. I was trying to help him."

"You're a regular Good Samaritan, aren't you? What did you do in the war, Iris?"

"I was a secretary and file clerk."

"Who knows how to pick locks," said Poppy. "That was the final test, not that I had any doubts before. I suspected Andrew, of course. Too many late nights, too many claims of staying at the club or coming back from the Continent days after the actual flight schedules said he did. I finally got sick of it and searched his office here. You haven't been to the office yet."

"No. Is it very nice?"

"It has an interesting old desk with a secret compartment behind the cubbyholes," said Poppy. "I found the lease for your flat in there, along with this very quiet little gun."

She pointed it at Iris's chest.

"Is that what you used to kill Helena?" asked Iris.

"Was that her name? I never knew."

"Then why did you—" began Iris.

Then she stopped, realisation dawning in her face.

"You thought she was me," she said.

"Unfortunately for her, I did," replied Poppy. "When I found the lease, I didn't know who it was for. I made some quiet enquiries, learned that the flat was occupied by a short brunette woman, but no one knew her name. It wasn't until last Tuesday that I found out."

"When you followed me to The Right Sort," said Iris.

"Exactly. I was going to corner you in the flat, but Tuesday night you came out with a valise and some man, and on Wednesday you met another woman in front and left with her. I didn't want to wait. Then on Thursday, I saw the light on in your window in the afternoon. I went in and knocked on the door. I was expecting a short brunette to open it, and fired the moment one did. I shot her again as she tried to run, and that's when I found out I killed the wrong woman."

"Bad luck all around," said Iris.

"Especially for you," said Poppy. "Fortunately, I managed to lure you here. I was hoping Gwen would suspect me and alert you. I was right. Now, here are you and Andrew, together again."

"Honestly, you can have him," said Iris. "It was over between us a while ago."

"How long did it last?" asked Poppy.

Iris didn't answer.

"I guess it doesn't matter," said Poppy. "Take off your dress."

"What?"

"I don't want to get blood on it. That would ruin the point of the little tableau I plan to leave for the police. The tragic lovers on the run culminating in a murder-suicide at their last illicit tryst while I was off visiting relatives up north. You'll be found in bed together, the gun still in his hand, just like that couple in that hunting lodge in Austria. I can never remember its name."

"Mayerling," said Iris.

"Aren't you the smart one?" said Poppy, smiling. "Take off that dress like a good girl and toss it on the floor. And the shoes, of course. You can keep the slip on."

Iris complied, looking for anything she could use as a weapon or a shield. She saw none.

"Now it's beddy-bye for you, young lady," said Poppy. "Climb in. Good. Put these on."

She tossed Iris the handcuffs.

"How are we supposed to kill each other while handcuffed?" asked Iris as she sat on the bed next to Andrew.

"I'll remove them after, of course," said Poppy. "I want to make sure I have you posed properly. I've been picturing this for a long time now."

"Since you're so set on killing your rivals, would you like to know the names of the others?" asked Iris.

Poppy froze.

"What are you talking about?" she asked.

"I told you I broke up with him," said Iris. "Why do you think I did? He was cheating on me, too."

"Sparks, don't," said Andrew.

"I'm sorry, but you don't have a say in what I do," said Iris. "If we're being frank, if I was going to die in bed with a man, you're the last one I'd want to be with."

"Who are they?" asked Poppy. "How many?"

"I can only tell you about the ones I know about," said Iris. "Turns out you got one of them already."

"The woman in the flat?"

"Helena," said Iris. "Helena Jablonska. She was the one in Poland, or one of the ones, I should say. That was part of his assignment there. There and Germany, of course. Find the vulnerable girls with the info, get them into bed, and all sorts of wonderful information comes spilling out."

"How do you know this?" demanded Poppy.

"My goodness, you don't think someone with my skills would actually waste her time running a marriage bureau, do you?" asked Iris. "It's all a front. You're right, I'm an operative, part of the same team Andrew's on. Getting Helena away from the Russkies was a major coup, then you cocked it up by killing her before we could get anything more out of her. Poor little fool—she was so set on settling down with Andrew and raising the baby—"

"The what?" cried Poppy, her face turning pale.

"Oh, didn't he tell you?" asked Iris. "Sad, that. Your righteous vengeance for his cheating was all very well and good, but that baby never did anything to you. It will never have the chance to do anything now that you've killed it."

"She was pregnant," said Poppy numbly. "I killed a pregnant woman."

She turned in Andrew's direction, pointing the gun at him.

"You miserable, heartless—"

Iris hurled the handcuffs at her face and dove off the bed, tucking her head under as she curled her body into a somersault. Poppy brought her left hand up to block the handcuffs as she fired, but the distraction of the spinning chain made her miss. She grabbed the bolt end of the gun and pulled it back, sending the spent casing flying.

Two seconds, thought Iris as she rolled onto her feet.

She sprang at the other woman, staying low. Poppy slammed the bolt home and raised the gun as Iris rammed into her side, wrapping her right arm around Poppy's wrist and bending it behind her own body, the gun pointing away.

Her Special Forces training on disarming opponents had focused on men, which would mean a knee to the groin at this point. That wasn't going to be as effective with another woman, especially one with the height advantage. Iris swept her left leg behind Poppy's, but the other woman clutched the top of the bureau and kept her footing. Iris jabbed at her face with her left, but Poppy took the blow and countered with one of her own. Iris could feel her grip on the gun hand loosen as the taller woman began to pull it away.

Bolt-action, Iris reminded herself. She reached behind her back with her free hand and felt for the pinioned gun. Then she grabbed Poppy's index finger and pressed hard.

The gun went off, which meant until it was reset, it was only a chunk of metal.

Which Poppy promptly pulled free and used to smack Iris in

the face, sending her reeling against the doorframe. Poppy stepped back and reached for the bolt to pull it back again. Iris stooped down, grabbed one end of the handcuffs, and swung them as hard as she could. The other end whipped through the air and caught bone somewhere on Poppy's gun hand. She cried out in pain as the gun fell onto the carpet between them.

Iris stood still, whirling the handcuffs, blood dripping from a gash opened up on her cheek, her eyes locked on Poppy's. The other woman glanced down at the gun, then back at Iris.

"Go ahead," said Iris. "Pick it up."

Poppy looked at the handcuffs as they spun.

"Sparks, stop," said Andrew. "It's over."

"Shut up, Andrew," said Iris. "This isn't about you. Try for that gun, Poppy. Let's see what happens."

"Everyone freeze," said a man behind her. "Hands in the air, ladies. Drop the cuffs, miss."

Iris immediately dropped the handcuffs and raised her hands. A moment later, Poppy slowly raised hers.

"I hope to God you're the police," said Iris. "If so, there is a gun on the floor there. I'm not taking my eyes off that woman until you've secured it."

"I would think after our night together, you'd recognise my voice," said Cavendish. "Stay still while I frisk you."

She felt him pat her down. Professionally, not taking advantage of it.

"Move towards the corner and stay there," he said.

She did, turning to face the room and watch.

"You, step away from that gun," he directed Poppy.

"I can explain," said Poppy.

"Explain further away from the gun," he said, motioning with his revolver. "Ian, you cover her. I'll cover Sparks."

Myrick slipped into the room behind him, gun drawn.

"All right," said Cavendish. "I'm listening."

"This woman broke into our house," said Poppy. "She threatened us. I think she may be insane."

"I'm inclined to agree with you on the last part," said Cavendish. "So what's she doing with her dress off, and how do you account for the gentleman handcuffed to your bed?"

"That may be more difficult to explain," conceded Poppy.

"Your turn," Cavendish said to Iris.

"That's the gun that killed Helena Jablonska," said Iris. "And that's the woman who fired it."

"Who's the gent?" asked Cavendish.

"Her husband. My ex."

"Why'd she kill her?"

"She thought Jablonska was me."

"What do you think?" Cavendish asked Myrick.

"I like the second story better," Myrick replied.

"So do I," said Cavendish. "Mrs. Sutton—am I correct in calling you that?"

Poppy nodded.

"You are hereby charged with the murder of Helena Jablonska. Please turn around and place your hands behind your back. We'll use our own handcuffs if you don't mind. Ian, take her down to the car. Oh, are the keys for those anywhere?"

"Top drawer of the bureau," said Poppy as Myrick handcuffed her. "Detective? Was the woman I killed really pregnant?"

"I'm afraid she was," said Cavendish.

"God help you," she said to Andrew.

"God help us both," he replied.

Myrick brought her out of the room. Cavendish rummaged through the bureau and found the keys. Then he took out his handkerchief and picked up the gun by the barrel.

"I've only seen pictures of these before," he said. "It's a quiet gun, they told us, because of the baffles in the barrel. Not exactly standard issue. Which one of you is the spy?"

"That would be me," said Andrew.

"You shouldn't leave these lying around," said Cavendish. "They can be dangerous."

"Are you going to unlock these or am I to lie here while you lecture me?" asked Andrew.

"I'm going to wait for more of my men to get here," said Cavendish. "You Intelligence types have a nasty habit of disappearing. You're coming down to the Yard in cuffs, and I will release you when you're done talking."

"Some calls will have to be made for that to happen," said Andrew.

"I'm certain of it," replied Cavendish. He turned to Iris. "You. Get dressed. We've got a first aid kit in the car. We'll get that cheek looked at."

"Thank you," said Iris, crossing to retrieve her dress. "Will I be coming with you in handcuffs as well?"

"I'm looking at you in that wig, and thinking we drove past a pretty blonde with a Polish flyer yesterday," he said.

"Small world," she said, slipping on her dress. "Your timing could have been better. I was almost killed."

"There are eleven Andrew Suttons in London," he said. "You're lucky we showed up at all. If it weren't for the tip from Mrs. Bainbridge—"

"Gwen? What did she tell you?"

"She figured it out, got word to the Yard along with the right address. We were checking in with the office, then drove like maniacs to get here. She's a smart one."

"Yes, she is," said Iris.

"How many shots did Mrs. Sutton get off at you?"

"Two," Iris replied, pointing to the bullet holes while she stepped into her shoes.

"Amazing," he said, looking at her with respect.

Sirens crescendoed outside.

"Right," said Cavendish. "Go on down, tell them where I am."

"Will do," she said, walking to the door.

"Sparks?" called Andrew.

"Music shop, eight thirty tomorrow morning," she replied without looking at him.

Then she left.

The fatigue hit her as she came out of the house. Myrick was standing by the Wolseley, speaking to a uniformed constable. Poppy sat in the rear seat, looking straight ahead with a lost expression. Three other marked police cars lined the street. The boys from the rugby game were lined up at the fence opposite, gawking.

Iris relayed Cavendish's message, and three constables went into the house while Myrick pulled out a first aid kit and tended to her cheek.

"Might need a stitch or two," he said as he dabbed iodine on it and applied a sticking plaster. "Better than a hole in the head, though."

"Much better," she agreed.

Another Wolseley, its sirens blaring, raced up to the house and screeched to a halt.

"Iris!" called Gwen through the window.

Henderson got out, then opened the rear door for her. She stepped out of the Wolseley, her hands cuffed in front of her.

"What's that all about?" asked Iris.

"Long story," said Gwen. "Are you all right?"

"Mostly intact," said Iris.

"Did they catch her?"

"I caught her," said Iris. "Then they showed up."

Cavendish came out of the house. Andrew followed him, his hands cuffed behind, a pair of constables holding each arm. Cavendish saw Gwen and came over.

"Why is Mrs. Bainbridge in handcuffs?" he asked.

"She's under arrest," replied Henderson.

"For what?"

"For assaulting a police officer."

"I slapped him," said Gwen. "Twice. It was the only way I could get his attention."

"Really? Good to know," said Cavendish. "We've been trying to get him to listen for years. Uncuff her."

"But—" began Henderson.

"She helped crack a murder case, she's a witness for the Crown, and you'll be the laughingstock of the office if you prosecute her for a slap."

"Two slaps," said Henderson sullenly.

"Would you like to make it three?" asked Cavendish.

"Fine," said Henderson, removing the cuffs. "What do you need here?"

"Take Miss Sparks to the nearest hospital to get stitched up, then bring her to my office. I'll need a statement."

"Not the same room as the last time," said Iris. "And I want tea."

"Done and done," said Cavendish. "Be seeing you. Thanks for the tip, Mrs. Bainbridge."

"You're welcome, Detective Inspector," she replied. "But you got one thing wrong."

"What's that?"

"I didn't help crack the case. I cracked it. Please put that in your reports."

"I'll think about it," he said. "Oh, almost forgot."

He reached into his pocket and pulled out some change.

"It's getting to be expensive hanging around with the pair of you," he said, handing two pennies to Iris.

Then he and Myrick got in their car and drove away.

Gwen glanced over to where Andrew was being put in a police car.

"That's him?" she asked Iris.

"That's him."

"He is handsome," observed Gwen. "I can see the attraction."

"It was more than his looks," said Iris.

"I know," said Gwen.

"How did you know this was the place?" asked Iris. "I never told you Andrew's last name. And there are several listings."

"I found out Penny's real name, looked her up in *Burke's*, saw that she married an Andrew Sutton, and everything snapped into place," said Gwen. "And there may be several Andrew Suttons listed, but there is only one Poppy Sutton."

"That bloody *Burke's*," said Iris.

"Come on, Miss Sparks," said Henderson.

"I'm coming with her," said Gwen.

"Naturally," he said.

The two women got into the rear of the car.

"So you caught Poppy before the police arrived," said Gwen, as they drove away. "Here I was, thinking I had rescued you."

Iris thought back to the moment when she and Poppy faced each other.

Try for that gun, Poppy. Let's see what happens.

"You did rescue me," she said, nestling into her friend's shoulder and closing her eyes.

CODA

MONDAY MORNING

The entrance to the Keith, Prowse and Company music shop on New Bond Street was set back ten feet from the sidewalk, with display windows on either side. Hand-lettered signs urged Londoners to "Make it a Musical Christmas for your Friends in the Forces!" Ukuleles hung from the ceilings; low risers held velvet-lined cases filled with rows of gleaming, silvery mouth organs; behind them were saxophones, piano accordions, violins, every maker of music whether serious or novelty. The other side was stacked with sheet music, much of it yellowed from long exposure to daylight.

Iris contemplated purchasing a pair of mouth organs for Ronnie and John. She was in the midst of wondering if the introduction of such easily produced cacophony to the Bainbridge household would be a welcome thing when she sensed someone come up behind her. Hovering behind her own reflection in the display window was Andrew's.

"What time did they let you out?" she asked without turning.

"Around midnight," he said. "Then I had to go into the shop to be debriefed. You?"

"Much earlier," she said. "Mostly filling in the gaps I had to leave open during my first stay there, then bringing them up to speed on my Sunday adventures. Nothing afterwards. I guess the shop has lost interest in me."

"Your name came up there," he said. "Your conversation with Burlakov was not appreciated. There was speculation that this operation was deliberately scotched by you succumbing to your radical tendencies."

"What was the operation, Andrew? I think you owe me an explanation, given everything I've been put through."

"I worked with Helena Jablonska during the war as I told you," he said. "Everything I said about that period was the truth."

"Including the relationship."

"Including that."

"Was she the real Helena Jablonska?"

"Maybe, maybe not. Only the Russians know the truth of it."

"Did you know that she was a Soviet spy when you met her?"

"I had my suspicions," he said. "But we were on the same side, so that didn't matter so much. Things became complicated after the war ended. By that time, we knew who she was working for. The plan was to let me appear vulnerable to seduction and being turned. That way, I could both feed them misinformation and gain their confidence enough to find out who their agents were here."

"How long was that going on?"

"I can't tell you that."

"But it was while you and I were—whatever we were."

She saw his reflection shrug.

"Helena was an assignment," he said.

"Then you brought your work home with you."

"I pretended to be so fearful of compromise that I had to ask for leave back home but had to hide both from their agents and Poppy. Hence the flat, and having her find me through you."

"But Poppy found out about the flat. And me."

"She did, unfortunately. I was out getting some provisions. Came back to find Helena dead. No idea who did it or why. I packed my things, grabbed everything that could be traced to Helena, and ran."

"Leaving me holding the bag. Why on earth did you go back home to Poppy after that?"

"After a day or two, I didn't see my name in the papers. I thought I should put up a normal front, so I came home to the wife and house. She was delighted to see me. Made me a drink right away. The next thing I knew, I was where you found me."

She still hadn't looked directly at him, but there was a haunted look in his eyes that was evident even in the reflection.

"All the dangers I faced during the war, and afterwards in Berlin and Poland," he said. "None were as terrifying as being held captive in my own house, on my own bed. You saved my life. Thank you, Iris."

"Oh, look, we're finally on a first-name basis," she said. "I wasn't saving your life, Andrew, I was saving mine. Saving yours was an unintended consequence."

"Nevertheless—"

"Nevertheless, what strikes me about all of this is that because you and I had an affair, Helena is dead and your wife is going to hang for her murder."

"Hopefully not," he said. "I'm going to get her a good barrister. The shop won't want this to go to a public trial, given the classified aspects, so there will be some pressure on the Crown to give her a life sentence instead."

"How nice," said Iris. "It doesn't mean we're not responsible."

"Don't take any of this on yourself," said Andrew. "I'm the one at fault."

"Don't you dare minimise my part," she said. "I entered into our affair because I wanted to, not because I was some little puppet whose strings you pulled. I was selfish and stupid, and now two other women are paying the price, not me."

"What will you do now?" he asked.

"Go home."

"Home? I thought you and your mother—"

"My home, Andrew. The flat. Cavendish gave me the all clear last night."

"You really want to live where Helena died?"

"She only haunted me when she was alive," said Iris. "Speaking of haunting, I want the other key. I can't have you showing up unexpectedly anymore."

He looked at her sadly, then reached into his pocket, removed his keys, and detached one.

"The lease runs out at the end of the year," he said as he placed it in her hand. "What will you do then?"

"I'll think of something. What about you?"

"My cover's blown as far as the Iron Curtain goes," he said. "A desk job lies in my future."

"Good luck," she said. "It's funny. Here we are at the music shop where we used to meet, and I still haven't heard you play the piano."

"Iris," he said. "Please look at me."

Reluctantly, she turned to face him.

"Even if Poppy avoids the gallows, she'll divorce me," he said. "I meant it when I said you were the best experience of my life. I'll be in London full-time, and I'll finally be free. What do you say?"

She looked down at the key in her hand, then back up at his face.

"This is the moment where we never see each other again," she said.

She put the key in her bag and walked away.

TUESDAY EVENING

The crowd spilled from the New Theatre onto St. Martin's Lane, buzzing about what they had just seen. Among them were Iris, Gwen, and Sally, the two women dressed to the nines and Sally in a tuxedo that had to predate the war given the amount of fabric needed to cover a man his height.

"That was stunning," said Gwen. "I'm still shaken."

"Do you think the picture he showed each of them was the same one?" asked Iris.

"I was wondering about that," said Sally. "Unbelievable. Priestley takes the detective story and the English family at the dinner table, two of the hoariest traditions we have, and blows everything to pieces. He rips our entire societal and economic structure to shreds in one evening."

"Richardson was absolutely chilling," said Gwen.

"Your friend Alec was terrific, too," said Iris.

"To think he's alternating this with the Fool to Olivier's Lear," said Sally. "He'll never look back."

"Where to now?" asked Gwen.

"I have a surprise," said Sally, reaching into his inside pocket and pulling out a pair of invitations. "We're going to the party."

"But there're only two," said Gwen. "Who is—oh. May I have a moment with Iris?"

"By all means," said Sally.

Gwen smiled, then grabbed Iris by the wrist and practically yanked her to the kerb.

"You promised me," she said.

"I promised you that the three of us would see the play together, and we have," said Iris. "I made no promises about the gala. Try to have some fun for a change."

"Sneak!"

"I don't want to go anywhere fancy with this little piece of frippery clinging to my cheek," said Iris, pointing to the plaster covering her recently acquired stitches. "Besides, I have a date."

"How can you have a date after—oh," said Gwen as a car pulled up by them.

Archie got out and came around to hold the door for Iris.

"Don't wear yourself out," she said to Gwen as she got in. "We still have to work in the morning."

"Likewise," said Gwen. "Hello, Archie. Nice to see you."

"Nice to be seen," said Archie. "Enjoy the gala."

He tossed off a quick salute to Sally, then got behind the wheel and drove off. Gwen walked back to where Sally was waiting.

"You're a sneak, too," she said.

"Only when it's for a worthy cause," he replied.

"I don't know if I'm in the best party mood," she said. "That play hit close to home. The girl is rejected by every member of the family, ends up pregnant, then dies. I kept thinking of poor Helena Jablonska and how I turned her away."

"Helena Jablonska had no intention of signing up with The Right Sort," said Sally. "She was only there to find Andrew through Iris."

"But I rejected her not knowing any of that."

"Nothing that happened to her was your fault," said Sally.

"Yes, but it's like that line of Inspector Goole's in the play. 'The girl's still dead, though.'"

"Yes, she's dead," said Sally. "But you and I are both still alive, in my case against very long odds. We're alive, we're young, and there is dancing to be had. So let's dance, Gwen."

He offered his arm. She hesitated, then took it.

"Italian food all right?" asked Archie. "I thought we'd pick up where we left off."

"Sounds good," said Iris.

He glanced over at the plaster on her cheek, a shadow of a bruise visible beneath the makeup.

"You win?" he asked.

"Yes," she replied.

"Does it 'urt much?"

"Some. The doctor said it might leave a scar."

Archie shrugged.

"We all got scars," he said.

THURSDAY EVENING

"How have you been since last week?" asked Dr. Milford. "Did you manage to get any socialising done?"

"I went to a party," said Gwen. "I danced with Ralph Richardson. Can you imagine?"

"I have never imagined myself dancing with Ralph Richardson," said Dr. Milford. "Did you make any new friends?"

"I had lunch with a woman I met at the V and A," said Gwen.

"That sounds promising," said Dr. Milford.

"She turned out to be a lying, manipulative murderess."

"That—that sounds extreme," said Dr. Milford, taken aback. "What do you mean by that?"

"Exactly what I said. Let me explain."

By the time she was done, he was shaking his head.

"How does this keep happening to you?" he asked.

"I wish I knew," she said. "I listened to you. I tried to keep out of it, I really did."

"So what happened?"

"Iris needed me," she said.

"How did that make you feel?"

"I had purpose," said Gwen. "It was frightening when it was happening, and I really, really don't want anything like this ever to happen again, but it felt good when all was said and done."

"Any conclusions about that?"

"You asked me if Ronnie's death was the reason I fell apart."

"Yes?"

"I think that happened because I had never been allowed to think I was anything but someone to take care of. There was this sense as I grew up of being useless and a burden, even though we had everything. I let myself believe that, and marrying Ronnie, as wonderful as he was, as much as I loved him, meant more of the same. When he died, I had already been cut loose by my family. I had nothing to shore me up."

"You thought you had nothing."

"Yes. Not the same thing at all."

"So?"

"So I'm not restoring my life, or my independence, by going to the Courts of Lunacy," she said. "I'm finally attaining it."

"You already have, for the most part. The petition is merely the next step."

"Right. About that. I don't want you to testify for me."

"Why not?"

"Because I want to keep working with you," she said. "There's more to be done. Besides, if I can't convince two other therapists that I'm ready, then maybe I'm not."

"Soundly reasoned," he said. "See you next week. And try harder not to get involved with any more murder investigations, all right?"

"I will," she promised.

Iris sat in the chair, her knees drawn up, her arms wrapped around them. Dr. Milford watched her quietly and waited. Finally, she looked up at him.

"I figured something out this week," she said.

"What?" he asked.

"I'm still in love with Mike Kinsey," she said.

"Ah," he said. "Good. Let's get to work."

ACKNOWLEDGMENTS

T he author would like to thank the following:

For matters Polish: Much of the history came from *The Eagle Unbowed: Poland and the Poles in the Second World War*, by Halik Kochanski. Information on Polish resettlement camps was found at www.polishresettlementcampsintheuk.co.uk/PRC/PRC .htm. Ania Mochlinska Rakowicz of Ognisko Polskie, London's oldest Polish restaurant, alerted the author to the Devonia neigh-bourhood. Asia Nowokunski and Justyna Mielczarek very kindly reviewed the use of the Polish language and found it acceptable.

Speaking of translations, Janis Gibbs provided the German.

For legal matters: Dr. Carmen Draghici of the City Law School of City, University of London, directed the author to the Courts of Lunacy and provided several articles on the topic. Authors of books and articles include Frederick John Smith, Alex Ruck Keene, Nuala B. Kane, Scott Y. H. Kim, Gareth S. Owen, and Chantal Stebbings.

For the *Britain Can Make It* exhibition: the University of Brighton Design Archives, Dr. Lesley Whitworth, deputy curator; "'Everything Is Made of Atoms': The Reprogramming of Space and Time in Post-war London," Richard Hornsey, from the *Journal of Historical Geography* (Jan. 2008); the many contributors to *Britain*

Can Make It: The 1946 Exhibition of Modern Design, Diane Bilbey, editor; and Brittany Riggs of Adam Matthew Digital for granting access to the Mass Observation Project archives.

The author takes full responsibility for any errors made. The author worked very, very hard to avoid such errors, so if you find any, remember that they are the results of very, very hard work.